CRIMINALS

CRIMINALS

a novel by

Margot Livesey

Alfred A. Knopf New York 1996

THIS IS A BORZOI BOOK
PUBLISHED BY ALFRED A. KNOPF, INC.

Copyright © 1995 by Margot Livesey
All rights reserved under International and Pan-American Copyright Conventions.
Published in the United States by Alfred A. Knopf, Inc., New York,
and simultaneously in Canada by Alfred A. Knopf Canada,
a division of Random House of Canada Limited, Toronto.
Distributed by Random House, Inc., New York.

Library of Congress Cataloging-in-Publication Data

Livesey, Margot.
Criminals : a novel / by Margot Livesey. — 1st ed.
p.   cm.
ISBN 0-679-44487-4 (alk. paper)
I. Title.
PR6062.I893C75   1996
813'.54—dc20   95-31512
CIP

Manufactured in the United States of America
First Edition

My thanks to the MacDowell Colony for two residencies during which much of
this novel was written. Also to Gerald Jonas, whose book *Stuttering: The Disorder
of Many Theories* (New York: Farrar, Straus & Giroux, 1976) gave me certain
insights.—ML

I would like to express my deep gratitude to the following friends for their invaluable suggestions on the manuscript: Tom Bahr, Carol Frost, Rig Hughes, Camille Smith, and Janet Sylvester. My greatest debt is to Andrea Barrett, without whom this novel would not exist.

I

Chapter 1

As the bus neared Loch Leven, Ewan studied the back of the seat in front of him, which more energetic travellers had used for self-expression. The sight of so many epithets, all that passion untidily scrawled in different pens, only deepened his exhaustion. He had worked late at the office the night before and taken the sleeper up from London to Edinburgh. Scotland greeted him with her dourest morning face. Princes Street, before the shops opened, had a gloomy, dishevelled air, and the castle squatted above the city like a toad. Now, through the bus window, the waters of the loch were a rumpled grey, the soft outlines of the Lomond Hills barely visible through the mist.

George loves Lindy forever. What kind of person, wondered Ewan, wrote such things to be read by strangers? *Sow your seed,* someone else had printed neatly. *Support the Greens.* On impulse Ewan took out a pen. If he wrote something, he would know how it felt. His hand hovered, but nothing came to mind. The long glittering snake of love slithered round the corner at the first sign of his approach. His political sentiments? That seemed easier, though how to choose amongst them? *Eat the rich,* by most standards, if not his, included him. *World peace? Give bankers a chance?*

This is what people don't like about me, Ewan thought. Even my spontaneity is calculated. His sister Mollie, for instance, whom he was on his way to see, could until recently have covered the back of this seat and several more with succinct advice. *Recycle for a better world. Say no to exams. Stop eating dead animals.*

For two pins Ewan would have put his pen away, but a faint cough drew his attention. Glancing across the aisle, he saw a young man—a boy, really—in a threadbare denim jacket, watching him. The cold curiosity on the boy's freckled face reminded Ewan he was wearing a suit, pin-striped no less. On his mettle now, he shook the pen a couple of times as if he had just been waiting for the flow of ink, leaned forward, and scrawled the least likely thing he could think of: *Remember the Krays.*

There, he thought, without looking over at the young man. He put the pen away and closed his eyes. He did not feel transformed, not remotely, into the energetic, passionate person he had imagined. Behind him in London, his desk overflowed with intricate financial transactions, and more sinister matters, which he could not bear to consider, threatened. Ahead in the Scottish countryside waited his neurotic sister. He opened his eyes. The words were still there; they might be his most lasting accomplishment of the year so far.

A quarter of an hour later the bus pulled into Perth station. On previous trips north, Mollie and Chae had come to meet him here, or sometimes in Edinburgh, where they could combine collecting him with a visit to Chae's children. But on the phone Mollie had sounded so frail that Ewan had announced he'd take the bus all the way to the local town. He even offered to take a taxi the final five miles to her house. This she brushed aside. "Of course I'll fetch you," she said, with a catch in her voice that made Ewan wish, for the first time in years, he had learned to drive. In London, and the other cities where he did business, taxis filled the streets yearning for the sight of his raised arm, but in rural Perthshire, his lack of skill became a noticeable handicap.

"Twenty minutes," the driver called.

Ewan stood up with his briefcase. Reluctantly, he eyed his bag in the overhead rack. He let the other passengers go ahead and went to ask the driver if it was safe to leave his luggage.

The driver paused in the midst of extricating his stout bulk from behind the wheel. "Safe as houses," he said with such conviction that to take the bag would've been an insult.

Ewan thanked him and stepped down onto the oily tarmac. A few yards away, the boy in the denim jacket was hawking and spitting. Ewan watched as he sauntered off, kicking an empty beer can along the gutter. He would have bet a hundred pounds the boy lived at home, another fifty that he was unemployed.

The station was no more than a single low building with a covered area down one side, where passengers could wait and be encouraged by a series of faded posters to take pleasure trips to the Trossachs, Oban, and Inverness. Ewan made his way to the cafeteria, thinking of coffee, but stopped short as soon as he opened the door and smelled the overwhelming odour of bacon. Coffee would be a disaster. The thing to order in these places was tea. No sugar, he had to say twice to the woman behind the counter to halt her automatic gesture.

He carried his cup to a round table, strewn with other cups, and perched there, trying to read a history of Mary Queen of Scots that Mollie had given him for Christmas. Now, four months later, he had brought it along, hoping to seem tactful. I can't do anything right, she had said on the phone, and he could suggest one small contradiction: look at the pleasure her gift was giving him. It was the autumn of 1542, and Mary's mother, Mary of Guise, was preparing for her accouchement at Linlithgow Palace. Ewan read a page. At the bottom he realised he had understood nothing. He read it again, to no greater effect. He was so tired that the sentences melted before his eyes; he could not keep one in mind long enough to grasp the next. Even the tea, thick as treacle, did not help.

An excruciatingly thin man in a shabby raincoat shuffled by, sat down at the next table, and began to devour a plate of baked beans, fried eggs, and toast. Forgetting Mary, Ewan stared at the man in surreptitious fascination. His Adam's apple heaved with every mouthful, and he clutched the knife and fork like weapons. There was something bizarre, Ewan thought, about this spectacle.

Suddenly he remembered the time. He stood up, downed the rest of his tea, and headed in search of the Gents. It was outside, halfway down the building, next to a poster of Loch Ness. He opened the door and once more was assailed by the smell of bacon, which here at least served to mask other, potentially less pleasant scents. Inside were one stall, its door a couple of inches ajar, and two urinals. Ewan had the place to himself. After using a urinal, he washed his hands at the surprisingly clean basin. There was no mirror, but on the cream-coloured wall someone had drawn a neat rectangle and printed MIRROR—12 × 16.

He was leaving, rubbing his hands dry on the legs of his trousers, when he heard a small sound behind him. Mice, he thought. Or something worse? The sound came again, a soft whimpering that did not seem rodent-like. Cautiously Ewan pushed open the stall door. On the floor, wrapped in yellow plastic, was a doll. No, not a doll. A baby.

Unthinkingly Ewan did what he often did at moments of crisis: he loosened his tie. He squatted down beside the bundle. "Goodness," he muttered. The baby looked past him with round dark eyes and whimpered again. The tile floor, unlike the basin, was not clean; an empty crisps wrapper lay in one corner, and pieces of paper clung damply to the base of the toilet.

The baby's skin had a coppery sheen, and its hair was silky black. Slowly, awkwardly, because there was nothing else to do, Ewan picked it up. He stood in the doorway of the stall, holding the baby, dumbfounded. Then from outside came the blaring of a horn, and he remembered his luggage in the rack above his seat. He bent down to grab his briefcase and stepped quickly through the door. A few yards away the grimy bus was already vibrating. A new driver, a prissy-faced woman, sat behind the wheel, writing in a notebook. When Ewan reached the top step she demanded his ticket without interrupting her task.

"I found this. My l-l-l-l-"

The driver closed her notebook and looked up. At the sight of Ewan's suit and the yellow bundle, her face lost some of its primness. "My, you've got your hands full. Just take a seat for now, sir." She almost smiled. "We're leaving."

Another late passenger was waiting behind him. As he moved down the aisle, Ewan heard a male voice ask for a day return. His luggage was still there. Ewan stepped into the cramped space in front of the seat. He caught a flash of red, a jacket or pullover, as the man passed him and took a seat a couple of rows further back. In a series of jerks, the bus pulled out of the station.

Later Ewan could never quite recapture his thoughts at this crucial moment. He had intended, hadn't he, simply to retrieve his bag and make his way to the police station. But the door closed, the bus started moving, and, to avoid falling, he sat down with the baby in his lap. Exhaustion clung to him like cobwebs. The bus passed beneath the railway bridge and accelerated towards a green light. The freckled boy, the main witness to his previous solitude, was gone, and the other passengers from before, three teenage girls in the back, would have found a sack of potatoes more interesting than a middle-aged, besuited banker.

As for the baby, the baby was no help. It stared at Ewan,

and Ewan stared back. He was much more familiar with millionaires than with infants. Although some of his friends had them, he glimpsed them only from afar, mysterious visitors; he could not remember when he had last held one. Now he studied this strange object. It was wrapped so neatly, a tiny mummy, with just the head visible. "Who are you?" said Ewan. "Where do you come from?"

The baby's eyes widened slightly. Ewan experienced a flicker of recognition. Not an object, he thought—a small, silent human. Presently he unwrapped the yellow plastic, which turned out to be a poncho of the kind worn by cyclists and hikers. Beneath was a clean blue blanket. There was no note, nothing saying *My name is David* or *I am Nell. Take good care of me.*

Vexed, perhaps, by the loss of its outer covering, the baby sent up a piercing wail. The sound, no worse than a dog barking or the teenagers in the back seat with their radio, made Ewan instantly desperate. If they had still been in Perth, he would have begged the driver to let him off and dialled 999 at the first phone he came to. But already they were passing by fields, ploughed on one side, grass on the other. The occasional cows and sheep promised no succour; they had their own knock-kneed offspring to deal with. He patted the blue blanket, uselessly. "Be quiet," he whispered. And then, "Shut up."

He had, he realised, nothing to offer by way of refreshment. What if the baby was hungry? But its plump cheeks did not speak of starvation so much as passionate aggravation. Finally Ewan raised it to his shoulder. He had seen people do this, men and women, in shops and parks, raise their babies and pat their backs. In his attempt to imitate them, he found that the baby's head fitted under his chin, snug as a violin. The wails continued for a few seconds and abruptly, in the middle of an especially loud outcry, ceased.

The bus slammed over a series of potholes, then entered a wood of beech trees. The new leaves, bright green even on this dull day, cast an aqueous light. Ewan felt his own breathing slow. The baby's head, crooked against his neck, was astonishingly warm, as if its entire life were happening just beneath the skin. He stared again at the graffiti on the seat in front. Children, he now noticed, were conspicuously absent. If his hands were empty, he would write something different. *Free childcare?*

Somehow that thought led him to his sister. He managed to reach into his briefcase, where he'd been carrying her letter since it arrived earlier in the week. She had written in pencil, on a page torn raggedly from a notebook. No date, no address.

Dear Ewan,

Black birds follow me. They wait for me in the treetops and swoop down when I leave the house. I'm afraid of their beaks. They hate my eyes. When I drive, they dive-bomb the car. I can't see where I'm going.

Or maybe they're bats.

Inside are voices. They ooze from the table and the tap. They say bitch cunt Penelope whore stupid mole-eyes snot yellow tongue. They know.

And at night poisonous gas fills the house. I'm afraid to lie down, afraid to breathe. Maybe there is something buried under the stone floors. I never used to think of bones but now the house is full of them. . . .

Rereading the jagged sentences, Ewan thought the only consolation was that Mollie had dealt successfully with all the business of posting a letter. The envelope was addressed clearly, a first-class stamp affixed. "I got your note," he had said when he phoned to announce his arrival. "My *cri de coeur*," she said with an embarrassed laugh, and thanked him.

He slipped the letter back into his briefcase and, like his small companion, closed his eyes. For a few minutes Mollie's dark words fluttered round his brain, then they gathered into a flock and flew away into a dreamless sleep.

He woke as the bus pulled into the narrow streets of the town. Something warm lay against his chest. Looking down, he discovered the baby still sleeping in his arms. Good God, he thought, what have I done? But in the confusion of getting off, there was no need to answer. By the time he'd lifted his bag down from the rack and packed the yellow poncho, the other passengers had departed. With his bag, briefcase, and the baby, Ewan manoeuvred down the aisle and off the bus. Behind him, the driver, who seemed to have forgotten all about his ticket, called goodbye.

In the street, a second, smaller shock awaited him. Rain had begun while he slept and was bucketing down—ricocheting off the pavement, sinking into his suit and hair, his bag, and the baby's blanket. Through his beaded glasses, Ewan searched the town square. Most of it was given over to parking, with a bronze war memorial in one quadrant. There was no sign of Mollie. He spotted several of his fellow passengers sheltering beneath the sizeable canopy of the old Odeon. The teenage girls were examining one another's earrings, and the man who'd followed him onto the bus, wearing what Ewan now saw was a red jacket, was smoking a cigarette. Ewan made his way over and stood on the top step, facing the street.

Cars passed, a baker's van, and one intrepid, black-clad cyclist, whose undulating progress Ewan followed attentively. Just as he began to worry that something had happened to Mollie, that she had been unable to drive after all, he heard a horn hooting. Across the road, from the open window of a blue car, an arm was waving. Once more Ewan gathered his belongings and hurried down the steps. Somehow he managed to get himself and everything else into the car and close the door.

"Sorry I'm late," Mollie said, leaning over to kiss his cheek. "Christ, what's that?"

"I should have thought it was obvious." As so often in childhood, her emotion calmed him. "A baby."

"But whose is it? Where did *you* get a baby?"

In a few sentences Ewan explained about the Gents, the bus leaving, his luggage. "I didn't know what to do," he said. "Maybe I should have left it there?" But the notion that he could have emerged from the Gents empty-handed was by now inconceivable. What if the freckle-faced boy had found the baby? Or the thin man in the cafeteria? Horrid newspaper visions flitted through his mind.

Mollie did not answer his question. Momentarily he forgot he was meant to be taking care of her and instead waited nervously for her to scold, then rescue, him. Surely he'd overlooked some practical thing that would be readily apparent to her, like the time he failed to put a filter in her and Chae's coffee machine. But Mollie was regarding him with an odd expression, one he did not know how to interpret. Her face was pale, and her hair, shorter than he had ever seen it, had an uneven, bitten quality. In their school production of *A Midsummer Night's Dream*, she had played Puck, and still, at thirty-five, she looked as if she ought to be flying through the trees, admonishing lovers and fairies alike.

"Is it a boy or a girl?"

"Not sure." And then, as Mollie reached towards the baby, "Careful, it's asleep."

"Well." She drew back. "You're certainly full of surprises, Ewan."

In the long pause, they all three simply breathed. Rain throbbed on the roof of the car and hazed the windscreen. The situation was urgent, Ewan reminded himself, but his nervousness had ebbed. He was experiencing an almost drowsy contentment, similar to what he often felt after swimming, when the chlorine of the pool took on narcotic properties. Mollie was cracking her knuckles, a dark, sinewy sound he recognised as the puzzling noise he had sometimes heard in the background during their last month of phone calls. The gesture signalled anxious thought but only reinforced his own lack of anxiety. She was his older sister; soon, he was certain, she would tell him what to do. They would deliver the baby to the proper authorities, go back to Mollie's house, and solve all her problems too. A lorry roared by, leaving the car rocking slightly in its wake.

"I think," said Mollie, "I think for now we should take it home. The police here won't have a clue how to deal with a baby. It's not even police plural, just Mr. Stevenson, using his parlour as an office. No, we'll have to drive back to Perth, and I'm not up to that in all this rain. Besides, I left soup on the stove."

Her voice was unexpectedly high, as if she hadn't spoken much recently, but what she said made sense. The baby was asleep, Ewan thought, and he was hungry. They would go home and eat; he would take a bath and change. Then they could return to Perth in a civilised fashion. An hour or two would make no difference. Mollie had described driving as difficult but not impossible, and that in itself seemed a good sign. The black birds were staying in the treetops. They could even have dinner in Perth, or see a film. After all, he was meant to be cheering her up. "Good idea," he said heartily, rousing himself. "I'm starving."

"I'll need to get one or two things." Before Ewan could ask what, she had opened her door and was running through the rain towards the row of shops.

He sat back and watched the pedestrians. Most, like Mollie, hurried to avoid getting wet, but near the war memorial two women dressed in anoraks, skirts, and Wellington boots were engaged in a lengthy conversation, seemingly oblivious to the rain. Only the white cairn belonging to the taller one kept tugging at his lead in an attempt to find shelter.

Presently Mollie returned with a large shopping bag. She put it in the boot, then came round to open Ewan's door. "You have to sit in the back," she said. "It's safer."

The back seat was untidy and covered with long fawn hairs: Sadie's domain. Ewan hunched over grumpily, the baby cradled on his knee, and waited for the five miles to pass. In the sodden fields were sheep, cattle, birds. He remembered Mollie whizzing down this road at sixty, laughing off his pleas for caution. "How would you know?" she'd said. "You don't even drive." Now she drove with irritating sedateness, signalling, changing gears at precisely the right moment.

At last they turned into the side road, along the track, and between the two stone gateposts. Mill of Fortune was a nineteenth-century farmhouse, a dignified version of the kind of house that children draw—a door and four windows, with a sloping slate roof and tall chimney stacks at either end. It boasted a duck pond, an apple orchard, and several outbuildings. Halfway up the drive, Mollie suddenly braked. "Sorry," she said. "The ducks." Over her shoulder Ewan glimpsed four brown ducks waddling towards the pond. During their early years in the house, Mollie and Chae had endlessly quoted Dylan Thomas and revelled in their wonderful crops of lettuces and raspberries. More recently, on the phone, Mollie had invited Ewan to Mill of Misfortune. Wouldn't it be better for her to come to London? he asked; apart from anything else, he was drowning in faxes. "Ewan," she said, "don't make me beg." Although she was already.

They pulled up at the back of the house. In the rain, the grey stone had darkened almost to charcoal, and the windows gave back nothing but the gloomy sky. The whole effect, to Ewan's eyes, was quintessentially Scottish. There was no effort, as on the part of English houses, to be welcoming; this was old-fashioned, uncompromising shelter. He sat waiting in the car while Mollie opened the back door, and noticed she'd left it unlocked. In London he had recently installed a burglar alarm and new window locks, and still he never came home without wondering if he'd been robbed. Finally, the baby in his arms, he climbed out of the car. Sadie, the Shetland collie, rushed to greet him and was intercepted by Mollie. Then they were all inside. Sadie nuzzled Ewan happily as he stood in the middle of the kitchen, looking round for changes.

They were everywhere. For years the large flagged kitchen had been his favourite room, the place he pictured whenever he needed an image of domestic happiness. He loved the deep windows, the whitewashed walls, the fabulous clutter. Every nook had held something strange and exotic: a tiny skull, a bird's egg, an antler, a plaster saint. Mollie used one corner for her loom, and hanks of coloured wool hung along the wall, an extended rainbow. Above the big window had dangled four mobiles made of heather roots, feathers, sticks—one each for Mollie, Chae, Daniel, and Rebecca. This morning the walls were empty save for two prints. The mobiles were gone. The skulls and stones. The loom, despite the work stretched on it, looked as if it hadn't been used for some time. Everything was too orderly. Only the blue budgerigar, Plato, uttered a familiar tweet from his cage to the left of the stove. Mollie was clearing the table, and it took barely a minute to remove the newspaper, the salt and pepper. Gone were the candles, incense, pots of herbs, table toys.

Ewan laid the baby down, and Mollie unwrapped the blanket. Beneath was a stretchy blue sleeper. "From Mothercare," she remarked. "Quite good quality."

The baby was a girl, about four months old, Mollie judged. At once Ewan saw her features leap into the feminine. A girl, he thought with pleasure, as if that made his picking the baby up off the lavatory floor a far greater accomplishment. He smiled, and briefly she forgot her interest in her own feet and smiled back. "Look," he said.

"Oh," Mollie murmured, setting aside the tin of formula she had been examining. Together they stood smiling down at their small visitor, and she beamed, broadly, at both of them.

Mollie changed her nappy and prepared a bottle. Ewan, his own hunger temporarily forgotten, watched the baby feed. Whatever her recent adventures, this skill remained intact. She sucked with such ferocity that several times her face darkened and she had to break off, reluctantly, to cough. Then, the bottle almost empty, she fell asleep.

Mollie wedged her in the armchair near the stove, and she and Ewan sat down at the table to have their own lunch. Over lentil soup, bread, cheese, and fruit, they made a plan. Rather than drive thirty rainy miles, they would phone the police to ask if a baby had been reported missing and find out what they should do.

Though it was Mollie who suggested the phone, the idea instantly appealed to Ewan. He did most of his business through machines and believed in the virtues of electronic communication. He had a vision of the three of them traipsing from one draughty office to the next, filling out innumerable forms like refugees. Yes, he thought, phoning was best. And it would be easier to explain what had happened. For now, as he reached for the brie, he suddenly understood an explanation would be required. The messenger was never entirely innocent. Mollie got up to make coffee, and the next thing he knew, he had nodded off over his empty soup bowl. She shook his shoulder and sent him to take a nap. "You're in Daniel's room," she said. "We'll go to Perth when you get up."

He climbed the crooked stairs, marvelling as he had before at the horrendous creaking. No wonder they didn't need a burglar alarm. When he opened the door of Daniel's room, he found it, like the kitchen, amazingly altered: every trace of the boy was gone. Ewan's visits to Mill of Fortune had seldom co-incided with those of Chae's children, but such was the impen-etrable state of their rooms that he had always slept in the parlour. Mollie had told him Chae regarded chaos as a sign of affection; his son and daughter wanted to leave their mark on his household. Now what remained was almost a parody of a guest room—the bed neatly made, with the counterpane smooth as an ice rink, the bedside light, the box of Kleenex, the radio, the stack of predictable books: Dick Francis, Georgette Heyer, something about Provence. Ewan brushed his teeth, got into bed, and was overwhelmed by the absence of noise. He missed the thunder of lorries, the chugging of taxis, the steady rumble of buses that formed his usual lullaby in London. He lay back between the stiff sheets listening hard, but all he heard was a faint quacking from the pond. A pause. And more, louder quacking.

He woke in panic, both feet already on the floor. Late for a meeting? Only when he caught sight of his suit draped over the chair did he remember where he was. He slumped on the edge of the bed, trying to follow the thread of alarm back into his dreams. Something to do with the office? Or Mollie? He saw yellow and blue. The baby. Before his apprehension could even take shape, he was rushing downstairs.

He burst into the kitchen, and the collie leapt upon him, her paws pressing against his thighs. She let out a volley of ex-cited barks.

"Down, Sadie," Mollie snapped, half rising from the chair near the stove, where she was sitting with the baby on her lap. "Ewan, are you all right?"

He stopped, sleepy and abashed, not knowing how to ex-plain. He came over and knelt beside the two of them. The baby's eyes were fluttering open and closed. "What," he asked, "did the police say?"

Mollie shook her head. "Once you'd gone upstairs, I realised it was pointless to phone. Nobody lost this little girl. They abandoned her." As she spoke, Ewan saw her arms tighten around the baby. "Abandoned" was the word she had used, over and over, on the phone to describe Chae's behaviour towards her. Usually it heralded a storm of tears.

"So what should we do?" he said carefully. He tried to think of anyone he knew who had been in a similar situation, and drew a profound blank. People found gloves and wallets, not babies.

"It's getting late," said Mollie.

"Late?" He turned from her to the clock above the sink. To his astonishment, it was four-thirty; he would have sworn he had slept no more than half an hour, an hour at most, yet nearly three hours had vanished in befuddled dreams. Outside the window, the overcast sky was already growing dark.

"I think we should wait until tomorrow," Mollie continued. "Wait until everyone's back in their offices. No reason to rush to throw her into the maw of social services. We might as well try to find the best place for her." She slid one pale finger into the baby's tiny, grasping hand. "Don't you think?"

Of course, Ewan said later, thinking was exactly what neither of us was doing. We were bandits scenting money, moles tunnelling towards light.

Chapter 2

That he agreed was the main thing: tomorrow was soon enough to deliver the baby to the authorities. Before Ewan could change his mind, Mollie sent him off to take a bath. Alone in the kitchen, she stood up, still holding the baby, and walked over to draw the curtains, heavy swaths of grey velvet that had come with the house when she and Chae moved in ten years ago and even then had been so old that the fabric was pleated into light and shadow. Looking out across the orchard, she could just distinguish the Youngs' garage, several hundred yards away; soon the leaves would entirely hide them from each other. During the last month, Mollie had come to dread this isolation. But now, as she pulled the curtains one-handed, she considered how lucky she was not to have to deal with curious neighbours.

For anyone to bring her a baby would have been amazing, but for her pedantic brother to do so was astounding. She had summoned him only because there was no one else. Bridget, their older sister, was hopelessly far away, in another country, where at this very moment she was probably enjoying a salad for lunch and saying "Gee." Occasionally, when she couldn't sleep, Mollie had dialled Bridget's number and been defeated by the insouciant chirp of her answering machine. She was even starting to sound American. In comparison, Ewan's greeting— "Hello, Ewan Munro"—was oddly reassuring. A couple of weeks ago she had rung late at night, and he, still half asleep, had answered the phone with that very phrase. "God, Ewan," she'd said. "Who did you think was going to be phoning at one in the morning?"

"People in the States sometimes forget," he replied. "Are you okay?"

"No," Mollie had said, and begun to weep.

She sat down again by the stove, and the baby squirmed and pouted. "Hush," Mollie said, "you're safe." She wanted to add "with me," but did not yet dare. Her joy must be kept secret a little longer. Instead she described how Mill of Fortune belonged to a family called Craig who had seven sons, each of whom hated farming worse than the last, rather like a fairy story. She remembered her friend Lorraine telling her that children learned to speak because people talked to them, and that the irritating habit of baby talk had a biological imperative in so far as babies were visibly more responsive to high-pitched sounds. As soon as the sons grew up, Mollie went on, one by one they ran away to Glasgow and broke their father's heart, leaving the house in need of tenants. "And that's us," she concluded, tapping first herself, then the baby, on the chest. The baby made a startled noise, as if she might not be quite ready for the responsibilities of paying rent.

From overhead came the tread of footsteps. Ewan. Oh dear, Mollie thought, if only he could be transported instantly back to London. Then she shook herself. His visit was a mere two days, a scant forty-eight hours; she could navigate that.

He came in, bringing with him the soapy aura of the bath. She knew, just from the way he opened and closed the door, that his earlier perturbation had passed. "Sorry to be such a sloth," he said. "What can I do to help?"

"Play with her while I cook?" Without waiting for an answer, she stood up, handed him the baby, and headed for the sink. As she filled a saucepan, she heard a squawk and a muttered "Bother." She stole a glance in their direction. Ewan was clutching the baby to his chest, eyeing her dubiously.

"Do I need to hold her?" he complained. "It makes everything so complicated."

"You can put her down if you want, but she'll probably cry." Mollie carried the pan to the stove and went to get the pheasant from the fridge. She was sure his efforts to discard the baby would be useless. After only a few hours in her company, Mollie believed absolutely in the baby's powers to be her own Circe, to transform Ewan not into a swine but into a less rigourous version of himself. Hadn't she already changed the house Mollie had grown to hate back into a home?

Mollie was cooking pheasant with roast potatoes, leeks, mushrooms, and rowan jelly. Following Ewan's phone call on Monday, she'd pulled out her cookbooks and sat at the table reading recipes for beef Wellington, Chateaubriand, oysters Rockefeller—delicacies she had never eaten, let alone prepared. She observed her own behaviour with bewilderment. Ewan wasn't difficult about food, even though he ate in restaurants all the time. But after six weeks of making nothing more complicated than a cheese sandwich or a bowl of cereal, the activity of cooking for others, once as natural as breathing, seemed part of a language she had forgotten. In the end she bought whatever looked good in the shops. The butcher urged the pheasant upon her. For years she and Chae had boycotted his shop, crossing the road to avoid the display of game dangling in the window; now Mr. Rae, his bald head shining, greeted her as if she'd been buying stewing steak once a week all along. He hefted the frozen bird in one hand and passed on the wisdom of his wife. "More versatile than hare, she always says."

As she moved between the stove and the table, Mollie studied her brother. He had changed into what she knew he regarded as casual clothes: grey slacks, a grey pullover, and a white shirt with one button cautiously undone at the neck. He'd dressed like this even at university. Involuntarily she found herself remembering Chae's reaction on first meeting Ewan—that he was a stuffed shirt and an old fart. And for years afterwards he had proved an irresistible source of humour. Ewan, meanwhile, had remained completely unmoved by Chae's charm, a fact Mollie had long held against him and which, in present circumstances, rendered him the ideal ally.

She began to peel onions. The plaits had been hanging up to dry in the garage since last autumn, and the filmy skins rustled like paper. She longed to talk about the baby, to praise her velvety eyes, her shell-like ears, her dimpled smile. But such conversation might be dangerous, leading Ewan toward law-abiding thoughts. No, instead she must lure him away, like the lapwings she and Sadie sometimes encountered in the meadow feigning injury to prevent discovery of their nests. She reached for a second onion and searched desperately for something to say. World events, local news—she could think of neither. When had she become so stupid? She spotted the pheasant in its roasting pan, smaller and more naked without Mr. Rae's praise. This would do. "I wonder why there isn't a word for pheasant when we eat it," she said. "Like beef and cow."

"I think they weren't common enough at the time names were being given out. Didn't the French bring them over— William the Conqueror and all that?"

He had sat down with the baby and was rocking her gently. Then, before Mollie could come up with another innocent topic, he said, "Who do you think her parents are? She looks as if she might be Indian, or Pakistani. It seems so nineteenth-century to leave a baby in the loo. And a bus station, no less—not even the train station or a fancy hotel."

"Presumably she was left by a man."

"Goodness," Ewan exclaimed, pausing in his rocking. "That never occurred to me, but of course. So would the mother know? She could've been kidnapped, or stolen for revenge." Bending to the baby, he said, "Perhaps somebody does want you after all."

Mollie held on to the edge of the table. She had staked her imagining on the baby's abandonment, on their need for each other being mutual. Now a mother rose before her—dark eyes, like her daughter's, arms outstretched in emptiness. A woman whose grief matched Mollie's own but who knew and had a name for what she lacked.

False tears saved her from true ones; the smell of onions pinched her nose. She blinked and was able to hustle the dark-eyed woman from the room. No decent mother would let such a small child out of her sight. For whatever reasons, the baby was alone in the world until Ewan stumbled along. She laid out four potatoes, added a fifth, and began to peel them in the extravagant fashion she had learned working in restaurants, lopping off a good quarter inch of skin. "I really appreciate your coming, Ewan. I know how busy you are."

"Thank you for asking me," he said, as if they hadn't argued for a month about this visit. "It does me good to get north of the border."

"Are you working on anything special?"

"Just the usual frantic boredom—chasing clients, going to meetings, faxing, phoning, discussing interest rates, trying to float companies. The trouble with doing business internationally is that someone, somewhere, is always awake and wanting something from you. Right now I'm fussing over an Italian company."

"Fussing?"

"Yes. The deal was all arranged, and then one of the major investors got cold feet. I'll probably have to go to Milan next week." He hesitated. "And there's, well, some kind of row . . ." He was frowning at the stone floor, and it was several seconds before he met Mollie's gaze. "Sorry," he said, forcing a smile. "I keep telling myself I'll retire when I'm forty-five and do something sensible."

"What could be more sensible than banking?"

"Working for Oxfam? Teaching? Translating masterpieces from the Sanskrit?"

"I didn't know you knew anything about Sanskrit. Down, Sadie." The collie had stationed herself beneath the table and was snuffling for scraps.

"I don't, yet. It's just an example of what I might be interested in, if I didn't work sixteen hours a day."

"And what about a family?" She picked up another potato.

"I have that: you, Bridget, Aunt Hester, and Uncle Godfrey. You're already enough trouble." He gave her a quick look, to see if it was all right to tease.

Mollie felt the power of hysteria. Ewan hated displays of emotion, other people's and his own, whereas she had always been ready to abandon the small boat of reason for the vast sea of feeling. She could persuade him to do whatever she wanted, Mollie thought, just by hinting she was about to shout or weep. "Ewan, you're being a prig. I mean girlfriends, sex. The only girl you ever brought to see us was Michelle. I remember she arrived wearing a beautiful white silk blouse. We were being macrobiotic and Daniel had just gotten his drum set and she hated the country."

"That was a disaster, start to finish. We argued the whole way back to London. Later there was a certain meagre consolation in being able to tell myself she'd bolted because of my mad family and their passion for brown rice."

"I'm sorry," Mollie said. "We were relentless. But there must be other people. At university several of my friends fancied you. Remember Charlotte? She kept begging me to bring you together. And I did, about twenty times, with zero results. She said you once kissed her cheek."

Ewan grinned. "She should've been thrilled. Cheek kissing was absolutely my outer limit in those days. Whatever became of her?"

"She moved to Malvern. Her husband works for a water company, those nice bottles we all drink. I haven't heard from her in years. But seriously—aren't women beating a trail to your door?"

"Don't be ridiculous. Women have better things to do these days than beat a trail to anyone's door."

Mollie looked up from the chopping board, surprised at his sudden crossness. She was about to ask what was the matter, but Ewan again turned the conversation back to the baby, hoisting her into the air and asking when such creatures started to crawl.

"Eight months? Ten?" Mollie tried to recall the age at which Lorraine's youngest daughter had started circling the kitchen. "She's probably due for another bottle. You can give it to her."

"I'm not sure I know how. You seem awfully well informed about babies. Weren't Daniel and Rebecca already at school by the time you met Chae?"

"Daniel was. He was six, and Rebecca started a year later. I wish I had known them when they were babies. I think we'd be much closer, but Chae says that's rubbish."

"Ah yes, Chae."

He let the name hang there, a ripe fruit waiting to be plucked. Not yet, Mollie almost whispered. She carried over a bottle and hovered longingly while Ewan struggled to manoeuvre the nipple into the baby's eager mouth. Then she made herself lay the table. As she set out the knives and forks, she thought, If the universe is full of lost objects and we each attract to ourselves the ones we need, Ewan must be among the least likely candidates to find a baby; it didn't even occur to him she was hungry. No, she corrected herself, as she folded the napkins. Wasn't he, in many ways, the best finder a baby could hope for? Honest, decent. And kind, she added penitently. He had attracted the baby out of the universe not for himself but for her.

Before the bottle was empty, the baby stopped sucking and turned her face away; she was asleep. Mollie took her from Ewan and put her back in the armchair. "Time for the grownups to eat," she said.

She served the food and Ewan poured a good burgundy he'd brought from London. Mollie had drunk no alcohol since the night Chae left, when she vaguely remembered a bottle of gin. Now she was delighted by the rich, smoky fragrance of the wine. She and Ewan clinked glasses, a little shyly, and he asked what she was weaving.

"Hangings," she said. "At least I was. Part of what I always liked about weaving was that I didn't need to shut myself away to do it; I could enjoy company." She took a mouthful of pheasant and was relieved to find it tender. "The trouble is, without *any* interruptions, I can't concentrate. Throwing a shuttle is both too finicky and too monotonous to do alone. Besides, I was in the middle of a present for Rebecca."

"This is d-d-d-d-"

As she waited, Mollie realised she had almost forgotten Ewan's stutter; it surfaced so seldom nowadays. When they were children it had been the sole thing about which she and Bridget were absolutely forbidden to tease him. After a few seconds he abandoned the struggle with "delicious." "Very good," he said, nodding towards his plate.

They talked about Bridget, her latest letter from Boston, and about Ewan's colleague Jack, who was becoming a daytime drunk. "Goodness knows," Ewan said, "I'm not one to complain about someone having a drink—whatever dulls the misery—but the other day he got so tipsy at lunch he called a client by the wrong name and couldn't figure out the exchange rate in dollars."

"Poor chap," said Mollie dryly. She could feel them inching up on the subject of her own misery, and wasn't that after all why she had summoned Ewan? She recalled saying on the phone, more than once, "I must talk to you." But now she saw that a large part of what she wanted was the mere act of his coming. She had needed to know there was one person in the world who would come if she asked. And he had. That it had been difficult, that his life was stuffed with appointments, only increased the value of the gesture. As soon as he'd agreed, she'd been able to leave the house again, say good morning and thank you, wave to the Youngs' children.

"So," said Ewan. "You were pretty fed up on the phone."

Mollie chewed, swallowed, sipped her wine. She had a terrible desire to go and pick up the baby. But instead she had to sit here and keep Ewan distracted. "Yes, I was fed up. I am."

"But what happened? It's only a few months since I got your glowing Christmas card. Did you have an argument?"

"You could call it that," she said, offering the words grudgingly, one by one.

"Did he leave the top off the toothpaste, or meet someone else? After all, you two have been together for over ten years. He can't just disappear. And what about the children?"

Mollie pushed back her chair and replied to the easiest of his questions. "The children aren't children anymore. Daniel's sixteen and Rebecca's nearly fifteen, and they'd both reached the stage when they hated coming here. I don't blame them. All their friends are in Edinburgh. Why should they spend their holidays going for walks and playing Scrabble? Last Christmas they only stayed for a week, under huge duress."

"Still," Ewan said, "I can't believe that's any reason for you and Chae to separate. People change—you both changed. There

are bound to be problems, but that doesn't mean it has to end."
He laughed and shook his head. "Sorry, I'm sounding like a
woman's magazine."

His laugh faded and he, too, edged his chair back from the
table. For a moment he seemed absorbed in adjusting the cuffs
of his shirt. Mollie watched him unobserved. His gold-framed
glasses glinted, and he must have shaved after his bath, because
along the jaw his skin shone. He reminded her of someone and,
as he twitched his left cuff link, Mollie realised who. In the
months since she'd last laid eyes on him, her little brother had
developed a remarkable resemblance to their father before his
first heart attack.

He looked up with an earnest expression. "I want you to
know," he said, "I'll help however I can. I thought you might
come and stay with me. You can have the top floor, your own
phone, plenty of privacy. You don't have to say anything now.
The house is there when you want it, for as long as you like. I
brought you a set of keys. And money, whatever you need."

Mollie could not speak. Jesus, what an idiotic reason to cry.
She fixed her gaze on Plato, trying to lose herself in the blueness
of his wings. The day after Chae left, she forgot to close the
door of his cage, and he had blundered, clumsy and panic-
stricken, from shelf to windowsill to lamp, while she pursued
him, calling his name, terrified. When he flew into the window
for the second time, she saw the mistake in her strategy. She
fetched his birdseed, sprinkled it noisily on the floor of his cage,
and sat down at the table to wait. Since then her fear of the
black birds had begun, and she sometimes had qualms even
about Plato. Now he kept his head tucked under his wing,
oblivious. His blueness did not help.

But Ewan came to her aid. "Do you still have the sheep?"
he asked. "I didn't notice them as we came in. Is there any more
to eat?"

"Yes, of course, there's seconds of everything." Mollie

jumped up and came round the table to get his plate, which gave her an excuse to see the baby. She bent down, putting her face close to that tiny one. A small breath wafted over her. There; she felt better. She filled Ewan's plate and set it before him. Then she fetched her own and helped herself to another slice of pheasant, a potato, and a spoonful of leeks.

He asked again about the sheep. "We had to get rid of them," she said. "Miss Havisham was a terrific bully. Always throwing her weight around. And Pip and Estella were boring. They just bleated and ate. Not that you can expect much of a sheep. But if they'd been nicer, we might have made more of an effort to hang on to them."

"I thought you kept them for the wool."

"We pretended to. Really, it was absurd. If you'd seen the accounts, if we'd kept accounts, you'd have torn your hair out."

"I'm afraid I don't have enough for that sort of gesture." He fingered his flimsy brown hair.

Mollie smiled and, picking up her glass again, drank determinedly. "What we were doing here," she continued, "I know it didn't make much sense to you, but it was an attempt to lead a correct life, a life consistent with the late twentieth century, dwindling resources, all of that. And we hit a wall. We couldn't grow enough food to be self-sufficient. We couldn't make enough money. Daniel and Rebecca weren't utopian children. Eventually, even to us, it became apparent we simply couldn't afford to go on. Our wool cost twice as much as in the shops. Our apples three times. The first few years we kept saying, Oh, it's part of the initial investment. But it wasn't true. If you do things on a small scale—four sheep, half a dozen hens, a small garden—the amount of time and money you expend is totally out of proportion. Those six hens cost a fortune to keep, and then they're eaten by foxes because you go out to supper and the children forget to shut them in for the night."

She stopped, taken aback by her own shrill tones.

Ewan was cutting up the last of his pheasant, nodding thoughtfully. "I wonder why?" he said. "After all, there used to be smallholders—two acres and a cow, or whatever. Somehow people managed. Maybe it's one of those situations where costs have mysteriously shifted. I remember Aunt Hester talking about the early days of their marriage; she and Godfrey had a servant the way you have a dishwasher."

"Yes," said Mollie. "Maybe it is shifting costs, but we felt like fools. It made this whole thing, this life we'd slaved over, into a joke."

"Is that why we're eating pheasant?" asked Ewan. "You practically threw me out once for bringing you a pâté from Harrods."

"That's exactly why. I'm tired of living a life of principle. Besides, I thought you'd enjoy it."

Soon they could respectably declare bedtime. Mollie let Sadie out for a last run. Together they stacked the dishes by the sink. Ewan ran himself a glass of water and bent to kiss her cheek. "Good night."

He was almost at the door when he stopped. "Oh, what about the baby? Will we hear her down here?"

"I'll take her to my room," Mollie said, trying to sound as if this were a hardship.

"Good," murmured Ewan. "I hope she's no trouble."

Chapter 3

Ewan adjusted his pillows and stared at the portrait of Mary Queen of Scots on the cover of his book. She did not look particularly regal, more like a housekeeper, with her long sharp nose and her eyes, two small brown fish swimming towards some object of disapproval—a smudge on the painter's chin, perhaps, or a spider's web in a corner of the window. Once, on a history outing, Ewan's class had visited Holyrood Palace. Fascinated by the ornate ceilings and faded tapestries, Ewan had loitered at the back of the group. He entered Mary's chambers just as the guide began her account of the death of Rizzio. "The Italian David Rizzio," she recited, "was the Queen's secretary and lute player. On Saturday the ninth of March, 1566, he was having a cosy supper with Mary and a few friends when her husband, Darnley, burst in with his followers, dragged Rizzio from the table, and stabbed him to death."

She had stressed "Italian" and "lute player" in a way that made clear these were not Rizzio's main crimes. Several of Ewan's classmates had snickered, as his sisters did when they discussed the S.A. of various boys. Sex appeal, you stupid berk, Bridget had said when he asked. Downstairs, the guide pointed out where the murderers had dumped Rizzio's body. Ewan remembered standing alone, after the rest of his class had trooped on, staring at the ragged bloodstain on the wide wooden floorboards. Now he wondered how the blood could have survived four hundred years of housework. Perhaps he had conjured the stain out of the guide's vivid descriptions. He must ask Mollie if she had ever seen it. Ewan let the book slide to the floor, unopened. He could barely figure out what was happening in his own life, or his sister's, let alone a difficult dinner party four centuries ago.

He shivered. All evening he had been trying not to yawn, but now he was too cold to sleep. He sat up and examined the pile of books on the bedside table. Between Dick Francis and a guide to the castles of Perthshire was a glossy purple spine. When he pulled out the book, he saw he was holding Chae's latest novel, *The Dark Forest*. His secretary, Yvonne, had mentioned seeing the book in Waterstone's a couple of months before, but this was Ewan's first sight of it. The cover showed a wood of twisted, menacing trees and, in the distance, a sunlit clearing towards which two figures of indeterminate sex were making their way.

Inside on the back flap was a picture of Chae, bearded and laughing. He looked as Ewan remembered him, the kind of person who could never enter a room unnoticed, not even buy a newspaper without making it a performance. "Chae Lafferty studied at Edinburgh University and the London School of Design. He has worked as a teacher, tree specialist, and journalist. He lives, ecologically, with his family, in a farmhouse in Perthshire. This is his fourth novel." The dedication page said, "For Mollie, always."

Chae had already published his first novel when he came into the vegetarian restaurant in the Grassmarket where Mollie was waitressing and befriended her over the nut rissoles. That Christmas she bought copies for everyone in the family and quizzed them afterwards. Ewan was still at university, finishing his degree in economics, and was suitably impressed by the whole notion of writing a book, that someone he knew had done such a thing. The actual novel, however, about teenage boys and petty crime around the Leith docks, had disappointed him. Was it true, he asked Mollie, there were boys who lived like this, hawking heroin in the toilets of pubs?

"Of course," she said impatiently. "Don't you read the newspapers? But that's not the point. It's a novel, Ewan, like *Great Expectations*."

"I understand that. It just seems so far-fetched. We both grew up in Edinburgh, and between us we don't know a single junkie."

"Exactly," Mollie said. "That's why Chae's book is so important."

He did not read the next two. Once she was living with Chae, Mollie became a less ardent proponent of his work, and anyway Ewan seldom read contemporary novels. Bridget said they were pretty good, and sometimes he gave them as presents to friends who claimed to like them. In a desultory, uncommitted fashion, trying to ignore his icy feet, he began to turn the pages.

The opening chapter described a man named Leo taking the train from London to Edinburgh, as Ewan had done the night before, although their approaches to travel were rather different. Leo kept moving from seat to seat until it became apparent that he was not simply exercising his good looks on various women but dodging the ticket collector. Past Newcastle he sat down beside a girl with short fair hair and a rather mannish jaw, a social worker named Sam. Leo told her he was an actor and was able to satisfy her curiosity about several of the stars of *East Enders*. When they arrived in Edinburgh, she invited him back to her flat off the Royal Mile.

Reading the description of their lovemaking, Ewan recalled

Bridget talking about the sex in Chae's books. "If I were Mollie," she had said, "I would be quite upset. It certainly sounds as if Chae is doing research."

"He's in his forties," Ewan protested. "He had a string of girlfriends and a wife before he met Mollie. I'm sure he just casts his mind back, or invents things."

"All right," Bridget said, and shrugged. "Contrary to the lessons of experience, let Chae be innocent until proven guilty."

Now, thought Ewan, events had vindicated her cynicism. What else but another woman could explain the way Mollie ducked his questions about Chae?

Next morning, Leo inveigled Sam into cashing a cheque for fifty pounds and promised to phone her when he returned to Edinburgh. He continued to his destination, which—although it had been moved thirty miles south, to outside Perth, and re-named Larch House—Ewan instantly recognised as Mill of Fortune. There were the gateposts, the duck pond, the apple trees, the sheep. And inside the house was Mollie, known as Maudie, married to Roman, who happened to be Leo's brother. So far Ewan had been reading slowly; as the book entered familiar territory, his attention quickened. Leo had hitchhiked from Perth and arrived late in the morning.

· · ·

Ever since Roman's weird phone call, I'd been imagining Larch House in a state of emergency. "Come at once," he'd whispered hoarsely, and the only thing I could think was that he was about to kick the bucket. Now I was here and everything seemed the same as usual: quiet, boring, rainy.

As I waited for someone to answer the door, I remembered our last meeting. Roman was down in London on business and invited me for a drink at the Russell Square Hotel. That afternoon I'd dropped in on my friend Josie.

She brought out some mushrooms she'd gathered at Glastonbury last summer, and I ended up nibbling a few, just to keep her company. We sat on the sofa watching *Coronation Street* and I felt fine. As soon as I left her flat, though, the mushrooms kicked in, and by the time I reached Russell Square I was well away. I'd happily have spent the evening in the revolving door of the hotel if the porter hadn't stepped forward and said, "Are you coming or going, sir?"

No surprise that Roman was already at the bar, he was always super-punctual. What I hadn't expected was the couple of colleagues he had in tow. Given my condition, I think I behaved astonishingly well with the old farts. Roman introduced me as an actor and there were the usual questions. I told them about famous people I knew and did my John Cleese imitation. I felt like a plastic bag, flapping in the breeze. Sometimes I was filled to overflowing and words spilled out of me, other times speech was impossible. At the end of the evening, Roman walked me round the corner to the tube station and gave me a pound twenty for my ticket home rather than the generous taxi fare I'd been angling for.

Remembering Roman's face as he watched me disappear into the station, I started to laugh. Then I heard him whispering on the phone and my glee faded. I knocked again, louder, and a brown and white dog appeared from behind the dustbin and trotted towards me, wagging her tail. "You're no watchdog," I scolded, sliding away from her eager nose. "What if I was a murderer or a thief?"

The dog gave a snort and that was all the encouragement I needed. I tried the door. It swung open and I stepped into the kitchen. I'd forgotten how large the room was and how shabby. The sofa looked as if an army of cats had used it as a scratching post and around the table stood six unmatched chairs. On one side of the room was the stove with a saucepan simmering away. I lifted the lid to discover spinach soup. Not bad. Some cream would help. A dash of nutmeg.

Could Roman be ill in bed upstairs? I imagined him, pale and skeletal, trying to smile at the sight of me, his darling little brother. I moved across the room, through the far door and up the creaking stairs. On the first-floor landing several doors stood open, including the master bedroom.

Like the other rooms, it was empty. I wandered over to the well-made bed and glanced through the books on Roman's bedside table; they were mostly about trains. On Maudie's side were a couple of novels and a box of Kleenex. I opened the drawer of her table.

"Holy moly," I exclaimed, taking in the pack of fancy condoms and the bottle of vanilla-flavored massage oil. What a slyboots. I hurried back round the bed. Roman's drawer yielded a well-thumbed copy of *The Joy of Sex*.

I shook my head in amazement. When we were growing up, Roman had always been the opposite of me: great at exams, hopeless at girls. And even now, deep in his second marriage, with two kids from the first, I found it hard to imagine him doing anything more than holding hands. I opened the book at random to a series of helpful diagrams. "Be sure to allow plenty of time for this one," the note said. Maybe it wasn't so out of character after all. Whatever Roman was up to, he was still doing it by the book.

I picked up the johnnies, not a kind I used, but for a moment I was tempted to pocket them. The idea of Roman discovering the theft weeks, or months, from now gave me a kick. He would suspect the children, who sometimes came for weekends. Then again, what if the old stick really was in trouble? I tossed the condoms back in the drawer and went to check out the bathroom. I was searching the medicine cabinet—the usual dull prescriptions—when from downstairs I heard a door open and close.

Maudie was in the kitchen, drinking a glass of water. As I came through the door, she stiffened with alarm. "Maudie," I said quickly, "it's me, Leo. I knocked but no one answered. I was just looking upstairs."

"Leo, what a surprise." She did not sound as if it were an entirely pleasant one. "Does Roman know you're here?"

Clearly he was not on his deathbed. I repeated the story I'd told Sam, that I had an audition in Edinburgh. "When I spoke to Roman on the phone he said I couldn't come all this way and not see you. Perhaps he was joking? Anyway I jumped on a bus and then one of your neighbours, a tall woman with stringy hair, gave me a lift."

"I'm sure he wasn't joking. That must have been Margaret." Maudie put the glass down, came across and kissed my cheek. I caught a whiff of her herbal shampoo. That she didn't know about my visit only made it more intriguing; I was Roman's sole confidant.

Maudie offered coffee. "Great," I said. "Where were you?"

"Out in my pottery. You haven't been here for ages, have you? We converted the milkshed two years ago. I'm waiting for the kiln to heat up so I can glaze a batch of bowls."

I watched her as she walked to the stove. She wore a faded red shirt and black leggings, but the contents of the bedside drawers had educated me. Beneath her baggy clothes and business-like manner, my sister-in-law was sexy.

•   •   •

Sexy, repeated Ewan, and felt a twinge of discomfort. Then he thought he was just being his usual fuddy-duddy self. Mollie was probably flattered. In the next chapter, Roman came home from work—he was head of marketing for a distillery—and the three of them had dinner. Only after Maudie had gone to bed did Roman begin to reveal his reasons for the urgent phone call. Far away in Boston, Aunt Helen, their father's sister, claimed to be dying.

. . .

"She's made me her heir," Roman announced. "Actually heir apparent."

"Shit," I said. "Do you mean I've come five hundred miles to hear that you're going to inherit more dosh? Roman, I thought you were dying. All that mystery on the phone. I was sure you had the big C." At that instant I really did hate him: his pudgy, comfortable job, his nice little wifey. "I didn't even have the money for the train," I told him.

Roman clapped his hand to his forehead. He ought to have been the actor in the family. "Why didn't you ask?"

"I told you. I thought it was a crisis. You phone for the first time in a year, whispering can I come at once. What am I going to say? I'm too sodding broke?"

"I'm sorry. I'm a thoughtless idiot." He started to laugh. In the candlelight his face glowed. I had never seen him look healthier.

"What's so funny?" I said at last.

"Us. You and me. As a matter of fact I'm tickled that you worried about me."

"Why don't you buy me a train ticket tomorrow and I'll get out of here?" I said crossly. "I know by your standards I'm wasting my life, but there's plenty of places I'd rather waste it." I finished my whisky and prepared to stand up.

"No, no, wait. I'm making a hash of this but I do have a good reason for inviting you—much better than what you so delicately call the big C. Here." He pushed the Glen Turret in my direction. "Have another drink."

Roman has always been a line-on-the-bottle kind of guy, so letting me loose on his best Scotch signalled something pretty serious. I poured myself a hefty measure and waited.

"Let me start again," he said. "Aunt Helen is eighty-seven. She's a wealthy woman, and out of some kind of sentiment and having no children of her own, she's made me her heir. I checked with her lawyer—you know how everyone in the States has a lawyer—and it's all above-board. Except for a couple of small bequests to charity, she's leaving everything to me."

"How much is everything?"

"Somewhere between five hundred thousand and a million dollars. It depends on house prices, stock prices. More than enough to take trouble over."

"And trouble, I suppose, signals my entrance."

"As a matter of fact it does. Unfortunately this turns out to be yet another example of the no free lunch philosophy. Helen has her price, and her price is—"

"A visit from the devoted heir."

"Not just a visit, a generous visit, demonstrating a proper desire to spend time in her company before the grim reaper shows up."

I gave up trying to guess ahead. I sipped my whisky and imagined what it would be like to sit in this kitchen night after night, drinking and talking, and then go upstairs to Maudie and the bedside drawers. It didn't seem so bad.

"So," said Roman, "how do you feel about a fortnight's holiday in Boston, all expenses paid?"

I set down my glass and gaped at him.

Now that he'd let the cat out of the bag, he couldn't shut up. He would pay my expenses, plus five hundred quid, to impersonate him. And when the inheritance came through, I'd get a cut. Finally I recovered sufficiently to interrupt. "Roman, have you gone starkers? Why would Helen think I was you for a second?"

"Because you'll say you are. She hasn't seen me in a dozen years and she's blind as a bat. We've sent her a few family photos but nothing recent, no close-ups. All you need to do is shave your beard, borrow my clothes and we're in business. You're an actor, right?" He smiled. "This role is tailor-made for you."

I asked why he didn't go himself and he explained if it was just a long weekend he'd go like a shot, but a fortnight off work was out of the question. The distillery was in the midst of a major reshuffle. Several senior managers had already been axed and he was afraid, if he gave them the slightest excuse, he'd be next. Of course only Roman would fret over his boring job after winning the pools. "I tried to tell Helen I'd come in April," he said. "She launched into a dirge about not lasting the winter. But according to her lawyer she's in excellent health; she might live another ten years."

He went on to list the airline reservations he'd made for me. I listened in amazement. It was a crazy scheme and the craziest part was that Roman, my pompous, proper brother, had dreamed it up. *The Joy of Sex* was just the start. "What on earth gave you this idea?" I asked.

Roman grinned. "Maudie and I saw a film on TV in which one brother impersonates another. When I said you and I could never do that, she said, nonsense, we were as alike as two peas in a pod, we just presented ourselves differently. That got me thinking. I realised maybe I didn't have to choose between my job and half a million dollars." Poor old Roman, what a heartbreaking choice.

He picked up the bottle of Glen Turret and spun it like you do in children's games. The neck of the bottle swung towards me. "I know it's a lot to ask," he said.

. . .

A creaking sound made Ewan glance up from the page. Someone was going downstairs; the kitchen door opened and closed.
He lay listening, trying to guess from the faint noises what
Mollie was doing. Having a stiff drink, perhaps? No, in that respect she was like him, too much of a puritan to turn to drink
in times of disaster. Then he remembered the baby and the
Dunkirk humour of colleagues, joking about the sleepless
nights of new parenthood. He wondered if he should offer assis-
tance, but the prospect of leaving the warmth he had, at last,
generated beneath the covers was not appealing. To justify his
decision, he closed *The Dark Forest* and turned out the light.

The baby had been a distraction, he thought; still, he was
glad he had rescued her. Tomorrow, first thing, they would return to Perth and hand her over to the police or the social services. Time enough then to figure out what to do about Mollie.
The room was very dark. He stretched out his arm and could
not see his hand. In London, even at three a.m. a reassuring twi-
light seeped through the curtains. What had Mollie said in her
letter? That the darkness was like gas. More like water, Ewan
pondered: a cold, black, saltless sea.

Chapter 4

As soon as she opened her eyes, Mollie knew it was still raining. She was murmuring her thanks to the gods of Scottish weather, when from the far side of the bed came a whimper. "Good morning," she whispered. She reached out her hand to stroke the small head. "Did you sleep well? What did you dream about?" The baby was quick to answer. "Baaa," she said. "Grrh." Before she could become committed to crying, Mollie slipped out of bed and carried her downstairs.

While waiting for the kettle to boil, she drew the grey curtains. Not only was it raining steadily, but the sky had the pitiless quality of steel wool that usually betokened rain until late in the day. When she opened the door to let Sadie out, the collie barely raised her head above the rim of her basket. Chae used to say that Sadie had weather announcers in her dreams, so surely could she divine bad weather without leaving her bed. Mollie let her be and settled into the armchair beside the stove, with the baby and a bottle. "We must give you a name," she said. "This business of your not having one is just too inconvenient."

The baby fluttered her dark eyelashes. Mollie stared down at the coppery face. "Robin," she said, "Daphne, Diana, Gretel, Jane, Hannah, Louise, Emma, Sally, Merril, Veronica." They all seemed wrong, because they were the names of people she knew. There were families, even entire religions, in which children were named after other people, living or dead, but to ask this baby, who already had so little, to share a name was intolerable.

The baby broke off feeding and calmly dribbled a stream of milk onto Mollie's shoulder. Olivia, thought Mollie. Something about the milky O of the tiny lips made the name spring to mind. She wiped her chin and perched her on the edge of the table so they were looking into each other's eyes.

"Olivia," she said. "What do you think of your name?"

Olivia smiled and reached out to pat Mollie's cheek.

Mollie had come downstairs shortly after six. Now several millennia passed as she waited for Ewan to appear. His lateness fitted perfectly with her plans, but with every decade of delay her frustration rose. She wanted matters settled, at least for today, and they couldn't be until she had dealt with Ewan. At ten-fifteen he opened the door, still in pyjamas, to ask if there was enough hot water for a bath. Plenty, said Mollie. Another half hour elapsed before he returned, wearing the same clothes as the day before.

"I don't know what came over me," he said, shaking his head. "I haven't slept this late in years."

"Not to worry. I'm glad you got some rest. If people from the States really do call at one in the morning, it must be hard to get a good night's sleep. Coffee?"

"Please."

Only once he had helped himself to coffee and was seated at the table did Ewan take notice of Olivia. "How is she? I hope she didn't keep you awake. I heard you come downstairs in the middle of the night."

Mollie ran her hand through her hair and felt the reassuring tug of the follicles. "Those damn stairs," she said. "I had to get her a bottle and change her. Afterwards she slept right through until six." She longed to try out Olivia's name on Ewan but managed to contain herself. What was the point of a name if they were taking her to Perth today? Careful, she said to herself, and then, aloud, "Cereal? Toast?"

"Cereal's fine." He went to the cupboard and, after a moment's deliberation, selected Chae's favourite muesli; Mollie felt vindicated in her parsimonious decision not to throw it out. The morning Chae left, she'd been tempted to eliminate everything he had touched or laid eyes on, a scorched-earth policy that would have meant her living, naked, in an empty house.

Ewan sat down at the table. A leaflet protesting a nearby bauxite mine lay against the salt and pepper. He picked it up. Mollie poured herself more coffee and took the chair opposite. As she watched him reading the leaflet and briskly spooning up cereal, she thought no one within a hundred miles would mistake her brother for anything other than a bachelor.

"I don't understand this," he said. "Why are people opposed to the mine? It sounds as if it's way up in the hills."

Hell's bells, thought Mollie. In an effort to conceal her impatience, she stood up and went over to the sink. She stared at the lilac bushes outside the window and explained that the mine lacked an access road. "They'd have to build one, and they estimate thirty lorries a day in the first year. No farmer wants that kind of traffic across his land."

"How strange that access wasn't part of the original mining rights."

"I suppose." Eat, she silently commanded. "It's an American company, so there wouldn't even be local jobs."

"You know, someone in the City was telling me that they've found gold on the west coast. They're digging a mine near Ullapool."

"A gold mine!" Mollie turned from the window. For a moment she was genuinely captivated. She pictured galleries veined with gold, leading to some dark chamber where the Picts had piled a gleaming hoard of cups and necklaces.

"I was amazed too," Ewan said. "Mining gold seems like growing oranges, something you oughtn't to be able to do in a cold climate. Do you remember that Easter holiday when we went to the gardens at Inverewe and saw the palm trees and pineapples?"

"Yes. I got a prize for an essay I wrote about it. And we each tried to grow date palms. Only Bridget's came up."

"She had the warmest bedroom, above the kitchen. No wonder."

"You sound grumpy." Mollie laughed.

"I am a bit. I mean, I was the youngest and yet they put me in the attic to freeze just because I was a boy. That's why I turned out such a recluse." He tried to join in her laughter, but she saw him tuck in his chin in a hurt gesture.

He carried his bowl to the sink and, ignoring the other dishes, rinsed it and placed it in the dishwasher. Mollie was reminded of Daniel and Rebecca, who had performed exactly these tasks at the end of every meal, irrespective of how many dishes, pots, and pans lay scattered around. Then she thought of her little brother lying shivering in the attic while downstairs she and Bridget scampered back and forth between each other's rooms, sharing barrettes and secrets. She had always blithely assumed that Ewan's childhood was more or less similar to her own. Now it came to her how vastly different their experiences might have been.

"Well," Ewan said, closing the dishwasher, "enough of this dawdling. Time to get under way." From his breast pocket he produced a notebook and pen. He flipped open the notebook and clicked the pen expectantly. "Did you have a chance to make any phone calls?"

Mollie's chest tightened. "No, no, I didn't. I'm sorry. I just . . . I didn't know where to start."

"Of course," Ewan said, instantly soothing. "No reason why you should. I'm the one who got us into this pickle. Do you have a phone book?"

"There's one in the study, and a phone too."

"Excellent. I'll get another cup of coffee and set to work. If that's all right with you?" His whole manner had changed. Chae used to joke about Ewan's ineptitude—he couldn't build a stone wall, plant a row of potatoes, prune an apple tree—but Mollie glimpsed that in his own territory, Ewan might be wonderfully effective. She could see him keeping track of facts and figures with dogged accuracy, analysing situations in penetrating detail. Stop, she wanted to say; go back to being incompetent.

He made a couple of notes. "Is there anything else we need to do for her?"

"Do?"

"Yes, for the baby. Once I've contacted the appropriate people, are we ready to leave? Does she need feeding?" He flapped a hand. "Whatever?"

There it was again, that misleading vagueness. I have to be very careful, thought Mollie. This isn't my bumbling younger brother. This is an international banker, a conservative who believes passionately in law, order, and private education. But two can play this game. He has his notebook; I have my neuroses. She wrung her hands and quavered that she would organise the baby.

At once Ewan grew soothing again. "There's no rush. I expect I'll have to call around to find the baby people."

Soon after he left the room, Olivia woke from sleep into bad temper. Perhaps, like Sadie, she received messages in her dreams, and sensed herself to be the subject of Ewan's phone calls. She began crying at twenty past eleven and was still going strong when he returned downstairs at quarter to twelve. By which time Mollie was wretched with fear. Suppose something was seriously wrong with Olivia. She could have caught some disease, lying on the lavatory floor. Or been abandoned in the first place because she was ill. What did she, Mollie, really know about babies? There wasn't even a book in the house to consult. Colic, croup, scarlet fever, diphtheria, pneumonia, on and on stretched the list of possible ailments she had never witnessed and had no idea how to treat. When at last the door opened and Ewan stepped into the room, she felt immense relief.

"What's this?" He frowned. "Is she hungry?"

"I don't think so. She refused a bottle, and her nappy is clean. My theory is she's out of sorts. . . . Aren't you?"

Ewan's presence made it easier to resume her facade of competence. She held up Olivia and peered into the small face, streaked with tears. At that moment, astonishingly, the crying stopped. Olivia hiccuped twice and grew quiet.

In the lull, Ewan reported his discoveries. The social services office was closed until Monday. As for the police, they'd kept him on hold for ten minutes. "I finally spoke to a sergeant with a Glaswegian accent you could cut with a knife. There didn't seem to be any reports of a missing baby."

Christ, thought Mollie. In all her intricate scheming, the possibility of his reporting Olivia over the phone had never occurred to her. This is Ewan Munro, she heard him saying. I found a baby girl, three or four months old. We're at my sister's. And then her name and address. "Ewan," she said hoarsely, "you didn't tell him, did you?"

"Not exactly. The sergeant was so brusque. I thought it would be easier to explain in person." He fiddled with his shirt cuffs, refusing to meet her gaze.

And suddenly Mollie guessed what must have happened: confronted by a rude stranger, Ewan had begun to stutter. She wanted to fling her arms around him. Instead she kissed Olivia.

"At this point," Ewan said, "I've no idea if we're Good Samaritans or criminals."

"Good Samaritans," said Mollie, laughing with relief.

They took turns holding Olivia and getting ready. When Ewan came downstairs, Mollie noticed he'd put on a tie and was carrying his briefcase. Perhaps he hoped these talismans of respectability would protect him from any charge of deviancy. She herself wore what Daniel and Rebecca used to call her uniform: black leggings, black lace-up boots, and a navy-blue sweater that came to mid-thigh, all topped off with a Burberry and a black beret. She wrapped Olivia in several blankets and packed a bag with a bottle and nappies.

Ewan opened the back door, and they stepped out into the blustery day. Instantly Mollie's face was wet with rain. She struggled to hold on to her beret with one hand and shield Olivia with the other. "Good grief," said Ewan. "You'd never know it was April."

They hurried to the car. He climbed into the back seat and did up his seat belt; she passed him Olivia. Then she got into the driver's seat, fastened her own seat belt, put the car in neutral, and turned the key. The engine spluttered. She pumped the accelerator and tried again. A fainter splutter. "It's the rain," she said. "I should've put the damn thing in the garage last night."

"Not to worry. Wait a minute and have another go." He started to hum "Waltzing Matilda." Mollie rubbed periodically at the windscreen, which was steaming up already. "Third time lucky," she offered.

The same subdued coughing greeted her efforts. "I'm not sure it's going to start in this downpour," she said in a small voice, not daring to glance at Ewan. She kept her eyes fixed on the mileage gauge: 53,496, she said to herself, 53,496. Ewan was right, there was something comforting about numbers, their firm, unchanging completeness.

"Not to worry," he repeated, in such even tones that she could not stop herself from turning around. At the sight of him sitting there, holding Olivia, his briefcase beside him, she realised to her amazement that Ewan was genuinely calm. Probably he'd read some time-and-motion study proving that anger was inefficient. In his place she would have been, however uselessly, enraged. "Let's go inside to strategise," he said. "It's stupid to sit out here in the cold."

Back in the kitchen, he handed Olivia to Mollie and wiped his glasses. "I'm freezing," he said, and went to stand beside the stove.

"Me too. I hope Ol—" she caught herself—"the baby is okay."

She unwrapped Olivia's blankets and put her down in the chair. Then she took off her own coat and beret. "I feel such an idiot," she said. "All winter I've been keeping the car in the garage, and now, the one time we need it, I forget."

"Let's phone the AA. Or your local garage? They'll have a tow service."

"No point. This has happened before, and there's nothing to be done. The mechanic told me it's a common problem with Fiats. All you can do is wait for the engine to dry out."

"Don't be upset," Ewan said. "Who knew the rain would keep up?" He paused to take off his glasses and polish them a second time. "Do you think between us we'd be able to push the car inside?"

"I'm sure we can. But let's get warm first?" She allowed her teeth to chatter a couple of times.

"Of course. Come and stand by the stove."

He made room for her, and they stood shoulder-to-shoulder. Now what? wondered Mollie. And quickly thought, Act feeble. Be frail. It's your best chance. The warmth of the stove was like a large hot hand against her back, yet she kept shivering for as long as possible. Beside her, Ewan again was humming "Waltzing Matilda." Beneath the table, Sadie whined in her sleep.

"I'd never really noticed what a sad song that is," said Ewan. "There must be some alternative. Could we borrow the Youngs' car for a couple of hours?"

"No," Mollie burst out, then embellished truthfully: "Last year Chae asked them for a loan of their car to pick up Daniel—ours was being serviced—and they got awfully stroppy. Mr. Young made a long speech about neither a borrower nor a lender be."

"How ridiculous. What did they think you were going to do—take it drag racing? Well, let's hire a car. There are a couple of places in the town, aren't there? I'll go and phone to see what's available."

He was already stepping away from the stove. "Ewan," she called.

He stopped to look at her, and she buried her face in her hands. "I can't fucking drive," she sobbed. "I can't. The birds will get us."

At once he was beside her, patting her awkwardly. "Mollie, don't cry. There's nothing to cry about. Hush, hush."

She felt him move away. Then he was back with a box of Kleenex and a glass of water. "Drink this," he said.

Gradually she let her sobs die down. She drank some water and blew her nose. "I can't drive," she repeated.

"No, of course not. No one's asking you to. I just wasn't thinking." He was gazing at her ruefully. "It seems daft that I never learned. I even took driving lessons for a while."

"You did?" Mollie exclaimed. "I always thought you had no interest. Chae said it was your sole ecological virtue, that you couldn't tell one end of a car from the other."

"I'm afraid it's nothing so laudable. On my third lesson, this elderly woman stepped into a zebra crossing in the Caledonian Road. I came within a hand's breadth of knocking her down. She had the most beautiful white hair. I can still see the fear on her face. She reminded me of Miss Gibson, the French teacher at school. After that I never wanted to drive again." He adjusted his cuffs. "No ecology involved, I'm afraid."

"But Ewan, everybody has narrow escapes. I think of myself as a fairly careful driver, and I've nearly hit a football stadium's worth of pedestrians by now."

"Other people say that too, but I'm just not up to it. I'll do my harm in other ways."

Mollie was still pondering these revelations when Ewan suggested a taxi. Isn't he ever going to give up? she thought. She blew her nose again and said that taxis for Perth had to be booked at least twenty-four hours in advance. Without waiting to see the effect of this fabrication, she carried the kettle to the sink, filled it, and brought it back to the stove.

She stared at the hot plate. If she didn't move, if she didn't speak, he would capitulate. She was so engrossed in her side of the bargain that her brother's words, when he at last uttered them, came to her wrapped in a warm, dark fog. Something about the best solution. Something about Monday. Abandoned. Won't be a bother. Make no difference.

Then the fog thinned and lightened. What was this? Oh, this was silence. Mollie realised he was expecting an answer. She let out her breath in a long, slow sigh. Don't show jubilation. Sound a bit put upon. "I suppose you're right," she said. "Fortunately I bought food for the whole weekend. And enough nappies."

"Jolly good. Let's get the car under cover so we can settle in."

Mollie put the soup on the stove for lunch and made sure Olivia was wedged safely in the chair. Taking the reluctant Sadie with them, they went out to push the car. Though the wind had picked up, Mollie no longer felt the cold. She wound down the driver's window and let off the hand brake. Then she joined Ewan to heave and strain against the back bumper. "One, two, three," he commanded. Slowly the car rolled forward through the mud.

The three of them spent the afternoon in the kitchen. Ewan took over the table and spread out the contents of his briefcase in neat piles. Olivia waved her arms and daydreamed. Mollie watched her and pretended to reread *Pride and Prejudice*, the safest book she could think of, but even Austen's felicitous wit could not hold her attention. What she wanted to do was talk to Olivia aloud. She had already spent too much time listening to her own voice inside her head; she needed to hear her words take shape in the air, travel towards another person. If she could have spoken, she would have told Olivia about the remarkable coincidence she had just become aware of, namely that they were both foundlings. Well, not quite a foundling in Mollie's case, no lavatory floors and police stations for her, but close enough. After Bridget was born, her mother had suffered a series of miscarriages and in despair had turned to adoption, only to find herself, a year later, carrying Ewan to term. Mollie thought about this so seldom that she had lived with Chae for three years before mentioning it to him; now, given Olivia's advent, it seemed hugely significant. We must bide our time, she murmured, and imagined the words floating into Olivia's sweetly coiled brain.

At four o'clock she made tea. When she carried a mug to Ewan, he roused himself from his papers and wandered to the window. "I think it's clearing up," he said. "Would you like to go for a walk?"

As soon as he spoke, he cut her one of his nervous glances—

remembering, she guessed, her earlier outburst. She was tempted to tell him that his mere presence would keep the birds away. Instead she said, "Good idea. We could use some fresh air."

When they'd finished their tea, Mollie loaned Ewan Chae's gardening boots. His feet were so small that he had to borrow a second pair of socks. She herself went out to the scullery to fetch her jacket and returned to tuck Olivia inside. "Oh, you're bringing her," Ewan remarked, sounding surprised.

Mollie stared. "What did you think we'd do with her?"

"I thought if Sadie was coming, she'd be fine on her own for a few minutes. I mean, it's not like she can set the house on fire." He smiled. "Don't listen to me. I don't know the first thing about babies. I just keep forgetting about her."

"As long as one of us remembers," said Mollie, and smiled back.

Sadie circled them excitedly. Without discussion, they took the path that led to St. David's Well. It zigzagged in wide bends up the hill behind the house, through the beech woods and rhododendrons. By the time they reached the well, half a mile away, Olivia was sound asleep. The small pool of water emerged, cold and clear, out of the rocks at the foot of a steep crag.

"Why is it called a well, again?" Ewan asked, and Mollie explained that according to local legend the pool was fed by an underground river from a lake far up in the hills. "The lake is the home of the old king's daughters, and if you throw in a coin and make a wish, they'll do their best to grant it. Last summer Daniel and Rebecca spent an afternoon here with a fishing net. They got about two quid, I think."

She held Olivia close with one arm and felt in her pocket for change, but before she could find any, Ewan handed her a fifty-pence piece. "We'd better take advantage of this," he said. "I need all the help I can get."

Silently, they threw. The coins slipped with two small

splashes into the water and disappeared in the leafy bottom. Mollie was too preoccupied with her own wishes to wonder what sort of help her brother might need. Later she recalled what she had failed to notice at the time: the earnest expression on his face and the utter seriousness with which he spoke.

They were nearly back at the house when Sadie, who had raced ahead, pranced up with something in her mouth. "What have you got?" said Ewan. "Here, drop it. Good dog."

At their feet Sadie let fall a limp mass of brown feathers.

Mollie was about to burst into her customary exhortations. Then she looked more closely. "Oh my God. It's Richard Tiger."

Clutching Olivia, she walked, almost running, across the grass to the duck pond, and there, scattered along the bank, lay the other three ducks. She stepped from bird to bird, bending down beside each one. "I left them out last night," she managed to say. "A fox must have got them."

Chapter 5

Although not given to optimism in any guise, Ewan had been cautiously pleased with the way his visit was unfolding. This highly inconvenient trip north seemed to be paying off. Mollie was fragile but not in the extreme state of wretchedness he had feared from her garbled letter, and even that letter was more understandable now that he'd witnessed her isolation and the odd jerky flight of the rooks and jackdaws swooping by the house. During the afternoon he had managed to draft a report, which gave him the illusion life at the office was somewhat under control, at least until Vanessa crossed his mind. Still, all of that was five hundred miles away. More immediately troubling was the business of the baby. There was, he knew, something wrong with what they were doing. They should've handed her over at once to the authorities, but given Mollie's condition and the various other constraints, he saw no way to accomplish this. That morning, when he tried to tell the Glaswegian sergeant about the baby, he had not been able to get past "I want to report a . . ." Then every letter he attempted reared up high as the deer fences behind Mill of Fortune. "Is this your idea of a joke, sonny?" the sergeant had demanded into his choked silence, and put down the phone.

Ewan had stood holding the empty receiver, instantly returned to the many humiliations of his childhood. Back then his stutter had plagued him to such an extent that his parents had given him extra money for the bus because he sometimes ended up paying more for the first stop his tongue would fit around. Now he stuttered only occasionally, and what he tended to lose was not bus stops but the vocabulary of his trade, for which he had a practised list of alternatives: "yearly" for "annual," "rate" for "percentage." On the phone, however, he had drawn a total blank on synonyms for "baby." Small person? he thought, after he hung up. Very young human? When the car failed to start, he had considered phoning back, only to feel himself grow mute at the mere memory of the sergeant's contempt. Surely, he repeated silently, another day's delay could not make much difference. And there was no doubt that the baby was helping his sister.

Then Sadie had shown up with a dead duck. Mollie began to weep profusely for the second time in a few hours and, between sobs, to blame herself. Ewan stood by helplessly on the muddy bank of the pond. "It's not your fault," he kept saying with transparent falsity. The amazing thing was that something like this had not happened sooner. Finally the baby began to cry too, and he told Mollie to take her inside. "I'll bury them," he said.

She stumbled off across the sodden grass, while he fetched a spade from the gardening shed. When he came back, Sadie was investigating another of the bodies. "No, Sadie, drop it," he said and, to his surprise, she did. He was tempted to throw the ducks on the compost heap, or simply bury them in the vegetable garden, where the soil was soft, but some obscure sense of duty made him carry them to the orchard. As he laid them under one of the apple trees, he noticed that they were more or less unmarked by their ordeal; the fox had broken their necks and made not the slightest effort to eat them. This had been done for sport, Ewan thought, with a mixture of admiration and disapproval.

He prospected, trying the ground, until he found a place, roughly equidistant between two trees, where the spade went in with relative ease. Sadie, after a second reprimand, left the bodies alone and settled down on the wet grass, her paws neatly crossed, to observe his labours. He measured out a small square and pushed down on the spade. What were they called, again? Richard Tiger, Albertine, Lucifer (known as Lucy) . . . and the fourth? For the life of him, Ewan was unable to bring the name to mind. Millie? Mabel? Marguerite, or maybe Marvin? The ducks had been named, without regard for gender, by Chae's children. The forgetfulness nagged at him, but he could not ask Mollie, at least for a while.

Other things, however, he would ask. In order to extricate her from this absurd house, he needed to know her financial situation. When their parents died, six years ago within a few months of one another, each of the three siblings had received a little over thirty thousand pounds. Ewan had offered to invest the sum on behalf of his sisters. Both had turned him down. Bridget had taken her share to the States to start a printing business, but he had no idea what Mollie had done with hers. She and Chae had gone to Tangiers for a holiday, but that could hardly have cost more than a few hundred pounds. Now he suspected the entire sum had been frittered away on livestock and Wellington boots. Was that the point of her long speech, last night, about the cost of hens? Whatever mismanagement was revealed, he promised himself, he would not lose his temper.

And a job must be found for Mollie, some satisfying occupation that would earn her a living, though he could certainly support her through this transitional period. Well, not certainly, he thought, touching the wooden handle of the spade for luck. She'd been so young when she met Chae, still muddling around in the temporary jobs of an ex-student. Then they'd moved to Mill of Fortune and she'd become a part-time stepmother, a gardener, a weaver, active in various local causes—a graceful, sensible life that had often made Ewan feel like a grubby materialist, but all of which, it now emerged, was based on her relationship with Chae. Without him, nothing was left. Even the weaving, at which Mollie was both skilled and successful, was somehow inextricably connected with her difficult mate.

He looked down at the hole and over at the pile of ducks. A little deeper, he decided, stooping to remove a stone. He'd forgotten what hard work digging was. Didn't children have some story about how you could dig through to China—no, it was Australia. And when you emerged on the other side of the earth, you would walk upside down. Ewan couldn't remember ever believing this; an Edinburgh childhood was inimical to such fantasies. He'd built towers out of Lego blocks and Meccano bridges—large, sensible structures—while his sisters painted and made papier-mâché animals and wrote plays. Suddenly he recalled *The Dark Forest*. The book seemed like a good way to broach the difficult topic of Chae.

He lifted out a few more stones and, judging the grave ready, laid in the ducks one by one. There was something melancholy about the brown plumage mingling with the dark soil, but by the time he'd shovelled the earth back in and piled the loose stones on top, his sadness had given way to satisfaction. The apple trees were just coming into leaf, and he remembered the excellent cider Mollie had used to make. As he returned the spade to the shed, he realised he was not yet ready to go back indoors. Inside lay difficulties and tears, the demands of the baby, Mollie's wobbly state, and his own problems, which might gain the upper hand at any moment.

"Come on, Sadie." He whistled, starting up the hill again.

The dog followed at heel until it was clear he was indeed going for a walk, then darted ahead.

This time Ewan ignored the path and climbed directly through the woods. He glimpsed Sadie as she nosed back and forth among the damp leaves that covered the ground. He heard rustling nearby and, once, further off, the sound of a branch breaking: a bird, perhaps, or a rabbit. Chae had told him the deer were plentiful, but you never saw them if you took the dog. He climbed on, breathing hard, until he reached the path and followed it west to the edge of the moors. On his last visit, the previous summer, he'd walked an entire day and met no one. To-day he went only a short distance, just far enough to experience the heather underfoot and hear the peculiar singing of the wind as it travelled mile after empty mile across the bare hills. Several small birds flew up from beneath his feet, and a pair of grouse hurtled into ungainly flight with their barking cries.

Back at the house, he was taking off Chae's boots in the scullery when Mollie flung open the inner door and seized his arm, nearly toppling him. "Where were you? I called and called, and you didn't come."

"I walked up the hill with Sadie. I'm sorry, I didn't think you'd notice. But it's all right, Mollie. I'm here. Everything's fine."

He took off his second boot and led her back into the kitchen, promising a fresh pot of tea. Mollie sat at the table without a word. Except for a livid blotch on each cheek, her face was pale as chalk. He could hear her tremulous breathing. "Last month," he said, swirling hot water into the teapot, "I was at a concert with Aunt Hester and Uncle Godfrey, and there was a man in the row behind us who'd been at Harrow with Godfrey." He ignored a gulping sound. "I wish you'd heard the two of them calling each other Tubby and Owl-eyes. But what was really interesting was that afterwards Godfrey was terribly upset at how ancient the other chap looked. Hester and I pointed out that his own hair is grey, that he uses a hearing aid, but it didn't help. He still felt Tubby had betrayed him. Here you are," he concluded, passing Mollie a mug of tea.

"Thanks." The hectic colour of her cheeks had faded a little. She took a sip and said, "I think we should name her Olivia."

"Name who?" For a confused second he thought she was referring to the ducks.

"The baby, of course. Just for the next twenty-four hours. I can't stand calling her it or she or baby."

"Won't she have a name? Even if her parents didn't want her, they must've called her something." He saw Mollie's eyes grow watery—was it at the notion of the baby being unwanted?

"Please," she said.

"Olivia is a lovely name," he said quickly. "I think it suits her." If his sister had suggested Quasimodo, Ewan would have praised her choice. He watched, baffled, as her face brightened. Such a small thing, but wasn't inappropriate affect one of the classic signs of disturbance? Not being able to distinguish the crucial from the trivial? He remembered his earlier plan of using Chae's novel to introduce awkward subjects and, with some idea of beginning on this task, said, "I started *The Dark Forest* last night. It's interesting to read about a place you know."

It was as if he had pressed a lever, ejecting Mollie from her chair. She shot to her feet. There was a crash, and the mug she'd been holding lay shattered on the stone floor. Ewan thought she might start to cry again, but her face, still pale, was set with fury.

At school Mollie had been famous for her temper. Once, she had brought her satchel down so hard on the head of a rival that the girl had fallen out of her desk. And at university, one time when Ewan met her for a drink, her left hand had been swathed in bandages. "Oh, Neal and I had a row," she'd said airily. Neal, her current boyfriend, was a burly young man from a Welsh mining family.

"But what about your hand?" Ewan demanded. "Did he hurt you?"

"No." Mollie blushed. "I smashed a window. It was either it or him."

Later, when he recounted this to Bridget, she had laughed and said, "Thank goodness Mollie isn't a boy. She'd always be getting into fights. You know," she added, "sometimes I wonder if it has to do with her being adopted. I've never heard Mum or Dad raise their voices, and you and I may sulk, but we don't shout. But Mollie, mostly she's quiet as a mouse and then, occasionally, it's just like fireworks. She scares me."

Now Ewan sat at the table, not moving or speaking, afraid of what she might do next.

"You can read the book," she said in a stifled voice. "In fact it's a good thing if you do. Then you'll know . . ." But she did not explain what his new knowledge would consist of.

He counted to thirty before fetching a dustpan and brush and kneeling at her feet to sweep up the pieces of blue pottery. Fortunately the baby, awoken by the crash, uttered a lusty yell. As Mollie bent over her, the frightening anger left her face. "Olivia," she cooed, "you're awake."

She picked her up and circled the room, talking softly. Had Olivia liked the walk? What would she like to do next? How about supper? A story? She was in the midst of this prattle when the phone rang. The sound startled Ewan almost as much as the fallen mug. Since his arrival there had been no phone calls. Mollie hesitated, as if of two minds whether to answer, then stepped out into the hall, still holding the baby.

If Ewan had been asked to justify why he listened so keenly, he would've claimed his deep concern for Mollie's well-being. He was hoping the caller was a friend, someone who would relieve his burdensome sense of being her sole support. He heard her say, "Hello" and "Yes, my brother. I'm afraid I didn't catch your name." Her voice was anxious, tentative. There was a pause. Then her tone changed. "Who is this?" she said sharply. "No, that won't be necessary." He heard the click of the phone being replaced, and silence.

Ewan stood holding the dustpan and brush, waiting for her to return. What was she doing out there—thinking about calling back? Crying? At last she stepped through the door, clasping the baby tightly with both arms. She was biting her lower lip. "Who was it?" he said, bending to retrieve a splinter of china.

"Brr, it's cold out there. I don't know—some crank."

"A salesman? A heavy breather?"

"No, no, nothing like that. A local farmer was having an argument with Chae about a right-of-way. I seem to have inherited the quarrel. I think you or Sadie must have walked across his land."

"We just walked up the forestry track to the moors."

"Probably it was Sadie. He's a bit mad on the subject. He wants us to keep her on a lead the whole time. Anyway, thanks for cleaning up the mess. The mug slipped through my fingers. I'm afraid any mention of Chae has a bad effect on me. And as for the book. Well . . ." She trailed off. "You'll see."

It was then that Ewan knew she was lying. She had a secret, a secret she wanted to keep from him so badly she was prepared even to talk about Chae. What could it be, he wondered, and should he press her? He fetched a floor cloth to wipe up the tea. As he reached for a distant splash, it occurred to him that perhaps her mendacity was a good sign, an indication of returning sanity, of independence. Yes, Mollie was prepared to lie to him.

That night he went up to bed as early as possible. He yawned and praised the country air in an effort to conceal his motives, but no advertisement could have made him as eager to read *The Dark Forest* as the mug his sister had dropped or, more likely, hurled at the kitchen floor. While putting the floor cloth away he had discovered a hot-water bottle—the British substitute for sex, one of his Italian clients had joked—and with this at his feet, he sat up in bed and gave the novel the kind of attention he usually reserved for financial reports. Of course Leo had agreed to his brother's proposition.

. . .

Next morning at breakfast Roman broke the news to Maudie. From his blustering tone I guessed he was edgy about her reaction. He thumped the table and at one point—tut-tut—even used the word *damn*. The night before he'd swept me along. Now, amidst the cornflakes and coffee, my older brother was turning into a certifiable nutter before my very eyes. As for Maudie, she didn't have a second's doubt. "What's got into you, Roman?" she said. "This is the stupidest thing I ever heard of."

"But it was your idea," he protested. "When we saw that film, you said Leo and I could easily pass for each other."

"I said the two of you weren't as different as you both like to pretend. You know perfectly well I wasn't suggesting anything like this. It's absurd, it's wrong, and, what's more, it won't work. People don't go around impersonating each other, or if they do, they don't fool anyone."

"The fact it's absurd is precisely why it will work. We're only trying to fool one person and she's eighty-seven. If Leo claims to be me, why would Helen doubt him for a second?" He glared at us in turn. Neither of us spoke. I pretended intense interest in the marmalade jar and Maudie stared back at him. "I know you like to rise above material things," he went on, "but half a million dollars would make quite a difference to us. Just because I'm not artistic, it doesn't follow I want to spend the rest of my life selling whisky."

Maudie blushed and I realised he was making a dig about supporting her. I heard her knuckles crack, clickety-click. "And you can't go yourself?" she asked in a low voice.

"Not in the way Helen wants. We've had three redundancies in my department in the last month. Even if I could talk David into letting me go, I wouldn't risk it."

She turned to me. "And what about you, Leo? What's your excuse for this insanity?"

"Money," I blurted out, not knowing what else to say.

I thought I'd really put my foot in it, but Maudie seemed to relent. "You're both cuckoo," she laughed. "It must run in the family. I'm off to the pottery. Call me when it's lunchtime."

Over coffee we set out to prepare my script. Roman was the worst possible collaborator. Helen took me to the museum, he said. She hates Whistler. Her lawyer's name is Art Savage. Oh, don't forget she still has porridge every morning. After an hour of this kind of scattershot information, I suggested we drive into Perth to buy a guidebook to Boston. Then I sat him down at the table and made him go through the important landmarks: the Charles River, the State House, Back Bay, the museum, a baseball stadium called Fenway Park, the various universities, Cambridge, and Arlington, the suburb where Aunt Helen clung to life.

"I don't suppose she'll remember everything either," I said, trying to cheer us both up.

"The trouble is, you can't count on her forgetfulness. Last time she phoned she suddenly mentioned the pistachio ice cream I ate after we went to the Fogg Museum."

"Pistachio, Fogg," I said, making a note. "Maybe you ought to be paying me more."

"Oh, come off it, Leo. I probably won't see a penny of my inheritance for years. Do you think you'll be ready to phone her tomorrow? We need to warn her she's getting what she asked for."

"More or less," I grinned.

For a moment Roman was glaring again, then he grinned back.

. . .

It was clever of Chae, Ewan thought, to put Aunt Helen in Boston, where he could check American details with Bridget. He reached to move the hot-water bottle and, as he did so, realised that Bridget had not been Chae's only source. A few years ago he had visited Mill of Fortune right after a trip to Boston; he remembered bringing American tee shirts for the children. The first evening, sitting at the table and drinking whisky, Chae had questioned him in a strangely naive way. What do the people look like? Did you find the money tricky? What sort of restaurants did you go to? Gratified by Chae's interest, he had rambled on about the quaint wooden houses, the unfenced gardens, the large portions in restaurants, the newspapers sold in boxes. Now he felt a delayed embarrassment at his own gullibility: he had mistaken one kind of interest for another. And why hadn't Chae told him what he was doing? He would've been flattered to be asked for his help. Grumpily he turned to the next chapter.

And found, tucked between the pages, a small piece of newspaper, from *The Scotsman*. "After his moving third novel, *Debts and Trespasses*, Chae Lafferty seeks to extend his fictional territory in *The Dark Forest*," Ewan read. He skimmed the review, waiting for praise or blame.

The plot has a somewhat old-fashioned flavour—wills play a more prominent part in nineteenth-century fiction than they do today—but Leo's masquerade of Roman is nicely rendered, though Mr. Lafferty makes comparatively little of the psychological aspects of impersonation, perhaps intimidated by such brilliant predecessors as Patricia Highsmith. Leo is a lively, if not particularly likeable, narrator. But being likeable is not the job of this novel, and perhaps the only truly sympathetic character is Maudie, Roman's wife. Let us hope that Mr. Lafferty, having shown that he can write about more exotic places, will now return to Edinburgh, the city he knows so well and has written about with such insight and energy.

How lucky no one reviews bankers, Ewan thought. There was an odd, scolding tone to the prose, which, although he had himself been annoyed with Chae only a moment ago, made him feel almost partisan. He returned to his lively (if unlikeable) narrator.

· · ·

By the third hour of the flight everything was boring. I had had my hopes about one of the stewardesses, a perky American blonde. I was sure she gave me the once over as she served my Bloody Mary, but when I asked about the nightlife in Boston, she recommended the aquarium. I blamed Roman's tweedy suit. In the seat next to me a middle-aged woman was slowly turning the pages of a book called *Birds of New England*. When her gaze wandered, I decided it was time for a rehearsal. I introduced myself as Roman. I was travelling on my own passport so this was my first chance to use my new name.

"How do you do. I'm Victoria. What an unusual name, Roman."

"My parents spent their honeymoon in Rome. Needless to say, they claim I was conceived there."

"Just as well they didn't go to Bognor."

Victoria chuckled and I glimpsed what it must really be like to be Roman and hear hundreds of people make this comment, each convinced of their originality. Victoria was visiting a nephew who taught at MIT. Thanks to Roman's coaching, I was able to nod intelligently. I explained that I was on my way to see an elderly aunt. "I am the nephew," I said, "but no scientific bent, I'm afraid."

"What do you do?"

I barely stopped myself saying actor. Roman and I had gone over his relationship with Aunt Helen in mind-boggling detail, but we hadn't bothered with the rest of his life. "I'm in marketing, for a distillery."

"Oh," said Victoria, sounding alarmingly interested. "My nephew and his wife are planning to do the Whisky Trail in the spring. Perhaps you have some suggestions?"

"I'm sure the Scottish Tourist Board can give them all the information they need," I said lamely.

"But what about your distillery?" pressed Victoria.

"It's in Perth—not particularly picturesque, alas, but we're always glad to have visitors." Before she could ask any more questions, I said I had to work on a report. Frowning, Victoria returned to the greater crested grebe.

The remainder of the flight, now I'd realised half the script was missing, rushed by. I unfolded the table and began to jot down the main facts about my brother. Or at least those I could come up with. For a quarter of an hour I drew a complete blank on the name of his first wife. Finally it came to me, Gretel. She never liked me. And then there was myself to consider. Aunt Helen's other nephew, I would surely rate some discussion. I decided not to mention my occasional adverts but stress the acting I'd done in schools and hospitals. Who knows, maybe Helen would leave me a legacy of my own.

By the time I got off the plane my head was buzzing. I was glad to have the mechanical tasks of immigration and customs to anchor me. As Helen had predicted there was no problem getting a taxi and the driver said, "Sure thing," when I asked him to take me to Arlington. Soon we were driving past gas tanks and factories, an industrial landscape not unlike parts of North London. Gradually this gave way to streets lined with wooden houses. But I was in too much of a funk to appreciate the scenery. I kept thinking what would happen if I fluffed my lines. Then we were pulling up in front of a large white house. I was on.

Aunt Helen met me at the door with her walker. She was wearing turquoise slacks, a sweatshirt, and a great deal of lipstick. Her glasses were splendidly thick. "Roman, welcome. Come in, come in," she said. On the phone she'd sounded American but in person, in spite of her garish clothes, she was every inch an Edinburgh matron. I embraced her carefully and said she was looking well.

"Rubbish. Now you'll be parched after your journey. Tea is all ready. You have the same room as last time."

I remembered Roman's instruction to take the back stairs and found myself in a large plain room with a view of the garden and its own bathroom. I washed my face and hands. In the mirror my skin where I had shaved off my beard still had a pale, unused look and somehow my eyes seemed different too. Smaller and darker, more like Roman's. Of course it was silly but I ran my hand over my thigh, searching for the dent left by a car that had knocked me down when I was eighteen. There it was, my secret identity mark, and my eyes were my own again. Before I could spook myself further, I went downstairs and made cheery conversation with Aunt Helen about my journey.

• • •

Ewan closed *The Dark Forest*. So far there seemed little to explain Mollie's intense reaction to the book. The portrait of her was mostly flattering; even the churlish reviewer thought she was sympathetic. As for the plot, he recognised it from the divinity classes of his childhood. Here were Jacob and Esau, the smooth and hairy brothers, disputing their birthright—a word that reminded him of Olivia. At least she was warm and well fed. He wondered what her real name was. At university there had been a brilliant Indian girl in one of his computer classes. He remembered meeting her one snowy afternoon standing on the library steps, both hands outstretched to catch the snow. Neera, he recalled; she came from Hyderabad. He had not thought of her in years.

Chapter 6

After the phone call, Mollie carried Olivia upstairs to the bathroom. She turned on the taps and sat on the lid of the toilet, watching the long porcelain bath fill with water and the room with steam. As usual after heavy rain, peat had filtered into the reservoir, and the water gushing from the taps was the same golden brown as the mountain burns. Mollie had always taken pleasure in this phenomenon—"Look at the peat," she would exclaim to Chae, holding up a tumbler—but now the little brown flecks seemed to dance with sinister life, the steam was far from innocent, and even the clawed feet of the bathtub curled with menace. She thought of the ducks, dead by her carelessness; in the silence, their voices were getting ready to denounce her.

Then Olivia gurgled, and Mollie found she did not have to listen to the ducks. Turning her back upon them, she tested the water several times before lowering Olivia into the bath. The day before, Olivia had cooed and splashed in the kitchen basin, but this larger expanse seemed to alarm her. Her mouth opened in protest. At the last moment, however, her expression changed and she welcomed the topaz water, whose colour mirrored her own.

For the first few minutes Mollie struggled just to keep hold of her slippery limbs. Soon she discovered the knack of cupping Olivia's head above the water with one hand while squeezing the sponge over her with the other. She began to sing:

> Rub-a-dub-dub, three men in a tub,
> And who do you think they were?
> The butcher, the baker, the candlestick maker,
> They all jumped out of a rotten potato.

As she sang she thought about the man on the phone: who was he? When he said hello, she'd assumed he was someone from the town, perhaps one of the men Chae used for odd jobs. He had called her Mollie Lafferty, a slip she hadn't bothered to correct.

"I'm sorry to trouble you," he said. "You have company."

"Yes, my brother. I'm afraid I didn't catch your name."

"A well-wisher." He paused. "Somebody wishing you well with your company."

Mollie's mild puzzlement turned to acute alarm. "Who is this?" she said. "No, that won't be necessary." And put down the phone. Then she went back into the kitchen and made up something to tell Ewan. In her state of agitation, it was astounding she could invent a convincing story. A week ago she'd been afraid to step out of the house, and here she was, deft as Ariadne, finding her way through a maze of crises, unanticipated crises.

But was she, she suddenly wondered as she reached for the soap, finding her way, or losing it? The phrase "unanticipated crises" sounded reassuring, like a large steel cage into which fierce animals could be herded. But this man—she pictured him bare-headed, bare-handed, his skin and eyes like Olivia's, perhaps a little stocky, wearing an Arran sweater the colour of oatmeal—it was not at all clear whether this man could be herded.

How could he have known their secret? No, not their secret; hers. As far as Ewan was concerned, they were waiting for the car to recover. He had no inkling that she had slipped out of the house the night before and loosened the distributor cap. Nor that she was already scheming how to get him to hurry back to London, leaving her to cope with the authorities.

Olivia waved her legs and splashed. "What are we going to do?" Mollie asked. She remembered Lorraine saying that small children, alone in their cribs, often talked to themselves, retelling the events of their day. The theory was that these crib narratives were an attempt at controlling experience. And now Mollie was doing the adult equivalent, trying to work out how to survive the remainder of her brother's visit, to calm herself, by talking to Olivia.

"Tomorrow's Sunday," she continued. "I'll have to talk to Ewan about Chae, et cetera, et cetera. He'd like us to leave Mill of Fortune as soon as possible. What do you think? Last week the house felt like a prison, but now you're here, it's all right." She tickled Olivia's toes, and Olivia squealed with glee. If only she hadn't sent Ewan that mad letter. But that was what had brought him to Mill of Fortune, and he in turn had brought Olivia. As for the man on the phone, briefly Mollie heard him again—"somebody wishing you well with your company"— then his voice, like those that spoke from the taps and the trees, receded.

She wrapped Olivia in a warm towel and carried her downstairs. Ewan was at the kitchen table, pushing buttons on his calculator. "How was the bath?" he said.

"We had fun. Would you hold her while I close the shutters? When it's windy like this, they make the house much warmer."

She handed him Olivia and went round the downstairs windows, checking the locks and closing the shutters; they creaked with disuse. Standing in the parlour window, she thought, Anyone could see me. Anyone could be looking in. But even this frightening notion fell far short of the vociferous terrors the darkness had used to hold. She made sure the front door was locked and quietly, so as not to rouse Ewan's attention, slid the bolt across the back door.

Later Mollie would remember that evening as the pleasantest part of his visit. By tacit agreement they put aside difficult conversations, and after supper settled in over the Scrabble board. At the end of the third game, Mollie emerged the victor by twenty-three points.

On Sunday morning Mollie knew from the moment Ewan entered the kitchen that the time for jokes about "umbrella" and "xylophone" was past. The word hovering over his head like a neon sign, lit by determination and self-reproach, was "talk." He gobbled up his cereal, then dashed upstairs to fetch his notebook. As he sat down, the notebook open before him, she saw he'd made a numbered list.

"Mollie," he said, "you know I'm not much use at the Sturm und Drang of love, but I am good at practical matters. We have to figure out your future." He glanced down at the notebook. "First off, can you tell me the legal situation about the house?"

Before his arrival Mollie had, in her occasional flashes of clarity, dreaded the revelation of what she knew Ewan would regard as massive incompetence. Now she welcomed it as exactly the sort of problem that would distract him from Olivia. Stumbling a little, she explained that everything was in Chae's name. "It didn't seem to matter," she said sheepishly.

"Not to worry. It won't be hard to establish your right to a share. After all, you lived together for ten years."

"So you keep saying," she snapped, and at once, as Ewan tucked in his chin, tortoise-like, found herself apologising. "Sorry. But actually, he doesn't own the house."

"He doesn't own it?" Ewan's eyebrows rose.

"We had a lease. I don't know the details, but the Craigs would never sell."

"Do you mean like a London leasehold, where you buy ninety-nine years for a hundred thousand pounds?"

"No, a regular lease, where you pay rent every month. I'm sorry," she said again. "Chae took care of all that."

He crossed off one item on his list. "So do you still have your inheritance?"

"Of course not. That was years ago, Ewan, and it wasn't very much. I bought a new loom. We put in central heating, paid Chae's child support, bought a car, and ate brown rice for a couple of years. Neither of us had a steady income; of course the money got spent. Now I feel like an idiot, but at the time it was such a relief to be able to contribute. We were so broke. I hated asking Chae for anything."

"But didn't he make money from his books, his journalism?"

Mollie laughed. "Those barely kept us in toothpaste. He got a hundred pounds for a piece in *Field and Stream*, fifty for a review in *The Scotsman*. The novels brought in more, though only every three or four years. And you know about my weaving. At that exhibition in Edinburgh last summer, the most expensive hanging went for two hundred and twenty pounds, and it took me three months to make. I tried to tell you the other night."

Ewan sighed, and Mollie felt the familiar pleasure of baiting her brother. He scribbled a note; she could see him almost visibly retrieve his sense of purpose, as if he were picking a shirt up off the floor. "Well, at least you're not tied to the house. Or even really to Chae." He paused and tapped his pen. "Do you consider the separation irrevocable? Are you ready to begin proceedings?"

"I'm not sure what you mean by 'proceedings,' but if they involve talking to him or seeing him, I'm never going to be ready. I just want to forget all this. Think of me as someone who's been hibernating for ten years. Now I'm awake."

"Hibernating," Ewan repeated, and, to Mollie's astonishment, wrote it down. "Where do you plan to be awake? How will you support yourself? I hate to sound like a Jeremiah, but you were very unsteady on the phone, even a few days ago."

Mollie saw that in the euphoria of anger she had gone too far; she had forgotten that, once more, she had something to lose. "You're right," she said penitently. "I do have to move, and I should take a training course. Learn a skill, not just muddle along in shops and restaurants like I used to."

"Weaving's a skill."

"But most people see it as a luxury. I want to do something necessary, like nursing, or carpentry."

"That's an excellent idea. Maybe computers? I remember you were good at maths. If you tell me the areas you're interested in, I'll make enquiries." He crossed off another item. I said the right thing, thought Mollie. I sounded sensible, practical.

"Now, about packing up the house," he went on. "You can put the furniture in storage until you're ready to make decisions, but there'll be a lot of organising. How about asking a friend to come and help?"

Her anger flooded back; she cracked her knuckles to contain it. "I don't have any friends," she said as calmly as she could. "That's what I kept trying to tell you on the phone. The people we saw round here, they're all Chae's friends. I can't face them now."

"Mollie, you're being Victorian. No one thinks twice about

people breaking up these days. I'm certain your neighbours would be happy to lend a hand."

"Yes, the phone's ringing off the hook." She gestured towards the hall. Later she could not understand what had driven her to talk about *The Dark Forest* except the same impulse that drove criminals to confess: solitude was too painful; worse than being known was being unknown. "You're reading Chae's book," she said.

"I haven't got very far. I'm a slow reader."

She stood up, went over to the stove, and pushed the kettle into the centre of the hot plate. "If you read the book, you'll see that what Chae did is scurrilous. He didn't make the slightest effort to conceal it. Everyone knows I'm Maudie. Maudie," she snorted. "It's not even a proper name, for Christ's sake." She came back to the table, her face hot from the stove, and sat down again opposite her meek, attentive brother.

"Of course I can see some similarities," he said, "but mostly the likeness is complimentary. Last night I found this review from *The Scotsman*. The bloke didn't seem to like the novel much, still he thought Maudie was by far the nicest character."

"Keep reading."

Her bitterness had derailed the conversation, but only briefly. Turning back to his list, Ewan said, "It's April the twelfth today. Why don't you aim to be out of here by the end of the month? That's a little less than three weeks. The first of May is a highly auspicious date for starting a new life."

"All right." Mollie raised her coffee cup in a mock toast. "A new life on the first of May."

Again Ewan made a note. "Do you think you might want to come to London?"

She nodded enthusiastically. "I was dreading Edinburgh, for all kinds of reasons—Chae, old friends, nowhere to live, no job. London's just what I need—a new start—and of course you'll be there, which is essential." She smiled and, to her relief, saw on

Ewan's face an answering smile. Her agenda had only one item, to keep the peace, though if she was going to move, London, with its famous promise of anonymity, did seem the ideal destination. Here, in the country, she had isolation without a shred of privacy. Everyone knew she was the woman from Mill of Fortune. Her promise of coming to London was, evidently, the last major item on Ewan's list. He made a final note and announced that he'd check the yellow pages for removal companies.

When he left the kitchen, she suspected him of sneaking off to read another chapter of *The Dark Forest*. But in ten minutes he was back, saying it was cold upstairs and naming two local companies that advertised both removal and storage. Later, on her way to the bathroom, she tiptoed into his room and looked at the book. The jacket flap was closed in Chapter Five. At least her brother had not succumbed to the propaganda that this was a book you couldn't put down.

They did what they had done the day before: ate, walked, worked, and read. On the walk Ewan asked about the right-of-way, and Mollie gestured vaguely up the hill. "It was Chae's battle," she said. "I'm not even certain where the property line runs." Late in the afternoon she went out to the garage and on her return pronounced the car to be running fine.

"That's good news," Ewan said.

He spoke so absently that Mollie stopped to study him. His eyes were shadowed, his mouth drawn, and in spite of their walks, his face seemed less ruddy than when he arrived. She recalled his remark about troubles of his own. Over supper she said, "The other night you mentioned a row at the office. Is it serious?"

"Y-y-y-y- quite."

"Can you tell me about it?"

He tore off a piece of bread. "It's complicated."

"I'd like to hear." Cunningly she added, "I need to know I'm not the only one who has problems. Please, Ewan."

"Okay—but I warn you, it's going to sound boring. You'll have to take my word that it's serious." He began to explain about his job, how he dealt with stocks and shares, how clients came to him. "A lot of the information I get is confidential," he said, "and people often try to pump me over lunch or cocktails. Fortunately I've cultivated a reputation as a dour Scot; it's one of the reasons clients trust me." He gave a small, unamused laugh.

"Anyway, to cut a long story short, I had dinner with someone and we were chatting about business. Vanessa made a remark that seemed to indicate we'd reached a new level of trust, that although we worked for different companies, we could be friends. I responded by letting fall a couple of details about this merger I was arranging. I didn't want to be standoffish, and to most people my comments would have meant very little. She asked one casual question. Then she said she was going over to New York soon and could I suggest a good hotel."

The lasagne was cooling, but Mollie hesitated to interrupt by eating, or by urging Ewan to do so.

"We had a date for a concert the following week, and she called to say she was stuck in the office, but that happens all the time in our line of work. I didn't give it a second thought. Then, the day before the merger went through, I got a phone call from Brian Ross, whom I used to work with at the Bank of Scotland. He'd just bought a large block of Gibson Group stock for one of his clients. He was calling because the client had been unusually vague about his sudden interest in the stock. Brian had gone ahead, of course, and made the transaction. Afterwards he remembered I was connected with the company, and he wanted to check it out with me." Ewan looked at Mollie. "Is this making any sense?"

"Yes, go on. What did you tell him?" She took a bite of lasagne. Now that Ewan was in the grip of his story, she noticed, his stutter had vanished.

"I said I'd no reason to think anything special was afoot, though the stock would probably hold steady. Fine, he said, so long as it wasn't a colossal blunder. Then, just before he hung up, he remarked again that it was an odd buy for this particular client—he'd worked for him for several years and never known him to be impulsive before.

"I got a strange feeling after that phone call. I kept going over my conversation with Vanessa, and it was obvious anybody who wanted to could make use of what I'd said. I felt like an idiot. It's one of the basic rules—never divulge sensitive information—and I babbled like a ten-year-old."

"I still don't see the problem. Maybe you were a little indiscreet. So what?"

"So nothing." Ewan meticulously straightened the cuffs of first his shirt, then his pullover. "Unless someone profited by my indiscretion. At which point I'm an accomplice to insider trading, like that American, Milken. It's a relatively new crime. People say that's how Rothschild made his fortune. He had spies at the Battle of Waterloo and used their information to manipulate the stock market in London. But it wasn't a crime in his day."

"Can't you just ask this Vanessa person?"

Ewan shook his head. "I doubt it. She's still in New York. And besides," he added gloomily, as if this were the last straw, "I'm fond of her."

Only Ewan, Mollie thought, would say fond when he meant dying of love. No wonder he'd been so upset when she asked about girlfriends. Across the empty plates she gazed at him, his misery blatant now to her unsealed eyes. "You're probably imagining the whole thing," she said. "No one will ever find out, and you can go back to being a dour Scotsman with a vengeance."

"Perhaps." He stared disconsolately at his lasagne, and Mollie saw that her platitudes about business were as convincing as his remarks about a new life. She stood up, went round the table, and hugged him.

A few minutes later, as she scraped their plates into Sadie's bowl, she moved into Machiavellian mode. "It sounds as if you're under a lot of pressure. Maybe you should fly down from Edinburgh? If we get up early you could make the nine o'clock shuttle and be in your office by eleven. I can always use your train ticket when I come to London."

"But what about the drive?" Ewan's forehead furrowed. "It's a long way to the airport. And there's Olivia to deal with."

Sadie hurried over, her nails clicking on the floor. "I'm sure I can manage the drive. I've been fine on our walks. The famous demons have flown. Of course you could take a taxi, if you prefer. And Olivia just needs to be handed over at Perth police station, doesn't she?"

Ewan nodded. "There'll be a statement to be made, though, and I am the one who found her."

"You can go to the police in London. They're all connected nowadays." She put the plates in the sink and turned on the taps. That's quite enough, she thought. I mustn't push any harder. She went to the cupboard to fetch the Scotch. "I'm having a nightcap," she said. "Do you want one?"

"Please. If you really think you're up to taking me to the airport, I have to admit it would be a relief. This business has me rattled. I have the stupid idea that as long as I'm at my desk, nothing terrible can happen."

"Nothing terrible will happen anyway," Mollie said, passing him a glass. "It's good for me to have projects. I got myself in a bit of a state this last month. Now, thanks to you, I'm okay. I can do whatever's necessary, even if I'm not wildly cheerful about it."

"No one's asking for wild cheerfulness," he said. "Such emotion would be quite unlike the Munros. Skol."

"Skol," said Mollie.

The alarm rang at five-thirty. No rain, Mollie thought as she slipped from the bed. She changed and fed Olivia, made coffee, and woke Ewan. Fifteen minutes after she knocked on his door, he came into the kitchen wearing his suit, carrying his bag in one hand and his briefcase in the other. Ten minutes later he was installed in the back seat of the car, Olivia on his lap.

The mist was rising over the fields and the country roads were quiet. The A9, however, was already busy. Mollie fell in behind a grey Volkswagen. She could not imagine why all these other people were up so early, but her claim to Ewan turned out to be true: the traffic did not bother her.

Soon after eight-thirty they pulled up at the airport. Mollie went round to open Ewan's door. He handed her Olivia, once again wrapped in the blue blanket, and climbed out.

"Are you sure you're all right?" he said.

"I'm fine. I know exactly what to do."

"You'll have to tell me what happens." He gestured at Olivia, squirming in Mollie's arms. "I've got quite attached to her in the last couple of days." He planted an awkward kiss on Olivia's forehead, then kissed Mollie. "Come soon," he said. "It'll be great having you in London."

"I will, and thank you. For everything. Good luck." She patted his shoulder and smiled.

He stepped through the glass doors and disappeared among the crowds of travellers. A loudspeaker announced no parking anywhere in the terminal. Mollie got the pillow she had brought out of the boot and put it on the floor below the passenger's seat. She wedged Olivia in place, secure and out of sight, then turned towards home.

II

Chapter 7

The part Kenneth remembered best, which had nothing to do with anything, was shaving that morning. Joan had left early, in a flurry of instructions about Grace: give her a bottle at nine, don't forget to change her, she likes her bear close by. He had nodded intelligently and been asleep again before her key turned in the door. A couple of hours later, he woke in the crumpled bed and knew instantly that he was in Joan's flat and that he had it to himself for five whole hours. This was one of his talents: never to wake in a lurch of terror, wondering where he was, but to surface seamlessly from the night before, no matter how many pints he'd had, into the morning after. The first night he'd gone home with Joan, she'd said, "Most people die when they're asleep. Not you. You're always here, alive." He wasn't sure what she meant, but his mother, an avid reader of dreams and horoscopes, whose lumpy sofa was at present his most permanent home, often commented with something close to horror on Kenneth's lack of dreams. He could no longer recall if his claim not to dream had been true at the time he made it, or if he'd simply wanted to wind her up. In any case, for years now his sleep had been empty. And so he was glad to be praised by Joan for something that came naturally.

He had gotten up, turned on the gas fire, made a cup of tea, and carried it into the bathroom, where he set it next to the radio, on the tank of the toilet. As he waited for the water to run hot, he caught sight of his face in the mirror. How peely-wally he looked, but didn't he always think that after a night with Joan? It was the contrast with her penny-coloured skin. Then he noticed her razor, a pink fiddley number, and a can of shaving foam perched on the edge of the bath. For no good reason he decided to shave. He squirted a blob of foam into one palm and smoothed it over his cheeks and chin, enjoying the cool, lemony smell. He liked using women's things.

Of course with the foam he couldn't drink his tea. Letting it go to waste, though, only added to his sense of luxury. He'd make another cup when he was done. He rubbed the mirror and leaned closer. Against the shaving foam, the whites of his eyes had a yellowish cast—not bad after five pints on an empty stomach. You have the eyes of a dog, Joan had said soon after they met, but he'd refused to take offence; that was just her being a foreigner. Instead he'd led her, jokingly, to the dogs he liked, Labs and setters. Now he peered deep into his brownish irises and appreciated the little flakes of light.

He had finished the left cheek and was at work on his chin, craning into the razor, when a sudden screech interrupted his pleasant task. What the hell was that? Oh yes, the bloody baby. Last night he'd agreed to watch her so that Joan's mother, who baby-sat on Fridays, would not arrive at seven-thirty this morning, thereby cutting short one of his few precious nights in a bed. You promise, Joan said. Cross my heart, he said, slipping his hand inside her blouse. He remembered now there'd been a pile of nappies and bottles on the kitchen table. Shut up, you little bugger, he thought, and switched on the radio. "Occasional showers, heavy in some areas," the weatherman said, in that singsongy way they had. "Inverness will have freezing rain, and in the north there may be snow on high ground."

"Snow on high ground," Kenneth echoed, and nicked himself in the soft fold of the jaw. He wasn't even sure he had broken the skin until he saw the red tinge in the foam. At once he felt a sting of pain.

He swore and moved on to the safety of the other cheek, where the razor swept sweetly through the foam. A few deft strokes and he was done. He patted his face with a towel from the rack behind the door and headed for the kitchen.

As he waited for the kettle to boil, Grace's cries from the living room rose steadily, until she was bawling fit to beat the band. How old was she? he wondered. If he counted from when he met her, three months; from her birth, just before Christmas, four. He'd been away in Arbroath, loading lorries—his first job after getting the sack from Perth Infirmary, but only temporary. It was late January when he ran into Joan at the supermarket. She was shopping with her mother. He hadn't seen her since that summer evening when they'd gone for a walk on the South Inch and she told him about the goddess of fertility. Already he'd forgotten her bright silky clothes and gleaming hair, the things that first caught his eye in the infirmary cafeteria. Here she was again, small and glittering in the tinned-goods aisle.

"Joan," he'd said, "you're looking awfie bonnie," knowing she wouldn't understand his phoney Scots.

He didn't notice the baby—the mother was carrying her—until Joan pointed her out. "This is Grace," she said, "your daughter."

They were beside the soups, and he'd backed away towards the oxtail. "Don't talk rubbish."

"I'm sorry," she whispered, staring sadly at the lino floor.

Well, that was what he liked about her: she did what he said. Maybe some men enjoyed a wildcat, but not him. When they shouted, he left. She stood there, eyes downcast, her mother, who knew no English, dandling the baby behind her, until he said he'd call round sometime.

A month later, after getting thrown out of the Perth Arms without so much as a coat on a rainy night, he'd made his way to her council flat. She had offered no reproaches and served shepherd's pie. While she was washing the dishes he took a keek at the baby. He saw not a vestige of likeness, except perhaps her brown eyes, though Joan had those too. He couldn't tell if she was his, nor if he wanted her to be. The thought of Joan playing nookie with anybody else gave him a slippery feeling, so he put it aside. He'd never had a dad. Why should this brat?

Since then he'd popped in on Joan half a dozen times, her flat being handy for the bus station, taking care to come without warning and leave without promises. But when he showed up last night at nine-thirty, Joan explained she'd been moved to the early shift at the infirmary, and a bit the worse for wear, imagining a quiet morning with the telly, he'd agreed to mind the baby until she got home at three.

Now, with a complete absence of her mother's docility, Grace howled. Kenneth drank his tea, shouted at her, tried to watch TV. He even resorted to one of the bottles Joan had left. That worked while she was actually sucking. Then she cried louder than ever. Finally, having smoked his last cigarette, he decided to take her to the shops. Probably she had some kind of outdoor gear, but he wasn't going to faff around. He took the blanket from her cot and a yellow cape he found hanging behind the kitchen door. He'd always had a knack for parcels, and in spite of the hullabaloo she was making, he soon had her turned into a neat papoose he could tuck under one arm. He pocketed the keys Joan had left him and set out.

Grace wailed the whole time, even when he shook her, until they were in the street. Then she quieted almost instantly and fell asleep even before they reached the corner shop. Kenneth bought his fags out of the seven quid his mother had given him to pay the newsagent. The question of how to replace the money flashed across his mind and vanished with the first cigarette. He wandered up Leonard Street, past the betting shop too early, though the two-fifteen at Newmarket might be worth keeping an eye on. A rabbity lad came by, kicking a can along the gutter. Kenneth sauntered towards the bus station.

He could not describe the inside of what happened next—perhaps the death that most people experienced in sleep came to him while awake—but the outside was like this. The tea was making itself felt. Kenneth eyed the long, low bus station and thought rather than endure, he could use the Gents. The mere idea gave him a small flare of satisfaction. He stepped through the door into a haze of bacon. Putting Grace down just inside the stall, he went over to the urinal and released a stream of urine. She was still being quiet, Christ almighty, as he zipped up and edged away. The room was small, and two steps took him to the door. He opened it and stepped out. Without any gesture on his part, the door thwapped shut. Maybe, he thought, she'd cry and bring him back; if she was really his daughter, she would claim him.

Several buses were lined up with their engines chugging, no problem for Grace, though, who—as she'd just shown him—could outyell any football fan. Yet she was silent. Somebody had left a copy of the *Sun* lying on a bench, and Kenneth sat down and glanced through it while waiting for Grace to summon him. A story about a family of illegal immigrants reminded him of Joan's brother: Lalit had come over last year and was sneaking around somewhere in Lancashire. Joan herself was mysteriously legal. The big news was that most football players were taking drugs. What a surprise. A bloke in a suit came hurrying down the platform. Kenneth gawked at his shiny shoes and briefcase. The man's eyes slid over him as if he were another plank in the bench, then he reached for the door of the Gents and disappeared inside.

A space opened in Kenneth's brain, and when it seemed he might be in danger of coming to the end of it, might actually have to open the toilet door, another space opened. A horn hooted. The bloke came out, looking stupid, carrying the yellow bundle that was Grace, and the next thing he was climbing onto one of the buses. Kenneth raced over and followed him up the steps.

As the bus pulled out of the station, Kenneth felt a panicky desire to ask the driver to let him off. Then they turned into North Methven Street and he caught sight of Harvey, one of the orderlies he'd met at the infirmary, gazing into the window of Dixon's. Somehow, that glimpse of old Harve in his tatty leather jacket, lusting after a CD player or a portable telly, made him feel better. He settled back to enjoy the journey. Just beyond the outskirts of Perth, past Dewar's distillery, Grace started to yell, but the time for summoning him was over. He watched the bloke getting annoyed, trying one thing and another, not daring to raise his voice. At last she calmed down in her unpredictable way, and the two of them nodded off. Kenneth stared out of the grimy window at the sheep and cows. In Arbroath his digs had been on the edge of town, a room overlooking a field, which he hated. Whatever else you could say about his mum's flat, at least it was on a nice busy street.

If someone had sat down beside him on the bus—Joan, for instance—he could've come up with a story, no problem. He'd felt dizzy in the toilet, put the baby down for fear he might drop her, and the bloke had nicked her while he was getting a breath of fresh air. And then, poor old Kenneth with his dodgy health, he'd got on that bus to prevent him making a getaway. Something like that. Nothing that'd happened so far had anything to do with him.

The part he was proudest of came when they all got off the bus. It was pouring cats and dogs. "Occasional showers," he thought contemptuously, and hurried to shelter in the doorway of the cinema. The bloke followed, squeezing Grace in one arm, clutching his luggage in the other. Kenneth got a good look at him—scanty hair, wishy-washy blue eyes, expensive specs, and, surprisingly, unshaven. Briefly he seemed to look back, registering Kenneth's existence in a way that was both flattering and alarming. Then a car hooted and the man stumbled towards it. He, his bags, and Grace disappeared into the blue Fiat. Nothing happened. It was too far and too rainy for Kenneth to see in. Were they talking? Necking? Having an argy-bargy about Grace? He stood at the corner of the cinema steps, listening to some girls gabbing, and waited.

Maybe five or ten minutes passed before the driver's door opened and a figure jumped out—a boy, he thought, until she began to run. And this was when his brain started working. Blessing the rain, which made haste natural, he hurried after her. Halfway down the main street, she turned into a shop. It was a chemists, the old-fashioned sort where you always had to ask a deaf assistant several times for anything embarrassing. Kenneth pretended to study the toothpaste while this woman— close up she wasn't bad-looking, with her spikey hair and black togs—whisked around buying armfuls of nappies and lotions and tinned milk. He saw her hold out a twenty-pound note to the assistant and say something, but he couldn't catch her words.

He waited until she'd left the shop before approaching the cash register with the cheapest tube of toothpaste, fifty-seven pence. "Was that Mrs. Mayall?" he asked, naming his mother's downstairs neighbour.

"No," said the assistant. Her dangly earrings sparkled as she put the toothpaste in a wee baggie. "That was Mrs. Lafferty from Mill of Fortune."

"What's that—a telly show?"

She laughed. You could probably whisper this one a request for a packet of Durex, not that it'd make it any easier. "No, a house. Out towards Glen Teall. Her husband's a writer, Chae Lafferty. Maybe you've seen him in *The Scotsman?*"

"Okey-dokey," Kenneth said. "That rings a bell."

As he came out of the shop, the blue car drove past, spraying him with water. Wankers, he muttered. He watched until they turned right at the crossroads and vanished. Then he noticed the pub across the street was open. He went in and asked for a phone book. Like his visit to the bog, this gesture was lit by satisfaction. No one can call me gormless now, he thought. That was what his mum called him, a gormless wonder, every time he lost a job. He paged through to the L's. Bingo, there was Chae Lafferty. He borrowed a pen from the barmaid and wrote down the number on the chemists' bag. Then he ran and caught the bus just as it swung through the square on its journey back to Perth.

This time it was his turn to sleep, and he woke, refreshed, only when they bumped into the station. He didn't exactly have a plan, but inspiration was lurking. The bloke with a suit had dough, that much was clear, and maybe a chunk of it could fly out of his pocket and into Kenneth's. Five hundred quid came to mind as a useful, liberating sum. That's all Kenneth was thinking—no harm to Grace, no harm to Joan.

Some people might have said he had things back to front: people paid to get babies back, not the other way round. But that was where the inspiration came in. Last week on the telly they'd been talking about this baby in the States, just an ordinary baby, as far as he could tell, not shitting gold or anything, and all these folk wanted her. They were spending thousands of dollars on solicitors, trying to prove what good parents they were, so a judge would say she belonged to them. Well, it was baffling—who in their right mind would want Grace bawling her head off?—but thank God Kenneth knew about it, because that gave him the antennae to pick up the secret little signals he might otherwise have missed. The bloke in the suit was a toff, so why hadn't he gone to the police or at least handed Grace in to Lost Property? And at the chemists, the woman had bought enough stuff to set up an orphanage.

No, they wanted that baby. And from his own long experience, Kenneth could see they were moving rapidly from behaviour that was merely a bit iffy, like when you carry a Walkman round the shop for half an hour, twiddling the knobs and reading the tiny print on the back about Taiwan, to the outright criminal moment when you absentmindedly slip the machine into your pocket and push out into the chilly street.

Chapter 8

The man seated next to Ewan was already at work, typing away on his laptop, and did not even glance up as Ewan sat down. Nor did the woman across the aisle, deep in her *Financial Times*. Nothing could have made him feel more welcome. Here was the world as he knew it, ready to receive him. He'd had time at the airport to phone the office and leave Yvonne a message that he should be in by eleven. Once the plane pushed back from the gate, the burdens of both his lives, brother and banker, fell away. Of course Mollie was still going to need a good deal of help, but the hard part, persuading her to leave Mill of Fortune, was behind him. Within a matter of weeks she would be installed in his top floor, making sense of the three-storey house he had bought as an investment when he joined Churchill and Rose and had since often regretted for its echoing rooms. As for the other business, he and Brian had been unnecessarily alarmist. People made unexpected purchases all the time; such was the nature of the market, and no cause for concern.

And Olivia, by the time he got to the office, would be safely in the hands of the police or, better still, some motherly social worker. In Mollie's company he had quickly grown accustomed to his unusual find; now, as the woman to his right turned to the European news and the man to his left studied a row of figures, he imagined himself politely interrupting them. Oh, by the way, guess what happened the other day? I found a baby in a bus station. He opened his briefcase and fished out his notebook. At the top of a blank page he wrote: *Banker finds Baby in Bus station*, pleased by the alliteration of his achievement. He must ask Mollie on the phone tonight if he needed to make a statement.

Even as he imagined telling his anonymous neighbours, the person he really wanted to tell appeared before him. All weekend he had done his best to keep thoughts of Vanessa at bay, but here she was, as vivid as if he had never forgotten her for an instant. I found a baby, he would say, and pictured her sitting a little straighter. The first thing he remembered noticing about her was not her dexterity with numbers, nor her smooth high forehead and marmalade-coloured hair, but her posture. Years of Victorian education—boards down the back, books on the head—must have gone into producing such easy, supple uprightness.

He reached up to direct the air nozzle into his face. Just as he'd overreacted to Brian's phone call, so he had read too much into not seeing Vanessa these last few weeks. Cancelled meetings happened eight days a week in the City. Given the possible dividends, it was stupid not to at least try to discover whether she might reciprocate his feelings. If the answer was no, then there would be plenty of time to dismantle his affection, to push it slowly back, like Zeno's arrow in reverse, until she again became a normal business acquaintance. Meanwhile, he thought briskly, nothing ventured, nothing gained. He jotted that down too.

As the plane lifted into the air and banked steeply over Arthur's Seat, it came to Ewan that his sister was right; he was thirty-three and in need of a wife. He raised his pen, tempted to add this to his list. *Install double glazing. Find a wife. Help Mollie move.* He remembered how she'd teased him about his propensity for list making. Instead he wrote *Phone Vanessa,* put an asterisk beside it, and took out his calculator.

Churchill and Rose had offices on the sixth floor of a newly renovated building near Finsbury Circus—within a stone's throw, Ewan had heard a colleague claim, of the Bank of England. A well-struck golf ball would've been more accurate, by his estimate, but he liked the narrow streets with their mixture of old and modern buildings and the sense of being part of the bustling mercantile history of London, a city he had long compared unfavourably to Edinburgh yet was gradually growing fond of. When he arrived, Yvonne was on the phone. "Mr. Munro is with a client, sir," she said as he hung up his jacket and tucked his bag between two filing cabinets. "Yes, I'll see he gets your message as soon as he's free." She pressed down the button and turned to Ewan, still holding the phone. "Mr. Lopez is in a state," she said. "For a change. How was Scotland?"

"Fine. It's a braw day," said Ewan, putting on an accent. He saw that Yvonne already had one pen emmeshed in her thick grey hair. Sometimes by the end of the day she would have three or four sticking out—like an Edward Lear character, Ewan teased her—and one of his duties was to remind her to remove them before leaving. "Any major blowups?" he asked.

"The usual. You have some faxes from Milan, and there's a meeting with Tony and Jack at two-thirty to discuss the budget for the Dryden account. Don't worry, Jack isn't having a business lunch. I checked."

The phone rang again, and Ewan went to fetch coffee. Nothing here could be so terrifying as his sister hurling a mug to the floor.

It was lunchtime before he had a chance to tell Yvonne about his weekend. She had been his secretary for nearly three years, and Ewan dimly recalled feeling sorry for her at the interview. She stood five foot ten and might be described as "Rubenesque." Now the idea of anyone pitying Yvonne was ludicrous. She spoke five languages, was dazzlingly efficient and the wife of a man who built violins; together they played in a chamber group. During the last month she'd spoken to Mollie several times on the phone and become privy to the whole mess. When Ewan announced he was thinking of going north, she immediately endorsed his decision, urging him to take Friday off and booking him a sleeper.

"So," she said, coming back from getting them tuna sandwiches and mineral water. "Any hope of a reconciliation?"

Ewan shook his head. "Absolute zero, I'm afraid. Mollie's so upset she can hardly bring herself to say Chae's name. Apparently he ran off with someone else, heaven knows who. I'm not even sure where he's living these days."

"Oh, I hate stories like this. I hope she sues him for every penny and the lint in his trouser pockets too."

"It turns out there aren't really any pennies. They all went on *la vie bohème*." He explained the plans for Mollie to stay with him and take a computer course. He kept expecting Yvonne to interrupt, to say this was precisely what Mollie needed, but she listened in silence, eating steadily. "Don't you think computers are a good idea?" he said at last. "Well paid and flexible?"

"Yes, yes, I do," Yvonne said. "Sorry, I was woolgathering." She drank some water. "I was remembering how desolate I was after I broke up with my first husband. I didn't want to be with him, but I found going home at night to an empty flat unbearable. I remember telling my sister my life was over. Then I signed up for French classes and met Jean-Pierre."

"Isn't Nick your first husband?" Taken aback by her casual admission, Ewan barely heard the rest of her remarks.

"Third." She smiled. "I'm a slow learner. Does Mollie have any friends here?"

"She claims to have no friends anywhere."

Yvonne popped the last of her sandwich into her mouth. "That can't be true, though she probably needs a few new ones. Oops, here we go." The fax machine was whirring again.

Later Ewan thought it was this conversation that had turned him into a criminal. Or more accurately, revealed him as one. If he was as innocent as he claimed, why didn't he mention finding the baby to Yvonne? It was an obvious piece of news and she, unlike his companions on the plane or the phantom Vanessa, was the obvious person to tell. No, at some level he had known all along what was happening. But he could not bear to confront his sister.

Whatever second chances there might have been for confiding were demolished by the message that awaited him after the budget meeting: Call Brian Ross. He glanced over to where Yvonne was typing up the report he'd written at Mill of Fortune. Never before had he found her proximity inhibiting. Sometimes he even waited for her to return to her desk before making difficult phone calls. He watched her lean forward to decipher a cryptic note and continue moving her nimble fingers. Reluctantly he dialled Brian's number.

"Ewan, hang on a sec. No, send it over pronto, two copies. Yes, right away. Sorry about that. Thanks for phoning back. How are you? Did you see the article on Japan in the *FT* last week?"

For several minutes they discussed individual versus corporate identity. Come on, come on, thought Ewan, his nervousness increasing with every meaningless phrase. "At least the Yamoto group is flourishing," Brian said. He cleared his throat. "I had David Coyle on the phone this morning."

Once Ewan had been in Oxford Street when an IRA bomb went off; only a small bomb, no one had been hurt, but the sensation of everything being briefly blown out of his mind was not dissimilar to the effect of Brian's remark. David Coyle worked for the Serious Fraud Office. "What did he want?" Ewan said, striving for calmness.

"The activities of one of my clients have come to his attention. In fact the one I mentioned to you, who invested so heavily in Gibson Group stock." Brian paused; somewhere a phone was ringing. "I thought maybe you'd like to know," he went on. "I suspect he'll be calling you soon, if he hasn't already, and it's always good, in these situations, to be prepared."

The Boy Scout motto, Ewan thought ironically. "No, he hasn't called me yet. Well, I'm much obliged to you, Brian. Frankly I've no idea what's going on." He trailed off. Just before the silence became truly awkward, he said, "I was north for the weekend. The home country is looking grand."

The conversation ended in a burst of Scottish nostalgia. "We're daft to live down here," Brian said. And Ewan agreed. Only after he hung up did it occur to him that he had got through this entire difficult dialogue without a trace of stuttering.

When Ewan finally got home to Barnsbury, it was past nine. He ate some toast, turned up his heating, and switched on the television without sound, then phoned Mollie. As he dialled, he thought of the solitary phone call of his visit; some kind of an argument, he guessed, judging from Mollie's demeanour, but with whom and about what remained a mystery. On the BBC news, several cars lay askew beside a road, and while he waited for her to answer—the phone rang at least a dozen times— Ewan had ample opportunity to imagine her blue car careening off the A9. "Hello," she said, much too loudly.

"Mollie, it's me. Sorry not to call sooner. How are you? You got home safely?"

"Yes, I've become an ace driver again. And I stuck a big sign on the back door: 'Have you put the car in the garage?' Pity I didn't do it sooner."

"Better late than never. What happened about the baby? Did they have a report of one missing?"

He heard her knuckles crack. "No, no one seems to have lost a baby. I think they were a bit taken aback—a baby, you know—but it all went smoothly."

Smoothly, pondered Ewan, and hoped this meant his earlier picture of a motherly social worker was true. "Do I need to make a statement?"

"Not at the moment. I gave them your name and address, and they said they'd be in touch if they needed more information. Was the flight okay? Your desk?"

"More or less. I do have to go to Milan tomorrow."

"Oh," said Mollie, and for a second he could have sworn it was an exclamation of relief. "For how long?"

"A couple of days. I'll be back on Friday at the latest. I'm mostly going to coddle the investors and eat osso bucco."

"Is this your famous row?"

"No, just the usual chaos." He stopped and found himself gazing through the window into the dark, dishevelled garden. He would've liked to confide in Mollie, to hear her burble well-meaning, ill-informed remarks, but even to mention Coyle seemed a dangerous act. The aptly named Coyle, Ewan thought, and imagined him like a cartoon character, growing larger with each utterance of his name.

"If I'd known you were going to Italy," Mollie said, "I'd never have made lasagne."

"Nonsense, your lasagne is delicious. Listen, I didn't get a chance to call the removal company today. Do you think next week will be soon enough?"

"That'll be fine. I'm not going to be ready for at least—"

There was a stifled cry, followed by total silence.

"Mollie! Mollie, are you all right?" Damn, that stupid isolated house.

"Sorry, Sadie went berserk. Maybe the fox is back, looking to see if we've anything else on offer. They say dogs can smell them over half a mile away."

"Although I don't remember her barking when the ducks were killed," Ewan said, then fearing he'd been tactless, quickly added, "If you're all right, I'd better go and pack for tomorrow. I'll try to give you a call from Milan. If you need to reach me, for any reason, call Yvonne. She'll have my number. I told her your plans, and she's looking forward to meeting you."

"I can't wait. She sounds terrific."

"Yes, she is," he said, pleased if a little startled by her enthusiasm. "Thanks for your hospitality. I know I made a fuss about coming, but I had a lovely time." Now the feeling of dread was like a light shining on all his other feelings, making them stronger and more vivid. He wanted to say something about how he understood she would miss the house, St. David's Well, the moors; that he would miss them too. Since their parents died, Mill of Fortune had been his home in Scotland. The scarcity of his visits had been in inverse proportion to his attachment. All this shimmered before him, hopelessly beyond speech. I'll write her a letter, he thought. They said their goodbyes, and he added it to his list of tasks.

Then he sat looking at the command he'd written when airborne that morning: *Phone Vanessa**. He was almost certain she was still in New York, and on the strength of that certainty he dialled her number. Her recorded voice was flat and brisk. He left a message—no more than that he would be away for a few days—and wanted, as soon as he hung up, to retrieve his awkward words. Too late.

He turned off the television and went to iron four shirts for the trip. Ironing was one of his favourite tasks, and he did his best to surrender to the pleasing scorched smell, which, along with stinginess, was the reason he did not have his shirts laundered. He hung them up on the pulley to air, and put four sets of underwear and four ties in his bag. He added pyjamas, a pullover, a spare pair of shoes. It was eleven-thirty before he got into bed in his own untidy bedroom. No sooner had he lain down than he recalled *The Dark Forest* in his briefcase downstairs.

So far Leo's impersonation was proceeding well. He and Aunt Helen had fallen into an easy bantering. In response to her enquiries about his "brother," he gave a glowing report of Leo's efforts on behalf of the underprivileged. Aunt Helen frowned. "If he wants to suffer for art, that's up to him," she said. "But if he wants money, let him work like the rest of us." Leo was tempted to ask what work she had ever done besides utter the onerous "I do"; instead he acted the tolerant older brother and said Leo would find himself one of these days. This allowed Aunt Helen to chime in that losing oneself was the height of carelessness. The following morning, Leo woke early and tiptoed downstairs.

• • •

One of the maddening things about Aunt Helen's was the number of phones. You'd have thought she was head of IBM—she had one in every room, including the loo. So even when I rang Maudie at the crack of dawn, I had to treat the conversation as part of my performance. I was always careful to identify myself as "Roman-in-America." After a week of avoiding four-letter words and saying "actually" and "as a matter of fact" as often as possible, I was losing a sense of where my voice ended and my brother's began. If I was ever lucky enough to be in the house alone, I planned to call and see if Maudie recognised me, unaided.

Today I said, "Maudie, it's me, Roman. I thought I'd give you a ring before Helen got up."

"Darling, how are you?"

"Excellent. Yesterday Helen took me out to Walden Pond. You know, where Thoreau lived."

Every other day Helen dreamed up an expedition. Over elevenses she'd announce our destination and estimated time of departure. Then it was up to me to come downstairs suitably dressed, back the car out of the garage, and escort Helen to it. The day before, I'd followed her directions west along Route 2 and down a winding country road to a car park in a grove of trees. There she settled herself with the Boston *Globe* and sent me traipsing off to look at Thoreau's hut. I'd never read a word the guy had written, still, just being alone for a few minutes was a relief. Walden Pond turned out to be a lake with amazingly clean water. The cabin had long since vanished but a reconstruction stood nearby. I peered dutifully in the windows.

I rabbited on about all this and Maudie finally said, "I'm glad Helen's well enough to take you places."

"Yes, she's full of vim and vigour. How are you?"

"Okay," she hesitated. "Not great."

I felt a little rush of warmth; it was the first remotely intimate thing she'd said to me. When I pressed her, she confessed she was still in the grip of last night's dream. She'd been wandering around in a flat, foggy, World War I wasteland. The air was filled with the cries of a dying elephant. Then she met an old man. He didn't seem upset so Maudie asked him why. "How can I be upset over one dying elephant," he said, "when there are so many?" As he spoke, the fog cleared and she saw that the wasteland was strewn with dying elephants, crying ceaselessly. "It was so sad," she said, "I could hardly stand it."

"Maybe you should make a gift for the elephants—a bowl or a vase?"

"I am already." Her voice lifted as if I'd said exactly the right thing. "Not just one—a series of bowls, that will fit inside each other like Russian dolls."

"Good, I'll admire them when I get home. A week today."

·   ·   ·

A movement caught Ewan's eye, and he looked up from the book to see the curtains drawn across the open window puffing in the breeze. The dream, he felt sure, was Mollie's. Suddenly all his fears for himself, about his career and Vanessa, seemed minor compared to the possibility that his sister might descend into the valley of despair and do something irreversible. He had always known Mollie lacked some of the ballast he and Bridget had had from birth. He must call her every day, must make sure the birds and the bones did not come back.

·   ·   ·

After I put the phone down I felt very weird. Maybe it was the remains of my jet lag but I stared round Aunt Helen's kitchen wondering what the hell I was doing there. If our scheme worked Roman stood to become a semi-millionaire, whereas I'd get enough for a cheap sofa. As if she were standing beside Aunt Helen's cooker, I heard my mother say, "Why can't you be more like Roman?" And my father by the monstrous fridge, "If only you studied like your brother." And echoing them an endless chorus saying, "I'm afraid you didn't get the part." I padded over to the coffee machine. I knew what I was going to do back in Scotland, and admiring a bunch of bowls was just the start. So far Roman's subterfuge had served his purposes. Next it would serve mine.

By noon the sun had come out. I figured I'd walk over to Arlington Center in the afternoon. Not that the shops were any great shakes—mostly fast food and stodgy clothes—but on non-expedition days there wasn't much else to do. Then at lunch Helen announced she had an appointment with her lawyer at three o'clock. "I have to take advantage of having a chauffeur," she smiled.

"Just let me get those hubcaps polished. Where is his office?"

"In Cambridge, near Harvard Square."

"In that case maybe I should pay another visit to the Fogg Museum." I was pleased with myself for using this detail at last.

"No, no," said Helen. "You're coming too. Art's really looking forward to meeting my nephew, one of my nephews."

Meeting me? The fluttery stage-fright feeling started up in my stomach. There was no way the old fart could discover me, but what if I'd overlooked some crucial thing? Something Roman had done at the age of ten that only he knew about, like only I knew who had put a bag of dog crap in Bill Hamilton's desk. Then I remembered the dreary production of *Twelfth Night* I'd been in last summer. If Viola could pass for Sebastian, what was my problem? I realised Aunt Helen was still waiting for a reply. "Art Savage," I said. "It's such a splendid name for a lawyer."

"As you've already remarked," she said, raising her napkin to her lips.

Another conversation Roman hadn't bothered to report. So much for any points I'd racked up for the Fogg, I thought, and asked if the chicken we were eating was free-range or battery.

The lawyer's office was on the ground floor of one of those wooden houses clustered around Harvard Square, and thank God there was a place to park in front. Aunt Helen negotiated the wheelchair ramp with aplomb and "Art" came out to the reception area to greet us, a small, dapper fellow with a ferocious tan and the inevitable bow tie. "So you're the famous nephew," he said, pumping my hand. "I'm pleased to meet you. I understand you had some problems getting away?"

"Actually, it was a bit of an effort." I was trying to sound extra-pompous. "However I'm hoping my absence will allow my colleagues to realise I'm irreplaceable."

"Good man," said Mr. Savage. "Stupid thing, yesterday I wanted to confirm our appointment and I had my secretary phone you in Scotland. Luckily the line was busy."

Jesus wept. I felt myself blush, something I don't remember happening offstage for a dozen years, and through her massive lenses, Aunt Helen seemed to check out every change of shade. I mumbled an incoherent comment about her being the perfect hostess.

"She sure is," said Mr. Savage. "Don't let her wear you out."

They both chuckled. Helen said she wouldn't be long and they shuffled off into his office. The receptionist, a nice-looking black woman in a cerise suit, asked if I'd like coffee and I said great and remembered to say with cream instead of white. "And may I use the phone for just a moment? I'm afraid it's long distance."

"Help yourself." She gestured to a phone on a table between two armchairs.

My fingers trembled as I pushed the buttons. What would I do if it was busy or no one was home? Maudie answered on the third ring. "Darling," I said, "it's me," forgetting all about identifying myself.

"Is everything all right?"

"As a matter of fact I'm at Mr. Savage's—Aunt Helen's lawyer. Apparently he tried to call me yesterday, in Scotland. The line was engaged."

"Goodness," Maudie exclaimed. "We never thought of that, did we? Well, don't worry. From now on no one but me answers the phone."

"You angel," I said and blurted out some nonsense about reminding her to pay the mortgage. My heart was still thumping as I hung up. Surreptitiously I wiped the sweaty handprint off the receiver.

The receptionist brought my coffee. "You're welcome," she said when I thanked her. I sat there, flicking through *Newsweek* and wondering about Aunt Helen's business. As I turned to the film reviews, it suddenly came to me: my campaign on Leo's behalf had paid off. She was going to make me a beneficiary. A hundred thousand, I daydreamed, two hundred? Beneath her desk the receptionist crossed and re-crossed her slender legs.

• • •

Ewan closed the book and got out of bed. Downstairs, he dialled Vanessa's number again. After four rings, her recording clicked on. Somewhere in the middle of his reading he had realised that David Coyle might also be phoning Vanessa and that he ought to let her know what was afoot. Hearing her voice, though, he had no idea what to say. The line between information and accusation seemed nonexistent. He let the tape run and hung up without saying a word.

Chapter 9

On her way home from the airport, Mollie stopped in Perth to buy supplies. In the chemists that first day, when Mrs. Tulliver had asked, she'd said some friends were visiting and had forgotten to bring their bag of baby things. "What a nuisance," said Mrs. Tulliver, and Mollie hadn't blushed or batted an eyelash. It was as if she had known even then, before fully laying eyes on Olivia or inhaling her downy fragrance, what she was going to do. But she had been acting solely on instinct, whereas now guile and cunning entered in. She went to the Boots on Perth High Street, a large, busy shop where no one paid her any attention, and walked up and down the baby aisle, buying whatever seemed remotely useful. Then she went to Mothercare and quickly chose a car seat, a sling, and half a dozen outfits. She wished there were time to linger over choices of colour and style, but glancing up as she wrote out her cheque in Boots, she thought she saw Mrs. Rae, the butcher's wife, at the cosmetics counter. When she looked again, the woman was a stranger; still, Mollie was reminded of how often she did run into people she knew in Perth. Later she realised she had ignored what should have been her worst fear: the possibility of meeting someone who knew not her but Olivia. After all, Perth was her hometown, and she was a distinctive baby who had already been missing for several days. To worry about that, however, would have required admitting the untenable facts: Olivia had parents, or a parent, and Mollie's joy was balanced against someone else's pain.

By the time Mollie finished, the back seat of the car was filled with purchases. Without stopping to install Olivia's seat, she tucked her back on the floor and began to drive through the busy streets. At the third red light, she launched into "I Love to Go a-Wandering." When she exhausted the verses she remembered, well outside Perth, she moved on to "Greensleeves." The only songs she knew were those she'd learned at school from Miss Luke, the music teacher.

> *"Greensleeves was all my joy,*
> *Greensleeves was my delight,*
> *Greensleeves was my heart of gold,*
> *And who but Lady Greensleeves?"*

she sang as she accelerated past two lorries. For once the motion of travel did not put Olivia to sleep; she lay gazing up from her pillow as if the ceiling of the car and Mollie singing behind the steering wheel were sights of infinite interest. Whenever the road straightened out, Mollie glanced down for a glimpse of her small face.

She came through the gates of Mill of Fortune, and there stood the house, foursquare and welcoming. The dark cloud of malevolence, which for the past month had hovered above the slate roof, was gone. Unlocking the back door, she was struck by how tattered the green paint had become; when the weather grew warmer, she would paint the door cerulean blue or perhaps a brighter green. Inside, Sadie pranced around, snorting her welcome, and Plato tapped his mirror so that the small bell hanging above it tinkled. On the table were a bunch of keys and a note. Bending down, Mollie read, *These will let you into the house. To turn off the burglar alarm press the first four digits of my phone number. Love, Ewan.* "How nice of him," she murmured, and, with no thought she would ever use them, slipped the keys into her bag.

That afternoon she put Olivia in the sling and walked up the hill to St. David's Well. She threw a coin for each of them and made the same wish twice—that they would never leave each other—as if repetition would convince the king's daughters of their sincerity and thus multiply the chances of success. Then she continued along the forestry track to the moors. She heard a lark singing, and a hundred yards ahead, a kestrel circled once, then again, before hurtling down with almost audible speed. As the bird rose clumsily out of the heather, its talons empty, Mollie registered with astonishment that she had forgotten to be afraid.

She stood gazing east down the valley. In the distance lay the town, with the river running through it and the fields spreading out on either side, some newly planted and already taking on that first cast of green, others still being used for livestock. Winter was safely past and spring was coming, hesitant but unmistakeable.

The last hurdle of the day was Ewan's phone call, and from seven o'clock onwards she waited anxiously. Once she went to call him, but even as she lifted the receiver she was letting it fall. Initiating the lies she planned to tell seemed fractionally worse than offering them in self-defence. When the phone did finally ring, she was so nervous she forgot most of her story. She'd planned to say something about a pleasant woman police constable, about a form she'd filled out. But Ewan seemed satisfied by her scant details. Then the kitchen door, which she had carefully closed, swung open, and Olivia let out a yell. Mollie jumped up to shut it, blamed the noise on the dog, and rattled on before he could ask any questions, not that he would have. His lack of curiosity, which she used to count a fault, now struck her as wonderfully fortunate. She was hard-pressed to conceal her delight at his news of Milan. Four days' reprieve, she thought, and counted them off on her fingers for sheer happiness. As soon as the call was over, she went back into the kitchen and, standing by the stove, drank a small tot of whisky in a single swallow.

After breakfast, when Olivia fell asleep, Mollie approached that corner of the kitchen where for weeks her loom had stood neglected. She was, or rather had been, in the middle of a hanging, a present for Rebecca, whose birthday had passed a fortnight ago. Studying the tapestry of grey and purple, Mollie thought, What an absurd gift. Rebecca wanted what she herself had wanted at that age: trendy clothes or brightly coloured cosmetics. She picked up a pair of scissors and began to cut a month's work out of the loom. In a more patient mood, she might have unravelled it. She had joked once with Chae that no one ever gave Penelope enough credit for the laborious work of unravelling. He had kissed her and had the hero of his next novel make the same remark.

As Mollie squeezed the scissors, she recalled a conversation with Bridget last autumn. Bridget had telephoned to wish her happy birthday and after the exchange of greetings gone on to expound her therapist's latest theory. "She thinks the reason I'm ambivalent about having children is because of our mother's difficulties," Bridget said, her voice growing shiny with self-importance.

"But you were much too young to know what was happening," Mollie exclaimed.

"Intellectually yes, but not emotionally. Don't you think it's strange that none of the three of us have children?"

"No," said Mollie. "You don't want them, Ewan hasn't met the right woman, and I have children."

"Stepchildren," Bridget corrected. "It's not the same."

"Of course it is," Mollie said. "Don't be reactionary."

Bridget in turn had accused her of repression, and the phone call ended in mutual irritation.

Watching the severed threads spring apart, Mollie thought she owed her sister an apology. Then another figure appeared, with an even greater claim on her remorse: Chae's ex-wife. Every summer she had phoned, begging to see Rebecca and Daniel just for a weekend. "I can't stand not seeing them for two months," she would say. But Chae insisted on sticking to their agreement; the children were hers during term, his over the holidays. And Mollie, finding her complaints incomprehensible, had supported him. Christ—she snipped vehemently—what a bitch I was! She had always believed she loved her stepchildren only a little less than their parents. Now, measured against her feelings for Olivia, she could see that love for what it was: a single strand of wool compared to the whole tapestry, a pine needle compared to the tree.

She picked up the weaving and carried it outside to the dustbin. A few scraps blew over towards the lilac bushes, where shortly they would merge with the purple flowers. Back indoors, Mollie began to dress the loom. She wanted to make a blanket for Olivia, something that combined the yellow of the poncho which had kept her safe on the floor of the Gents, the grey of Ewan's suit, and the brown of the baby's own eyes. A couple of years ago she would've insisted on dyeing the wool herself—gathering the lichens and roots, carefully boiling and distilling until, after perhaps a dozen attempts, she had the ideal shade. Today she simply scanned her rows of wool, lifted down a skein of moss-brown yarn, finely spun, and began to measure out the weft.

As she wound the wool, she caught sight of the postcard

pinned to one end of the loom: the three Fates at work, spinning, measuring, and cutting. She didn't have to look to remember the brief message on the back. *Darling Mollie,* Chae had written, *keep spinning.* And for a long time she had thought of their life as something they were spinning together. Recently, however, she had suffered the fierce attentions of the third Fate. Snip, snip. Now she was weaving the new life she wanted, a life with Olivia, of which the blanket was a promise.

When the knock came on Wednesday afternoon, Mollie was sitting by the stove, feeding Olivia. For a few seconds she was paralysed. She hadn't locked the back door, and it was quite possible, according to country manners, that the caller would feel free to try the latch and step inside. At the second knock, Mollie jumped up with Olivia and raced from the room. Not daring to venture the stairs, she went into the parlour, pulling the door behind her. The shutters, still closed since last Saturday, gave the room the dim quality of a dirty aquarium; the overstuffed furniture floated like slow fish.

Crouched behind the sofa, Mollie heard the back door open and a voice call, "Anyone home?"

It was Lorraine. When Mollie told Ewan she had no friends, she was, in her bitterness, discounting several people, of whom Lorraine was the most significant. She and Taylor had moved up from Gloucester five years ago and bought a house on the outskirts of town; together they ran an antiquarian book business, and Lorraine knitted intricate cardigans and jumpers, no two alike. Soon after she arrived, she had phoned Mollie to ask where to buy wool, and their similar interests had blossomed into friendship.

"Mollie," Lorraine called again. "It's me."

Mollie stared at the faded beige print of the sofa and did her best to hold the bottle steady in Olivia's mouth. She heard Lorraine moving around, a chair scraping, the trickle of water, the clink of a glass or cup being replaced on the draining board, and, at last, the precious sound of the back door closing. In the ensuing silence Mollie sank to the floor and simply sat there, her back to the sofa and her eyes closed.

She was rescued by Olivia, who needed burping. Her attention, as usual, was perfectly focused on the lineaments of her small world. Mollie patted her and, on her own behalf, tried vainly to resurrect the breathing techniques of a long-ago yoga class—blue, red, yellow, green. She stood up and tiptoed into the kitchen. Just as Olivia burst into wails, she raced to the back door and slid the bolt across.

For a few minutes Mollie could do nothing but sit at the table, crying inconsolably, while on her lap Olivia wailed away. At last they both fell quiet. Mollie dried her eyes and drank a glass of water. Lorraine had left a note beneath the pepper grinder, flecks of pepper dotting her words like additional punctuation.

> *Mollie,*
>   *I was driving by and stopped in to say hello. Sorry not to have been in touch. School holidays! Let's talk soon.*
> *Love, Lorraine*
> *P.S. I like your new piece—great colours!*

"Love," sneered Mollie. She crumpled the paper and hurled it to the floor. For a month Lorraine had neglected her. No calls, no trips to Perth. Now she strolled into the house without so much as a by-your-leave. Swollen, angry thoughts buzzed in Mollie's brain, making it easy to forget their last meeting, the week after Chae left, when Lorraine had urged her to take him back and Mollie had screamed that she never wanted to see either her or Taylor again.

Gradually the buzzing subsided. Lorraine wasn't important,

but what she had shown Mollie was. Stopping occasionally to run a hand through her hair, or adjust her grip on Olivia, Mollie paced back and forth in front of the stove. This was not simply a matter of being more careful; she had to be more clever. To think she could keep Olivia a secret was madness. Sooner or later someone would discover her, and then even the best explanation would seem suspicious. She had to invent a story that explained this baby's presence.

She put Olivia down in the chair and from among her cookbooks retrieved a notebook of recipes, only half filled. Armed with this, a pen, and a cup of coffee, she settled herself at the kitchen table, just as Ewan would have done. Could she have adopted a foundling? For a moment, given her own history, the idea was immensely appealing. But no, she thought. That would be fraught with problems. She didn't know enough about the mechanics of adoption; and if anyone enquired, her ignorance would be plain and some local social worker might hear rumours and investigate. How did people get babies—from friends? Rather unlikely. She recalled a girl at school, Heather, who had lived with her aunt and uncle. Mollie couldn't imagine why; it had not seemed to her, or anyone else, worth enquiring. Bridget, she thought. Her faraway sister was the answer.

At once everything seemed possible. Bridget had visited Mill of Fortune a few times, although not for several years, and people still remembered her. Sometimes they'd ask Mollie about events in the States—Clinton, Waco, the World Trade Center—as if she might have special information. Yes, Bridget had had a baby. The father was black, of course; that fitted perfectly with life over there. But why had she given her daughter to Mollie?

Against her will, *The Dark Forest* came to mind. She recalled Leo's assumption at the beginning of the novel that Roman was ill. People were always ready to believe in illness, the worse the better. *Bridget,* she wrote, *cancer.* After a pause, she added *breast,* then stared, slightly horrified, at what she had done. Briefly she felt the tug of superstition, as if her words could cause the cells in Bridget's breasts to become malignant. She raised a hand to her own chest. Once again she'd forgotten to check. Next month, she swore, and wrote down *Check breasts* in a separate column.

So Olivia was Bridget's daughter, but how had she got to Mill of Fortune? She'd sent the baby over with a nurse to the one person she could trust. No, that was a wartime fantasy, when people had dispatched neatly labelled children on enormous journeys. The logical thing would've been for Mollie to go to Boston, where she could care for both her sister and the baby.

Mollie tapped her pencil against the table. Was this, she wondered, what it was like for Chae when he wrote his books? One event leading to the next, almost without volition, much more like life than she had supposed. And for an instant, seeing how blithely she'd given her dear sister cancer, Mollie felt a feather of sympathy drift down onto the vast stony landscape of her fury. Then she turned back to her task. She needed to get the details straight so she could tell the same story to everyone and believe it herself.

Suppose Bridget were in London. Perhaps she'd come back to see her old doctor, in whom she had tremendous faith. And Ewan had brought the baby up from London. "You should've seen him," Mollie heard herself say, "carrying a baby in his pin-stripe suit." Yes, yes, this was good. Didn't they say in crime novels that the best alibi was the one closest to the truth, alter only what you absolutely have to? There had, after all, been other passengers on the bus. So Olivia had come to stay with her Scottish aunt. "It does me good," Mollie would say. "I've been down in the dumps since, well, since that business with Chae. Nothing like a baby to cheer you up."

This way they could go into town together, take walks, talk to people; they would no longer need to live like outcasts. Mollie did not consider her promise to Ewan of coming to London, nor the dwindling bank account on which she'd already written several large cheques. Most especially she did not think of Olivia's true origins, and of the man with a local accent who knew the phone number at Mill of Fortune. None of these quibbles disturbed her pleasure as she went over the details one more time. The one thing she did not quite like was the naming of her relation to Olivia: "Aunt" had an unappealing, Dickensian ring.

That afternoon she took Olivia into town to meet Mrs. Tulliver. If she could tell the story successfully to her, she could tell it to anyone. She parked opposite the chemists and hurried in with Olivia. Mrs. Tulliver wasn't behind the counter, and for a moment Mollie thought it must be her day off. Then she spotted her in the corner, arranging the shampoos. Hastily Mollie chose two kinds of lotion and approached. "Excuse me?"

Mrs. Tulliver turned, a green bottle in each hand. "Hello, Mollie. How are you keeping?" she said, then her eyes widened. "What's this, a baby?"

"It's my niece, Olivia. I was so flustered the other day I didn't get to tell you what had happened. My brother, Ewan, showed up with her unexpectedly, from London."

Mrs. Tulliver was bending over Olivia, stroking her cheek. Olivia smiled her best smile. "She's Ewan's bairn?" she said, sounding puzzled.

"No, no. He's still the swinging bachelor. She's my sister Bridget's daughter."

She fluttered the coat-tails of her story, just enough for Mrs. Tulliver to say how dreadful but try not to worry. "I've a cousin in Dalkeith. Ten years since he was diagnosed, and he's fit as a fiddle. It's wonderful what they can do nowadays."

Mollie agreed. "Which of these is best?" she said, holding out the two bottles. Mrs. Tulliver explained that she herself favoured the one with lanolin.

Back in the car, Mollie burst out laughing. "We did it!" she said to Olivia. But Olivia's good humour had fled, and all the way home she cried as if every bump and sway of the car were taking her further from where she wanted to be.

Chapter 10

Walking back from the bus station, Kenneth stopped at the betting shop on Leonard Street and put two quid, all that was left of his mum's money, on Easy Does It to place in the two-fifteen. Then he drifted round the corner to the pub. He had just enough change for a pint. The last time he'd been here, a Saturday night a couple of months ago, the room was crowded with people his age, in their twenties. He'd got into a heated argument about euthanasia and gone home, his head jangling with comments about deep freezes and villages in China. Now, the lunch hour rush over, it was almost empty, with only a few old dossers reading the paper and some kids at the video machines. Skiving off, Kenneth thought, recalling his own school days. One of the few things he missed about the infirmary was that puffy sense of self-importance when you had to get out of the pub and go to work, telling people and complaining all the while. He'd enjoyed that part, maybe a bit too much, and been fired for being late three times in a single week and having beer on his breath. "Reeking" was the word the supervisor used, sounding not angry but—and Kenneth found this infinitely more upsetting—bored.

He leaned on the bar and sipped his beer. The bartender, a beefy bloke whose face and neck were the same shade of pink from his scrubby brown hair to his collar, was checking the fridges. When he handed Kenneth his pint, he spilled a little and made a tired remark about the weather. Don't I even rate Princess Di? Kenneth wanted to ask.

The clock above the bar read ten to two. In a little over an hour, Joan would be home from work, and he'd need some excuse for Grace's absence. He wished he could remember more about that baby in America, but you didn't have to be Sherlock Holmes to know that the longer these people hung on to Grace, the better. If they gave her back right away, they'd just be doing their duty. They had to keep her at least a night or two to be good and guilty. He heard himself saying, "You kept the baby for how long?" He could make that wee sentence sound full of big, sinister suggestions.

Meanwhile, what to say to Joan? He thought longingly of those places where women still obeyed men—Egypt? Iran? He wasn't sure, but he knew there were countries where he could simply have told Joan not to bother him about Grace and bring him his bloody tea, and that would be that. Even though she was a foreigner, she wasn't that kind. Still, the situation was easier than if she'd been a Perth girl. He remembered his old girlfriend Brenda, who had thrown his clothes out of the window just because he came home two hours late one night and then, when she caught him with Margaret, had followed him from pub to pub, playing "Tainted Love" on the jukebox. Joan would never do anything like that, but in her quiet way she might make a stink. She could go to the police, he thought. Or tell people at the infirmary. He had a vision of the bored supervisor pricking up his ears at her story.

What was an okay thing to do with a baby? You couldn't lend or lose her. A friend wanted her? Fat chance. Research?

Beyond the pale. He tried to recall what Joan did with Grace when she was at work. As far as he knew, either her mother came round—she worked odd hours as a live-in laundress at the Salutation Hotel—or Joan took the baby downstairs to Mrs. Kemp. Well, they were both useless as excuses. He drank some beer. It had lost that first bite of coldness and slid down effortlessly. On the telly behind the bar, his race was coming up, the horses prancing round the enclosure. The grass was a nasty shade of green. "Can you fix that?" he asked the bartender.

" 'Fraid not. Been that way since Wimbledon." He guffawed, and his overall pinkness deepened.

"What about sound?"

"That we can do." He turned up the volume. Easy Does It was a chestnut filly whose jockey wore a custard-yellow outfit. Kenneth was instantly depressed. No one who wore togs like that could ride a decent race. He stared gloomily at the screen. The next horse, Pretty Thing, now there was a good-looking beast; her jockey had a nice blue and purple outfit and was promisingly small. "Do you have anything on it?" asked the bartender.

"Pretty Thing, to place."

"Pretty Thing? Never heard of her. Not that that means much these days. I promised my missis I wouldn't bet in any way, shape, or form until my birthday. A month and four days to go."

"How would she know?" said Kenneth, interested in spite of himself.

"She'd know. If I win, I foam at the mouth. If I lose, I weep. Wouldn't be any fun having to keep it to myself."

"Why'd she make you promise?"

"Last year Lester Piggott came to me in a dream and told me the winner of the Derby. I bet a week's wages. Didn't even place. Daft, really."

"I never dream."

"May be as well." The bartender shook his head and wiped his hands on the dish towel slung over one shoulder.

The race was off, and they both leaned towards the screen. As the horses accelerated, so did the announcer's voice, slurring the names into an endless sentence. After a slow start, Easy Does It, with her bilious-yellow rider, began to move forward, past High Noon and Christopher Columbus. Kenneth cheered wildly, pounding the bar so hard the ashtrays rattled. The horse came in second, while Pretty Thing lagged home in sixth place.

He became aware of the bartender watching him, fish-mouthed. "Didn't you bet on Pretty Thing?"

"I just said that not to jinx things. Easy Does It! Look, there she is, the beauty." He raised his glass to the screen, where Easy Does It was walking nimbly behind a chap in one of those sheepskin jackets.

He went next door to collect his winnings. To his delight the cashier gave him four fivers, still crisp from the wrapper. He had always loved new money; it seemed worth more before a thousand sweaty fingers faded the pictures of Walter Scott and the Queen. As he strolled down the street, patting his pocket from time to time, he thought he might take Joan out for a meal. Or maybe a take-away? No, a restaurant. And then it came to him: his mum.

She sometimes baby-sat for the brat downstairs. Why could she not baby-sit for Grace, in fact keep her for the night? After all, she was the other granny. In one fell swoop he embraced paternity, at least for now.

He let himself into the flat and heard the radio on in the bathroom. He wished he'd been here first, but not to worry. He went to the kitchen sink and bent over the faucet, rinsing the beer out of his mouth. The water beaded on the gleaming metal. He felt slightly sick and realised he'd had nothing to eat all day. Two bus journeys, and not a single bacon roll. He reached into the bread bin, took out a slice of bread—brown, unfortunately—and ate it dry, in quick bites, not wanting Joan to catch him. She emerged as he swallowed the last mouthful. "Kenneth," she called.

"I'm in here."

She came in wearing billowy trousers and a black cardigan he'd watched her buy last spring from the Oxfam Shop. Her hair was down in the girlish way he liked. At the infirmary, she had to wear one of those stupid paper bonnets, pink or blue, for hygiene. It was when he saw her without the hat, in the cafeteria, her hair hanging nearly to her waist, that he'd asked her for a drink. "Joan," he said, edging round the table to meet her.

"Where's Grace?"

"I've a wee surprise for you." He had made a mistake. Her mouth was opening, and he could feel her scream coming, like the gust of air from an onrushing train. "Grace's spending the night at Mum's," he said quickly. "I thought it was time they got acquainted. No use having a granny you never see."

"Your mother," she said, not quite a question but not acceptance either.

"Yes, you know, my mum—like your mum, only Scottish." God, what a blithering idiot! He went over and put his arms around her. He was nearly six inches taller, another thing he liked. Nuzzling her spicy hair, he could tell from her stiffness that she had not yet succumbed to his story. He glimpsed the road ahead, hard work. "Joan," he said softly, "don't you want Grace to get to know her Scottish gran? My mum's brilliant with kids, better than that old bag Kemp. All the kids are mad about my mum."

She interrupted. "But you took nothing for her." She was pointing at the pile of gear she'd left on the table—nappies and bottles, mostly.

Shit. "Like I told you, she looks after kids all the time. She has everything."

"Milk?" Joan asked. "Nappies?"

"The whole cafuffle. A pram, a cot." He racked his brains. "One of those nice chairs she can sit in."

Gradually Joan shed her suspicion. Of course she believed everyone was as daft about the baby as she was. The part that wanted explaining was not why his mum wanted to look after the little snot but how he could bear to give Grace up, even for a few hours. "So what about going out for a meal," he suggested.

She argued at first—she'd bought groceries on the way home—then giggled and agreed. Kenneth began to name restaurants, ticking them off on his fingers: the Peking Palace, the Gondoliers, the Koh-i-Noor, Benny's. The Koh-i-Noor, she said happily, and went off to tell Mrs. Kemp she wouldn't need to mind Grace tomorrow. He sat at the kitchen table, eating slice after slice of dry bread, trying to prepare his stomach for the curry and get his brain in order. It was ages since he'd had a scheme, not since he and his mate Duncan had jobs at the off-licence and carefully whittled away a few bottles a week in breakages. At two quid an hour, a couple of bottles of Scotch made quite a difference. Kids' stuff, he thought now. He'd been too modest, thinking in terms of five hundred pounds. He should squeeze them for a grand, at least.

He stood up, suddenly wondering if Joan might have bought him a beer. The small fridge was covered with snaps, all of Grace, except for one of Joan with her mother and some young lad beside the river Tay. Now, who could this be? Then he remembered Joan telling him her brother, Lalit, had come up to Perth for a holiday right after he arrived in Britain. Not a bad-looking bloke, Kenneth thought, with his white shirt and dark hair. On impulse he peeled off a photo of Grace in her cot and slipped it into his pocket. You never could tell what might come in handy.

He was contemplating the fridge, disappointingly full of yoghurt and orange juice, when he heard the tap of Joan's sandals. She had changed into a long, silky blue top and sleek black trousers, with gold combs in her hair and a row of different-coloured bracelets up her arm (he knew from the time he'd broken one they were made of glass). She stood in the doorway, smiling at him, a toothy, nervous smile that ignited a little spark in his brain—compliment, he thought.

"Hey, good-lookin', what you got cookin'?" he said, and went to kiss her.

He was glad the Koh-i-Noor lay the other way from the bus station. To walk on those same pavements with Joan, he felt, would be a mistake. There might be some lingering trace of his earlier passage with Grace. As they headed down the High Street past Boots and Woolworth's, Joan told him how they'd been cleaning a storeroom at the infirmary, when a frog hopped out from under the radiator. "The poor creature was terrified," she said. "Three people chasing it with brooms. At last we got it into a box, and I carried it outside and let it go on the grass. It was a sign. I have to ask my mother."

"A sign of what?" Kenneth said, steering her into George Street.

"Oh, the gods, you know." She paused in front of a shop window full of dresses. "Pretty," she murmured, pointing to a nifty red number.

Inside the Koh-i-Noor, a waiter with a bushy moustache led them to a corner table. He poured water into their glasses from a great height, as if he were doing a conjuring trick and the water would come out as something else. Kenneth ordered papadums and a lager and let Joan do the rest. While she and the waiter yakked in some wog language, he sank back into his own thoughts.

What was hard, which he hadn't expected, was keeping his trap shut. He was dying to tell her—or anybody, for that matter—about his cleverness, to have a toff pick up the baby and then sniff out his name and phone number. Bloody brilliant, but he knew it would be a mistake to blab. When Mr. Moustache returned with a plate of papadums, Kenneth ate one in a single greedy swoop and another more slowly. His lager came in a glass streaming with condensation, and he took a long draught. Joan was saying something about Deirdre at work's retirement party. "We had a cake shaped like a cat. My brother's girlfriend also is called Deirdre."

"Your brother?" For a moment Kenneth was thrown—had she seen him nicking Grace's photo?—but no, it was just Joanie blethering on.

"Lalit," she said. "Down in Preston. He wrote to tell me about her. She cuts hair."

He nodded and grabbed another papadum. Something about the conversation was nudging at him, though he couldn't reel it in. "And what does he do, Lalit? Does he have a job?"

"Of course. Lalit is not lazy. He is here to work, so he works, making batteries." She outlined an invisible box with her hands. "Not healthy, I think. The hours are very long."

Lazy, thought Kenneth.

It was touch-and-go whether he would stand up and walk away, tugging the tablecloth with him, just to hear everything crash to the floor. He'd done that before in restaurants, and no one had lifted a finger. In one place the waiter had even held the door open. Now he did his best to keep the lid on it. Who cares what the little bitch thinks? He tore his paper table mat in half and then in quarters. He'd never told Joan that he was fired from the infirmary. They were cutting back, he explained vaguely. Maybe they'd need him later. Lazy, gormless, daft, cretin, idiot, berk—all the words they'd sent hurling his way; they wouldn't be able to take them back fast enough when they heard about Grace. And in the midst of his anger, he landed the dim thought of a few minutes before.

"Your brother's an illegal immigrant, isn't he?"

Joan shook her head.

"Come on," he coaxed. "I'm Grace's dad. I'm family."

"There is some problem," she said in a low voice. "My uncle is sorting the business out."

He reached across and patted her hand. "Good luck to him. Have a papadum. Anyway, so why'd you call the baby Grace?"

She laughed shyly. "The first job I had in this country was for a very nice woman, Mrs. Lawson. I cleaned her house. She had a big picture over her fireplace of a girl in a boat, rowing on a stormy sea. I looked at the picture every day, and one day I asked her about it. She told me this girl was Grace Darling and that she was famous for rowing out from her father's lighthouse to a ship and rescuing people. They would have drowned if she hadn't saved them. So when Grace was born I decided to call her after that girl, that it was a brave name."

"Here's to Grace." He raised his glass and clinked it against Joan's. As usual she had asked for water and then giggled compliantly when he ordered her a shandy. A lighthouse keeper, he thought; now there was a dead-end job.

Their curries came, and Joan served them. Once they were eating, she said she wanted to ask him something. "In the w.c. at work, someone has written, 'Betty is a wanker.' She is not pleased. What is a wanker?"

Kenneth grinned. "Poor old Betty. A wanker is—" He broke off. How to explain in a way that wasn't chronically confusing? He took a swig of lager and had an inspiration. "Forget about wanker. What you want to say when you're cross is 'shitty bastard.' "

"Which means?"

"Something nasty and terrible. Have a go."

"Shitty bastard," she said slowly. "Was that right?"

"Perfect. You need to practise ten times a day."

"Shitty bastard," she repeated. "Shitty bastard." She raised her glass of shandy, and the bracelets tinkled.

They made good use of the bed that night, and in the morning, when he woke, Joan had once again left for the infirmary. She worked overtime every other weekend. Filled with feverish excitement, Kenneth made a cup of tea and carried it back to bed. When he was seventeen, he and Duncan had hitchhiked down to London. They had had no clear plan of action, no exact goal, but Kenneth had nursed the sure conviction that he had only to present himself in the capital city for fame and fortune to accost him. He'd been keeping them waiting.

They ended up living in a broken-down car, which they pushed nightly round the streets of Camden in order to avoid being harassed by the police, or by the residents in whose gardens they sometimes peed. During the day they would beg and in the evening try to pick up women in pubs in order to have a place to sleep. Neither of them ever scored. Finally, one night, facing yet another closing time alone, Kenneth announced to Duncan that he was thinking of going home to see his mum. She'd been poorly recently.

Duncan could be slow, but he caught on immediately. Though neither of their families had phones—and who would have written to where?—he didn't question how Kenneth got his information, only chimed in that his dad, too, had been under the weather. By seven the next morning they were heading out to Finchley, as presentable as they could make themselves, to stand fifty feet apart by the roadside. Kenneth couldn't help being chuffed that he got a lift before Duncan. A black lorry had pulled up. See you in the Perth Arms, he'd shouted as he ran towards it.

By silent agreement neither of them ever admitted the gloom of those weeks. In memory they made them shine. But what was not invented, what Kenneth had missed for months afterwards, was the energy and excitement pulsing through him, especially the first few days, when it was as if the little pills they bought in a pub off Piccadilly Circus had taken up permanent residence in his veins. Now, in Joan's bed with his cuppa, he had that same feeling of his blood flowing faster and brighter. Ideas, he thought. I am an ideas man.

Today he would make the first phone call. The soft creepy one where you didn't ask for anything, didn't threaten anybody; just let them know you knew. He drank some tea and closed his eyes to picture all over again the bloke in the suit, walking towards the cinema with Grace. With his specs and his cack-handedness, he had looked like an easy touch. Some of those suits had killer instincts, took no prisoners, and would sell their grannies for a bob, but this bloke could barely get on and off a bus by himself—and why had he taken Grace out of her poncho in the rain, the stupid bugger?

There was money, no question. Even the name of the house, Mill of Fortune, had a wealthy sound. The more he thought about it, the larger grew his notions of what he ought to ask for. Every hour, every day, they held on to Grace upped the ante, if only he could keep Joan quiet. His mum wasn't going to wash much longer. He needed something else: not an excuse, a threat. He tugged the sheet tight around him. Ideas, he crooned, ideas. Then he caught sight of the blue top she'd worn the night before and remembered her squirming at the question about Lalit. Maybe that was the answer: he could threaten to report her brother, the illegal immigrant. Taking jobs away from us local lads with his blasted batteries.

But what if the Laffertys had already handed Grace over to

the police? He closed his eyes and sat very still, trying to divine if this awful thing had happened. He climbed out of bed and found a ten-pence piece on the dresser. Heads they had, tails they hadn't. Best of three. He stood there shivering slightly in his tee shirt, trying to tell the coin its job: how it must read the signals he couldn't. Then he tossed the coin three times, and three times tails lay gleaming in his palm.

He left Joan a note saying he was off to see Grace and her granny and would be back later. Keep her calm, he thought, writing, "Love, K." Miraculously he had just enough left from Easy Does It to pay the newsagents. His mum greeted him with a stream of accusations. He let her go on until he felt sure he'd earned a fiver, then he slammed the receipt down on the table. Right enough, she looked taken aback and offered a cup of tea. While he waited, he glanced through the magazine she'd been reading. Food, food, shopping, some kind of kitchen gizmo. He paused at an article called "Taking Care of Company." The first sentence said, "Company can be anyone—an aunt, a sister, a baby, a best friend." Company, he thought, that had a nice ring to it, of fear, of money. His mother put the tea in front of him and announced that Venus was moving into alignment with Saturn, which meant they were going to have a grand week. Romance and finance, she explained, would both flourish. "Okeydokey," said Kenneth. He downed his tea and got up to go.

He was passing the newsagents when he remembered the phone he and Harve had discovered last autumn at The Blind Beggar. The machine took one-pence pieces for twenty, and for a while they'd met there a couple of times a week for Harve to phone a mate in Glasgow. Kenneth didn't really know people in other places, except his mum's sister in Braemar, but he phoned radio stations and the off-licence where he and Duncan had worked. Now he changed direction, making his way to The Blind Beggar. Ideas, he was swimming in them.

A woman answered. Although he hadn't caught her exact words at the chemists, he recognised the voice. "Mrs. Lafferty?" he asked, and she said yes, hesitantly, as if he might be talking about someone else. In the pause that followed came a high-pitched squeak, a sound so faint he would've missed it if he hadn't had the phone jammed to his ear. Grace, he thought. Bloody fantastic. "I'm sorry to trouble you," he said smoothly. "You have company."

She said something about a brother and then, "I'm afraid I didn't catch your name."

"A well-wisher." He stared at the grubby phonebook. "Somebody wishing you well with your company."

"Who is this?" she demanded. "No, that won't be necessary," and slammed the phone down.

I got to her, he thought gleefully. Step one.

Then back to deal with Joan, who pounced the instant he came through the door. "Grace," she said. "Where is Grace?"

"Joanie, she's with Mum. I thought you'd like some p and q. A nice quiet evening by the telly with your old man."

"Take me there," she said, slipping off her mules and reaching for her outdoor shoes.

"She's fine. You don't want to disturb her. She'll be getting ready for beddie-bye. I just came from seeing her. She and my mum are getting on famously. Come on, this is a treat not to have her yelling the place down."

Joan stopped and looked at him. She was catching on. Her eyes went watery. "Please, Kenneth. I want to see her."

He liked that. He liked her saying please and her voice going tiny. "Let me take my coat off," he said, "and I'll tell you what's what."

At the kitchen table he explained he needed to borrow

Grace for a few days. That she was vital to his plans. "If all goes well," he said, "she'll earn us a pretty penny. I'll be proud of my daughter."

When Joan spoke again it was in a tone that suggested that English, the language in which she now conducted her life, had suddenly deserted her, the meaning emptied out and gone like water into the sand. "She is with your mother. Grace is with her Scottish granny."

"Yes, yes, of course she's with my mum, but she's there for a reason. I can't explain it to you. You have to trust me."

Joan stood up. "I must go and get her," she said carefully. "It is kind of your mother, very kind, but it is too long for Grace to be away from home. I need her here. She needs me. I will explain, and your mother will understand."

Kenneth took her wrist and pulled her back into the chair. These fucking women, he thought. Since when had his life got to be ruled by women—shouting, crying, telling him what to do? "Shut up and listen. Grace is with my mum, okay? She stays there till I say, okay? It's only a few days. She'll be fine. Right now you've got me to take care of."

He wouldn't have thought she could grow pale, not with her skin, dark as strong tea, but unmistakeably her colour faded, and tears began to slip down her cheeks. "Kenneth, please."

"Aren't you listening?" he said. "It's not a question of please and thank you. Grace is doing a job, like you at the infirmary. When it's done, she'll be home. Meanwhile, you do what I say. Okey-dokey?"

"I will go to the po-lice," she said softly, giving the word its Scottish pronunciation.

"No you bloody won't. Your brother, Lalit—if you go to the police, I'll have him shipped back to Bombay."

He had not the faintest clue how to implement his threat—he didn't even have the guy's address—but his words had gone home. Joan was rooted, appalled. He was still holding her wrist, and he gave it a good shake. "Come on. Say you understand. Your brother's fine, your baby's fine. So just be patient."

"Why? Why do this to Grace? She is not with your mother The Scottish granny. Your mother is no more Grace's granny than you are her father."

Her scorn was for both his duplicity and her own innocence. And then she did something, he realised, she hardly ever did—she stared right into his eyes, and he found himself struggling not to look away. "Is she dead?" she asked. "Is that it? Tell me now."

"Of course she's not dead, you idiot." He was about to say again that Grace was with his mother, but he could not bring himself to repeat the lie uselessly. "Do what I tell you," he said, "and everything will be grand. Now what about some grub? I'm starving."

He gave her another little shake, meaning cook, meaning where's your sense of humour? For a few more seconds Joan stared at him, her eyes so dark that he could barely distinguish iris from pupil, then she turned away. She bent to pick something off the floor, and Kenneth watched her, the swoop of her breasts, the curve of her waist. Plenty more where Grace came from, he thought.

Chapter 11

In Milan, Ewan made a presentation to various investors and surprised himself by achieving a fluency he had not previously believed lay within his repertoire. On these occasions he usually felt no more than competent, and sometimes, especially when he was tired, his stutter reasserted itself. But in the boardroom of Ginestra and Sedara—with its arched ceiling, and green and black oil paintings by some contemporary Italian artist—the words he needed flowed easily. The men and women around the table studied various charts and graphs, took notes, and nodded. "There are risks, of course," Ewan reported. "The currency situation is volatile. Nevertheless we project a steady yield over the next three years, with accelerated profits in the second half of the decade."

He watched his own performance with a kind of breathless cynicism. At home he was approaching ruin and dishonour, and here he was, not exactly fiddling while Rome burned, which suggested genuine delight on Nero's part, but maybe organising his wardrobe while the house fell down. At the end of the session, several people shook his hand, including a crucial bank manager who had been swithering for weeks about underwriting a loan and now conveyed, in a few laconic phrases, that he was ready to do so. Marco Ginestra, one of the directors, a slight, fair man of invincible charm, congratulated Ewan and invited him to dinner. "An informal meal," he said. "Just family."

When Ewan arrived in his taxi from the hotel, he found a dozen people gathered in the large house on the Via Umberto. He'd been there once before, last summer, when they dined in the garden by candlelight and Marco's children had serenaded them with flute and violin. Tonight it was raining and they were indoors, in a room panelled with blue silk up to the moulded ceiling, where scantily clad putti disported themselves amongst fulsome clouds. A vase of daffodils on the table reminded Ewan of his walk across the moors. Was it only three days ago? Marco led him to one corner of the room and showed him a high-backed wooden chair. "We believe it belonged to Lucrezia Borgia," he said. "One of our great patrons of the arts."

"We tend to think she patronised pharmacy a bit too much," Ewan said.

"Rumours." Marco shrugged. "She was beautiful and had three husbands. People were certain to say unkind things. Like your own Mary, Queen of the Scots."

Ewan bent over the chair, admiring the curving arms, the surprisingly delicate, gazelle-like legs.

"You may sit in it," Marco said, "for a moment. We all need Lucrezia's skills these days, even Scottish bankers."

Gingerly Ewan lowered himself into the seat. He kept both feet on the floor and closed his eyes, waiting to see who or what would come to him. Might he catch a swish of skirts, a few notes on the lute, some lines from Dante?

When he opened his eyes, a woman was standing before him, holding a baby. "I'm Sophie," she reminded him. "Marco's wife. And this is Carolina."

She held out the baby, perhaps merely for inspection, but

Ewan unthinkingly reached for her. He recognised at once her warm, sleepy fragrance, the same as Olivia's. Carolina was fair-haired, like her father, and dark-eyed, like her mother; she regarded him solemnly as if she foresaw serious matters in the night ahead. "Hello, Carolina," he said, bouncing her up and down. "How old is she?"

"Six months, and already she rules the house."

"She's very pretty." Then he began to say "I found a baby," but either the words were not spoken aloud or Sophie, in spite of her excellent English, did not catch their meaning, for she was already thanking him for the compliment and whisking her daughter away to another group of guests.

Ewan sat there, in the chair of Lucrezia Borgia, over-whelmed with thoughts of Olivia: here was another area of life where he had failed to behave as he ought. He had seen her as interrupting his plans, but now it occurred to him that he had interrupted hers. He could have kept watch over her at the bus station, in case anyone came looking for her. Instead he'd carried her off and, save for one abortive phone call, made not the slightest effort to find her parents. He hadn't even checked the *Perthshire Advertiser*. Remembering the times she cried, he wondered if she'd been trying to let her parents know where she was. And where was she now? he thought, picturing her alone in some grim institution.

He squeezed the arms of the chair and vowed, the moment he got back to London, to phone the police in Perth. He would have written a note if his briefcase had been to hand, but a promise to Lucrezia seemed almost as good.

At eight o'clock Sophie summoned them to the table, placing Ewan on her right. To his right was Nina, a family friend, who confessed charmingly that she was a pianist and knew nothing of business. They made their way through six courses, from calamari to tiramisu. As Ewan ate, the intensity he had felt during the presentation returned. Though he was used to foreign travel and exotic places, tonight his journey from the genteel suburbs of Edinburgh to this room, complete with a chair from the court of the Borgias sitting casually in one corner, seemed astonishing. Was this how Bridget felt in the States, her life lived at the edge of a waterfall, at that pent-up moment before everything cascades over the edge? He abandoned his normal reticence and chatted lavishly to Nina. He had not a second to waste. And at the end of the evening, with a slow smile, she offered to drive him back to his hotel.

In the lift of the hotel he put his arms around her, buoyed by this amazing new urgency. Nina sighed. How was it that he had not known sooner how to do these things? In the room, he set the door key down on the chest of drawers and turned to find her unbuttoning her blouse; a moment later she was naked, her nipples very dark. He came across and kissed her, enjoying the mild perversity of being fully clothed with a naked woman in his arms. "Ewan," she whispered. "You are so proper."

While they made love she spoke Italian and he spoke nothing, simply tried to lose himself in her articulate body. He had drunk more than usual—he could taste the grappa in his mouth and hers—but that only lent him courage. Nina laughed, a high, joyous sound. Would she have laughed to learn how few lovers he'd had? And that some of them had been paid for, back in the days when he did business in Amsterdam and such arrangements were safer? He suspected there was little he could do or say that would surprise her.

He kissed her ear and gently bit it. That the heart did not necessarily follow the body was a discovery he had made in his twenties and still not entirely come to terms with. The guilt he had felt, looking down on a woman whom he did not love, had cast a long shadow. If he could've stopped wanting women, as he had stopped learning to drive after his near accident, he would have. Now Nina cried out words of which he was thrilled not to know the meaning, and he said "Oh, darling" and pushed harder.

Afterwards she lay beside him for a decent interval, then slipped from the bed. There came the muffled sound of water running in the bathroom, followed by the nearby rustle of her dressing. Ewan kept his face hidden in the pillow and imagined her clothes flying on as easily as they had fallen off. She kissed his cheek. "Sleep well," she said, and was gone. Without getting up to brush his teeth or draw the curtains, he obeyed.

He woke, startled, not knowing why. Then he saw the message light on his phone glowing; the sound had pulled him from sleep, but too slowly. He fumbled on the bedside light and rang the operator.

"Room 902," she said in English. "You have a message, sir."

"Wait, I'll get a pen."

"No need. It says, 'Vanessa phoned. Will phone again.' You understand?"

"Yes, perfectly. Vanessa."

"Good night, sir."

He got up and went to the bathroom. In the mirror he saw his cheeks still flushed and his hair sticking up in little tufts. The smell of sex rose around him. He stepped into the shower, turned the water as hot as he could stand it, and, seizing the little bar of soap, scrubbed furiously at every part of himself, even shampooing his hair. He wanted to be rid of everything that had happened since he arrived at Linate airport: his own mysterious efficiency; Marco, who had urged him to follow in the footsteps of Lucrezia; Nina, who had played him as if he were her piano.

When he emerged from the bathroom, the bedside clock showed quarter to four. What would Vanessa have thought of his not answering at such an hour? If she was phoning from London it was three in the morning; if from New York, then ten at night. He wished he knew which, since one implied desperate urgency and the other perhaps mere absentmindedness. He considered trying her London number but was loath to do anything so melodramatic. His whole respectable self protested any more unusual activity. To acknowledge that they were in the midst of a crisis would merely fan the flames. Instead he tidied the bed, meticulously smoothing out the signs of lovemaking, fetched his briefcase, put on his glasses, and got back between the sheets.

In his notebook he wrote, *Vanessa called,* plus the day and the hour. Then he added a question mark. *Olivia,* he wrote in large letters. And, quite unnecessarily, *Phone Yvonne.* He tried to think of something else to write down. In Latin class at school he'd mastered Cicero's trick of remembering a speech by placing the paragraphs in a house he knew. To calm himself now, he went through his house in Barnsbury, room by room, listing preparations for Mollie. *New linen,* he wrote. *Fix the upstairs tap. Toaster.*

At four-thirty he turned to *The Dark Forest.* Wasn't this what novels were for, to fend off the dark night of the soul, or at least to offer solace in that night? Ewan looked at the familiar cover—the wood, the clearing, the two figures—and was peculiarly pleased that he'd carried the book from Mill of Fortune to London to Milan. It suggested, despite the great distances, a kind of continuity. He skimmed the remainder of Leo's time in Boston and jumped ahead to the next chapter.

• • •

At Edinburgh airport I hired a flimsy black Maestro, very different from Helen's stolid Volvo, and drove into the city. I hadn't had a chance to use the credit card Roman had lent me. Now I snapped up three shirts and a pair of jeans in a pleasant half hour. In the loo of the Caledonian Hotel I finally shed the obnoxious tweedy suit and put on a new shirt and my old jeans. By this time it was just after eleven. A quickie for the road was definitely in order.

In Boston no day had passed without my thinking only X days before I'm free. I'd assumed that as soon as the taxi pulled away from Aunt Helen's, I would cease to be Roman. Now, sitting sipping vodka in the almost empty bar, I felt oddly stranded between my two identities. Getting rid of Roman was not quite as easy as changing clothes or growing back my beard. On the flight I had got up in the middle of the night and put the moves on a tall, giggly stewardess. When she asked my name, I answered Roman. And the car was hired in his name. Beneath the table I ran my hand down my thigh until I found the dent. It was all pretty weird.

Fortunately two businessmen sat down at the next table and began a noisy argument about golf. Glen Eagles either was or was not the best course in Scotland. Forget the existentialism, I told myself. What I had to focus on was getting my brother to cough up. He might call our agreement a contract, but what could I do if he reneged— take him to the small claims court? So just one drink and another visit to the Gents to brush my teeth and splash water on my face. Walking across the thickly carpeted lobby, I felt more cheerful. Soon I would see Maudie.

I drove out past Fettes and Blackhall. Near the Forth Road Bridge the rain started. I trundled along in my little metal coffin, windscreen wipers swishing back and forth. The sound reminded me of an Indonesian lover I had once. She told me the Indonesian word for sex was *mik-mek* and offered a properly energetic demonstration.

•   •   •

Ewan stopped in amazement. Years ago in Amsterdam, a woman had told him this very thing as she led him to her room. He still remembered the Van Gogh print above her bed: *A Starry Night in Arles*. He could not envisage any route by which a conversation with Chae would have reached such a topic, but apparently it had. Further proof of my indiscretion, he thought bitterly.

•   •   •

I arrived at Larch House around one. Again no one answered my knock, not even the pointy-nosed dog, so I went directly to the pottery and banged on the door. "Who is it?" called Maudie.

"Me." I was still grinning at the ambiguity, when the door opened. Before she could say anything I kissed her on the mouth. "Honey, I'm home."

"Leo," she exclaimed. There was a smudge of clay on her forehead and she wore a baggy grey sweatshirt and jeans. "Leo," she said again. "This is so strange. I don't even know what to call you anymore. I talked to you on the phone as if you were Roman, then I had to turn around and tell him what you said. It was like having two husbands." She looked down at my hand. "See, you're even wearing my ring."

"So is your second hubby hard at work on the whisky?"

"He'll be back later tonight or first thing tomorrow."

I've done enough of those Shakespeare plays where characters claim their actions are governed by the stars to occasionally find myself thinking along those lines. When Maudie explained that my brother was at a meeting in Glasgow, I metaphorically hitched up my toga, forgot about the risks of being ripped off, and settled down to business.

"Come in for a moment," she said. "I need to wrap the clay. Then I can be a proper hostess."

"An improper one is fine with me," I joked. She turned away as if she hadn't heard.

Inside, while she covered the clay, I drifted over to the shelves where the finished plates, vases, and bowls were stored. I'm no judge of such things but they looked just like the stuff you see in shops. I was examining a small grey and purple bowl when she came up behind me. "It's the first of the elephant series. You can look later. Let's go and get some lunch."

As we ate our omelettes, Maudie asked about Aunt Helen. "I was afraid the sight of her beloved nephew might send her into decline. That your visit was all she'd been hanging on for."

"Not a chance," I said, reaching for the bread. "She's a feisty old bird—she'll probably make the century. We had some ding-dong rows about politics. I did worry once or twice I'd gone too far, but when I was leaving she told me she'd enjoyed our discussions."

"And how was it for you, living as someone else? Roman said actors were used to that, killing Claudius every night. But I thought this was a bit different."

I nodded emphatically. "Totally different. *Hamlet*'s a doddle compared to the last fortnight. After all, everyone knows you're acting. Whereas the tricky thing was that Helen mustn't guess I was giving a performance. If I hadn't been able to talk to you I'd have floated right off the planet."

Maudie smiled. "Can I get you anything else?"

After lunch I went to take a nap. I woke at five, had a bath, and came downstairs to find Maudie reading in the kitchen. She'd changed into a black tunic and leggings, much better. "Roman just phoned," she said. "He won't be back 'til tomorrow morning."

"Oh, that's too bad." I did my best to frown and offered to take her out to dinner, but she said it was already organised. In my honour we were having an American meal: steak and baked potatoes. Meanwhile what about a walk? We put on our jackets and boots. Of course the dog went bonkers. Outside it was a mild autumn evening and the swallows were flying low, because of the rain earlier, Maudie said. As we climbed the hill behind the house, she told me the story of The Little Swallow. I listened happily. In my experience it's a good sign when women embark on this kind of conversation.

"Eventually," she concluded, "the prince has the swallow pluck out his sapphire eyes. Winter comes and they both die."

"And the moral is altruism doesn't pay," I said lightly.

We were passing a chestnut tree and I picked up one of the spikey green nuts and cracked it open. I held out the single glossy kernel to Maudie, then asked about the steak for supper. "I thought you two were die-hard vegetarians."

"He is, but when he's not around I lapse. For all I know, he does too. You end up with lots of secrets after ten years of marriage." She gave me a sidelong glance. "How come you're not married, Leo? Or the equivalent?"

"I'm not sure." I'd been about twelve when I realised confiding in Roman was a mistake, and I'd applied the same rule to Maudie. Now I said something vague indicating heartbreak in the not too distant past. "I suppose we had different priorities." I let my voice fade.

We came out from beneath the trees onto a ridge. Below us lay the town of Perth and the river Tay winding slowly towards Dundee. Two sailboats tacked back and forth on the water. "Sometimes," I said, "I think I must be mad to live in London."

"But look at all the things the city has to offer," said Maudie. "Work. Pleasure."

"Of course, but it's so easy to lose sight of what matters. Remember that sonnet?

The world is too much with us; late and soon,
Getting and spending, we lay waste our powers;
Little we see in Nature that is ours;
We have given our hearts away, a sordid boon!

I saw Maudie's mouth open in surprise—nothing like the odd poem—and didn't mention the gig I'd done on the Romantics. Instead I said those lines haunted me. She assured me that even in the country they had angst.

Back at the house, while she cooked the steak I made a salad and set the table. Soon we were eating by candlelight. I began to ply her with wine and questions. She gave the usual story about developing late, her older sister being effortlessly popular. (Somehow I never do meet those older sisters.) Then, to her amazement, boys started paying attention to her. "That led to a lot of bad behaviour."

"You're probably exaggerating."

"No, quite the reverse." She smiled and pushed back her hair. "I must be tipsy to be talking this much."

"So what happened?"

"I started going out with a rich old man called Tom Patterson. He wore purple shirts and leather trousers and drove a vintage Rolls. We went to fancy restaurants where I drank too much. Then he'd drive me home. One time he was going down to Durham and I asked if he'd give me a lift to visit some friends. We went out to dinner and back to his house. He had a castle, a modest castle, just south of Edinburgh. I was staying the night so we could get an early start.

"And this is where it gets impossible. I was sharing Tom's bed, you know. He was forty years older than me. I trusted him. Suddenly he was climbing on top of me—he was huge, six foot, sixteen stone—and forcing his way inside me. I wish I could say I kicked and screamed but I don't really remember."

I was about to offer sympathy but Maudie rushed on.

"Really, though, that wasn't the worst thing. The worst was driving with him next day. The whole two hundred miles to Durham I shrank against the door of the car in terror. At one point he asked about my period. I thought he was worried because he hadn't used anything but it turned out he wanted to make me pregnant. Some macho kick. When we finally got to Durham, I fled. I never heard from him again. A couple of years later I ran into him at the cinema. With an even younger woman."

"Oh, my dear," I said. Her face had grown ugly telling the story and I had a fleeting pang at what I was about to do. I carried our dishes to the sink. Then I came back and bent over Maudie. I kissed her neck. She leaned against me and I slid my hands inside her tunic. Presently I straightened up. I reached for her hand and led the way upstairs to the guest room. The bed was still rumpled from my nap.

As we lay down I remembered the johnnies I'd found on my last visit. Should I use one? but then Maudie's hand was inside my jeans and I forgot. "You're so sexy," I whispered. "Tell me what to do. Tell me what pleases you."

"Touch me," she said. "Not there, further back. Do you mind?"

Then she was climbing on top of me and I was fucking her and fingering her until we both came in a clamorous rush.

Afterwards I lay beside her, feeling our breathing slow, our bodies cool. "Maudie," I murmured.

"Oh, Leo. I love you."

The words hung there, my trophy. "I love you too." I touched her breast. "Tell me a secret."

"I just did."

• • •

It was the end of the chapter, and Ewan set the book aside, with relief. This was too similar to his own recent activities. And even without that immediate association he would have felt a voyeuristic grubbiness. While he was reading, the sky had lightened. He got up and went to the window. In the street, nine stories below, a small figure was walking two brown dogs.

Another figure bicycled by. Had his sister really been forced to have sex with an elderly man and he, Ewan, living in the same city, known nothing about it? He shuddered, and at that moment the phone rang.

"Ewan, it's me, Vanessa. Are you awake?"

"Yes. I was reading." He stopped, not knowing how to explain his earlier failure to answer the phone. "Where are you?"

"London. I got back yesterday morning." She paused.

Ewan reached again for his notebook. Whatever was coming, he felt fractionally more able to face it with a piece of paper and a pen. He turned to a clean page and waited. A question, he thought, a question could reveal nothing and still be helpful. "Is something wrong?" he said at last.

"Didn't he speak to you? I was sure he would."

"Who?"

"Coyle, for Christ's sake."

Ewan stared at the blank page; it was as if David Coyle's name was suddenly written all over it. "I've heard rumours he's been trying to reach me. Brian Ross telephoned me, twice. Oh, Vanessa . . ." He trailed off miserably.

"But he hasn't actually talked to you?" Her voice was brisk, like her answering machine.

"No."

"When are you coming back?"

"This afternoon."

"Why don't I meet your plane? We need to talk. And whatever happens, don't speak to Coyle today. Can you do that?"

"Of course. There's no reason to think he'd phone me here. What's going on?"

"We'll talk this afternoon. Tell me your flight number."

He found his ticket and gave her the details. No, it was no trouble to come to Heathrow. She lived in Chiswick, and even at rush hour, the journey was manageable. "Remember," she said, "don't speak to Coyle."

"All right, all right," he said. "I've got it."

In the silence after he put down the phone, Ewan heard the dim, digestive rumbling of the hotel lift. For no reason he could name, he found himself remembering an incident that had occurred the previous summer. He had been early to meet some friends and, to pass the time, had wandered into Regent's Park to read the paper. He was sitting on a bench, studying the cricket scores, when a small girl rushed by. Just as he registered that she seemed to be alone, a woman on the next bench shouted, "Whose child is this? Whose child is this?"

Up and down the benches, people stopped chattering and eyed one another warily. No one spoke. The woman ran after the little girl and caught her; the child burst into tears. Then, from a group of picnickers a hundred yards away, rose a long-haired girl in torn jeans. Ewan was near enough to overhear her conversation with the woman. "I'm sorry she's upset," the woman had said, "but what if she were abducted?"

"Abducted?" said the girl, tossing her hair indignantly. "I was right here."

The woman slumped back to her bench. After a few minutes she got up and walked away. Ewan could still hear her strong voice crying—"Whose child is this?"—as he went into the bathroom and took his second shower of the night.

Chapter 12

Mollie woke to the ringing of the telephone. She had lain down on the bed beside Olivia and dropped off into a companionable slumber. Now she rose, heavy-headed, and, ignoring the phone in Chae's study, a room she had not entered since he left, made her way downstairs. She kept telling herself there was no need to answer. But it was only eight in the evening, and something about the shrill sound curdling the silence demanded a response. Perhaps Ewan, nearing the end of his working day in Milan, was checking up on her, and for several sorts of reasons, Mollie did not wish to cause him unnecessary concern. The receiver, when she picked it up, was chilly with disuse.

"Hello," she croaked. She cleared her throat and said again, more robustly, "Hello."

"Hello, Mrs. Lafferty."

She recognised his voice instantly. From the noises—a babble of conversation and a sixties song—she guessed he was calling from a pub. In the background another man said, "Hey, knock it off, mate."

"I want to speak to the bloke in the suit. The pinstripe suit," he added, as if there might be several to choose from.

"He's not here," Mollie said. And wanted to scream at her own stupidity. "I can take a message."

"A message? This is bloody urgent. I don't have time to mess around with messages. Fetch him."

"Who are you?"

"Who am I?" He sounded taken aback. "That's not the point. I'm the one asking questions. Get the bloke. He and I need to talk business."

"He doesn't have any business with you," she said. "None of us do."

"Don't get high-and-mighty with me, bitch," he shouted. "I know you've got—"

Before he could say the final, incriminating word, Mollie replaced the receiver and took it off the hook again. If she had found herself standing next to the man on a railway platform, she would gladly have pushed him into the path of an oncoming train. If she had known where the pub was, she would have broken every bottle in the place over his head.

She ran upstairs, two at a time, to where Olivia lay still curled in sleep, and knelt beside the bed. "Olivia," she said. "What are we going to do?"

Olivia did not stir.

Mollie kissed her cheek and stroked her silky hair. She's mine, she thought. And then, No, she isn't. Bitterness rose inside her, like ink into the petals of the daffodils she'd dyed for a biology experiment at school. It had been too good to be true: the baby Chae would never give her coming just when he left her, a magical resolution to her pain, as if suffering really did earn you some kind of reward instead of leading on to more suffering. She threw herself down on the bed and lay there, sobbing out her indignation. Beside her, Olivia slept on, lulled by her grief as by the sweetest lullaby.

Gradually the interval between sobs grew longer, until Mollie realised she was crying out of habit and stopped. She performed a mental equivalent of the gestures she made at the loom when the selvages or the warp grew slack and she lost the rhythm of the shuttle: she pulled herself together. Tears are useless, she admonished, gazing up at the soft wedge of light from the hall that fell across the ceiling. The only other time she'd gotten an anonymous phone call had been when she was living in Edinburgh, sharing a flat with two other girls. She had been there alone one morning, when the phone rang and a man asked for David, the previous tenant. Mollie explained he had moved back to Kirkcaldy.

"Oh," said the man, "and who are you?"

"I'm Mollie Munro. I live here now."

"Mollie Munro, like the song."

"No, that's Malone," she corrected.

"I can see you, Mollie. I can see what you do all alone in your room. Do you like touching yourself? Pretty thing."

"Who are you?" Mollie asked.

"I love you," he said, and put down the phone.

She had told her friends about the call, claiming, of course, to have been the one to hang up, and they had waxed indignant on her behalf. In truth there was something fascinating about the man, something that made her believe his profession of love. For days afterwards she would turn around in the street, looking for someone who might be looking for her, and if an attractive man was in sight, even if he was pretending to be otherwise occupied, he would become the caller.

A month later, Chae had appeared at the restaurant. He chatted to her while she served his food, and left a note inviting her to meet him at Deacon Brodie's. It was signed with a name she had never seen before. When she came into the pub, the first thing she asked was what Chae meant.

He smiled and patted the stool beside him. "My mother called me after a character in a novel she read while she was pregnant: *Sunset Song*, by Lewis Grassic Gibbon." Mollie told him her name, and he said, "Maybe you're named after a character too. Moll Flanders, Molly Bloom, lots of pretty women to choose from."

"No." Mollie blushed. "It was my grandmother's name." She was blushing because Chae had pronounced pretty exactly like the anonymous caller. From that moment, she no longer needed to search the streets.

Now she thought the two phone calls did not have much in common—there was nothing lover-like about the man who rang about Olivia—but she did sense the same dark power emanating from the receiver. The shutters were all closed, the doors locked. He was calling from a pub, and the nearest one was in the town five miles away. Still, Mollie felt he could mysteriously see her, not in the ordinary way, but with X-ray vision that permitted him to view her thoughts, her very soul. Even his ignorance about Ewan's movements did not lessen her belief in his omniscience; for she knew it was Ewan he wanted, not Chae.

She stood up and went to the bathroom. The mirror showed a wild-faced woman she wished were a stranger. But no, it was herself before Olivia arrived. Her cheeks, creased from sleeping against the patchwork quilt, were blotched red, and her eyelids puffy with tears. She bent over the basin, scooping warm water onto her face, and dried herself with Olivia's towel. At the end of these ablutions she looked, if anything, slightly more bedraggled. She went back to the bedroom and gently picked up Olivia, without waking her, and carried her downstairs to sit by the stove.

Only the day before she had been congratulating herself on inventing a credible history for Olivia. Mrs. Tulliver had seemed to believe her unquestioningly; other people would fall into line. Now she was reminded that there was at least one person who would not believe any story about Olivia, however credible, however carefully invented. And that person was losing his temper.

In her sleep Olivia made a gurgling sound, and above them in his cage Plato began to sing, something he seldom did after dusk. He puffed out his chest and warbled away with especial brio. As she listened, Mollie felt her mind grow smooth and clean as a freshly laundered sheet.

What exactly had Ewan told her about finding Olivia? He had used the public conveniences at Perth bus station and been on the point of leaving when she caught his attention with a little sound; perhaps the same sound that had just caught Plato's. He had picked her up. Then he was afraid his bus was going to drive off, with his luggage and without him. So he climbed on board carrying Olivia, and the bus had left immediately. Once in the town, he had probably waited for less than five minutes at the Odeon before Mollie appeared.

Anyone seeing Ewan in Perth, Mollie thought, would have had no way of connecting him with her. She stood up, leaving Olivia tucked in the chair, and moved to the table. In the notebook she had used to work out her story for Mrs. Tulliver, she wrote down the few facts she knew. After his first phone call she had imagined the man as an older version of Olivia—Indian, dark-eyed, sinister in a polite way. Now she began to glimpse the outlines of a younger, ruder man, who had followed Ewan and Olivia onto the bus, who had seen her meet them, who phoned calling her bitch.

Her immediate thought, her greatest fear, was that he wanted Olivia. But if that was the case, why didn't he just ask? Or tell the police? For the first time since Ewan's arrival, Mollie admitted to herself that there was an angle from which her actions could be viewed as culpable. So what did he want? she wondered.

Suddenly it seemed it would be better to know. That keeping the phone off the hook was merely a delaying tactic, not likely to solve anything. If he couldn't reach her by phone, he would try some other method. She went out into the hall and replaced the receiver. She lingered, thinking it might ring at once. Nothing happened. The man in the suit, she thought. The man in the suit is money.

Back in the kitchen, Plato had stopped singing and was pecking at his cuttlebone in an irritating fashion. "Shut up, Plato," she said, to no effect. She sat down. What she needed was not another story but a plan. A few hours ago she had believed this house could be their sanctuary; the utopia she had failed to create here with Chae would belong to her and Olivia. Now that ambition struck her as ludicrous. Apart from anything else there was money, of which Mollie had none, or at least an amount so small that it could easily be measured out in nappies and formula. Even if she wove night and day, the wool would not turn into silver and gold.

Forget utopia, she told herself. She stood up again and went to look at Olivia. The baby's eyelashes quivered, and one of her hands, lying outside the blanket, reached for a handful of air. The idea of Olivia being taken away, of their being separated, was insupportable. She was still mouthing the five syllables, in-sup-por-ta-ble, when there came a knock at the door, a single loud thwack, more like a blow than a request for admission.

Mollie's hair rose as if an icy hand had passed over her scalp. Her feet were bolted to the floor. She could not move, even to save Olivia.

There was a gaping silence, during which she imagined mayhem and terror. Plato was quiet and Sadie stood at alert, looking at the door. Then came a volley of blows.

"Mollie, it's me. Let me in," Chae shouted.

Quickly she carried Olivia upstairs. She put her in the guest room where Ewan had slept, wedged against the wall with a pillow. She closed the door and turned on the radio in her bedroom. In the bathroom she swept all signs of Olivia into the airing cupboard, then raced back downstairs to the kitchen and put the formula and bottles under the sink. She couldn't keep Chae out. He would see the car in the garage, and he would not, like Lorraine, leave a note and disappear. She pictured him battering the door down, breaking a window, not so much out of a desire to reach her as from an absolute dislike of being foiled. She hated him. She poured a glass of whisky, set it on the table, and hid her notebook in among the cookbooks on the windowsill above the sink. Finally she opened the door. Sadie pushed past her. Without looking down, Chae bent to fondle the dog's ears.

Seeing him was like being hit by a tornado. The rush of adrenaline, the emotion of whatever unnameable kind, was so all-encompassing that Mollie felt herself momentarily and absolutely lifted free from the terrible history that had occurred between them. Here was the person she knew best in the world.

Then the tornado deposited her, just where she had been, on the doorstep of the house she had until recently shared with this man from whom she had separated in bitter anger.

"Mollie," he said, "can I come in?" She smelled beer on his breath and something else, a faint mintiness.

Not saying anything, she led the way into the kitchen. He followed, forgetting to close either the outer or the inner door and then, noticing the draft, going back to shut them. While he came and went, Mollie made a decision. She would admit the presence of a baby; she was baby-sitting for these friends of Ewan's. They needed somewhere to leave their daughter for twenty-four hours, and she had volunteered. This was far safer than outright denial.

He was wearing a red tee shirt, black jeans, and a black jacket. His boots were caked with mud, but Mollie did not plan to ask him to remove a single piece of clothing for any reason. Not knowing what else to do, she sat down again at the table. She wondered if the signs of her tears had faded, and the thought that Chae would assume she'd been crying over him was galling. He was about to sit down opposite when he caught sight of the glass of whisky in front of her and stepped back, obviously intending to help himself, before he remembered. "May I have a drink?" he said hoarsely.

"Go ahead."

They were the first words she had spoken to him in a month, and they came out just as she would have hoped: calm, composed, careless. But her hands were shaking so much she did not dare to raise her glass. She watched Chae shamble around the kitchen. He had always been, in spite of his stocky build, a rather graceful man, competent in his movements. Now he stumbled across the room. She watched him fumble with the bottle, the glass, rummage around in search of ice. When, finally, he sat down, she said nothing. She would not give him even the small satisfaction of her curiosity.

He looked, she thought, a little rough. Unshaven but not glamorously so. His thick, dark hair was too long, his eyes bloodshot and heavily shadowed. He looked old, older.

He drank some whisky, cleared his throat. "There's something different about the room," he said at last.

"I got rid of the junk."

"Junk?"

"The postcards, the ornaments, the stones, the mobiles, the bits of pottery. All that glorious memorabilia."

"What did you do with it?"

"I gave whatever was useful to the Girl Guides for their jumble sale. The rest I burned. I assumed you didn't want anything you left."

"So my study," Chae started to say, and then smacked the side of his head. "Christ, that's what I hate about myself. I come here to talk to you, and the first thing I do is ask about my papers, as if they were the Holy Grail. Don't answer that. Whatever you've done, it doesn't matter. You did what you had to do."

"I didn't do what I had to do," Mollie said contemptuously. "I did what I wanted. Wasn't that your message? Be spontaneous. Acting decently only clogs the arteries, like cholesterol."

"Yes, yes." Chae buried his head in his hands as if to fend off her blows. Then he stood up, took off his jacket, and slung it over the back of his chair. She noticed, not wanting to, that he had lost weight. "I'm a little drunk," he announced. "I was worried I'd get stopped, so I drove like a driving instructor the whole way. It took three hours to get here. I had a pint at the Melville to recover."

The Melville, Mollie almost gasped. Was it possible that that was the pub from which the man had phoned? Maybe he, too, was on his way here and had stopped for a quick drink before the final leg of the journey. The purpose of his call had been not to talk to Ewan but simply to ascertain her presence. Then she shook herself free. She was being ridiculous. This was much too far-fetched.

"A bloke at the bar told me a joke," Chae said. "How did the—" He glanced at her face. "Never mind."

He got up again and wandered around the room. "Why do you have the shutters closed?" he asked. "What are you weaving?"

"It's warmer. A blanket."

While his back was turned, she picked up her glass and managed a quick, shaky swallow. She could feel the words brewing up inside her. She had fought so hard to get rid of the desire to talk to him, to have nothing at all in the world that she wanted to say to him, and yet here it was, as strong as ever.

"Nice colours," he said, bending over the loom. "I wish I did something like weaving. Something where you don't have to think. I haven't been able to write for two months. Well, just one or two reviews with a gun at my head."

Mollie wanted to say six things at once. Go home. My heart

bleeds for you. Won't you ever get it into your thick skull that weaving is an art too? You need a haircut. Stop pawing at my work. What the hell are you doing here? And said nothing.

Chae circled round again and sat down. He put his elbows on the table and looked her full in the face. "Have you been crying?"

"No."

He held his gaze steady. The first time they made love, he had told her Sartre's theory that every intimacy originated with the gaze which acknowledges the other as separate and distinct from the self. He had kept the light on and watched her as he moved first above her, then beneath her. Now he put his hands on the table, and she saw the slight dryness fanning across the knuckles, the long straight fingers and square-cut nails. He had played the piano as a boy. "I've missed you," he said.

"What are you doing here?" Mollie said, forgetting her resolution not to question him.

"I was walking down the Royal Mile and I passed Deacon Brodie's. I was walking down Dundas Street and I passed the shop where you bought me that Art Nouveau lamp for Christmas the first year we knew each other. Wherever I am, you appear. Last week I went into Colin's and he told me he'd sold all the pieces you'd given him except two. I bought one of them—a lovely brown and purple hanging. I remembered us walking on the moors and then you picking out the colours when we came home."

"Oh, yes," Mollie exclaimed. "It was the last piece I wove from our own wool. Dear Miss Havisham."

"Dear? Think of all the times she broke into the Youngs' garden. She was a pest."

"I suppose. Pip and Estella weren't much better. Oh, Chae, the ducks are dead. I forgot to put them in one night, and a fox grabbed them."

"I'm sorry," he said. "I'm sure it wasn't your fault. They'd had long, happy, fat duck lives already." He reached across the table. "Mollie, I miss you."

"You should've thought of that sooner."

His face puckered. "Aren't you ever going to forgive me?"

"I doubt it." She put down her glass, dreading the familiar conversation. "I've tried to explain, it's not a question of forgiveness. It's a question of who you are. I trusted you, more than I trusted myself. When I read the book, that vanished utterly. I realised you weren't the person I thought you were. Maybe you never had been."

"But you always seemed glad to be in my books before. You were so pleased when I borrowed that remark you'd made about Penelope."

"Chae, we've been through this." She began to crack her knuckles, ferociously. "It's one thing to use the odd quotation, quite another to make me a central character and tell everyone my secrets." All my secrets, she thought. "In fifteen years you're the only person I've ever told about Edward, and what did you do? You put it in your book for everyone to see."

"Edward? Who the hell is Edward?"

"The old guy who raped me in a castle. You changed his name, but that's the only thing you did change." She squeezed her knuckles harder. "And then when Leo and Maudie screw, fuck, whatever, it's as if you'd taken notes while you and I were doing it."

Chae's eyes were swimming. For a moment she yearned to comfort him. Then she reminded herself he'd always been an emotional drunk. "Don't you understand?" she went on. "What Edward did was bad, but what you did was much worse. You stole from me twice over, once by telling my secrets and a second time by destroying my idea of you. I didn't just lose our life together, I lost the whole foundation upon which it was built. Can't you see how painful that is?"

The tears overflowed his brown eyes and ran down his cheeks, but he did not blink or move or shift his gaze. He kept his eyes fixed on her until Mollie felt her hands unfold. She saw one hand reach across the table to touch his cheek. And the other reach for his hand. She stood up and leaned to kiss him.

Chae was still moving in her, the last dreamy motions of sex, when Olivia started to cry. "What on earth is that?" he said, pausing.

"Don't worry." She arched against him to finish him sooner. "It's just the baby I'm looking after."

He was slipping away, away from her, away from the waking world. "Baby," he murmured, and disappeared into the vortex of sleep.

Downstairs, Mollie changed and fed Olivia. The edges of everything were softened, blurred, and as she gazed at Olivia's face, Mollie knew now the answer to the question she had asked a few hours earlier about what they should do.

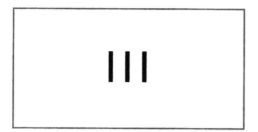

III

Chapter 13

After his shower, Ewan shaved and brushed his teeth. He had slept for only two hours, but in the mirror he regarded his reflection approvingly: his eyes were clear, his cheeks rosy, his hair, responding to being shampooed twice in a single night, fuller and sleeker. He whistled as he dressed, a chorus from *The Mikado*, and chose the raciest of the four ties he'd packed, a vivid paisley bought during the Christmas sales. To hear from Vanessa, under any circumstances, made him glad. The easiest way to follow her injunction, he decided, was to check out of the hotel; then no one could even leave a message for him. The point was not merely to avoid Coyle but to do so without appearing to. To slip through the net without seeming to notice it was there.

He picked up his notebook from the bed and saw *Call Yvonne*. Of course any attempt at normality must include letting her know his whereabouts; how to explain his brief absence? He paced up and down. Business? No. Everywhere he went, phones and faxes embraced him in their many tentacles. An old school friend, he thought. An image of Sophie and Carolina appeared before him. An old school friend with a baby. He had to go to the house to see the baby. His sixth-form tennis partner, Martin Pettitt, came to mind. He and his wife, Valerie, lived in Dorset; their first child was born in November. Briskly, Ewan moved them to Milan and gave Martin a job at the university for a year.

No, on second thoughts, Yvonne might be rather too interested in an academic. Only a few months ago she had asked if he knew anyone who could translate some medieval French verses that her husband was setting to music. A software consultant, he thought. She respected his terrific vagueness about computers. He sat down on the bed and rang the office answering machine.

"Yvonne, it's me. Things are winding up here. I'll be hard to reach today. I'm seeing an old school friend later this morning. Then I'm being met at Heathrow and going straight to dinner. If you need me, the best bet's probably a message on the machine at home. I'll be in by nine tomorrow. Bye."

He ticked off *Call Yvonne,* slipped the notebook into his briefcase, and whisked out of the room. The lift was in use, so he took the emergency stairs two at a time to the lobby. At the front desk only one couple was ahead of him, a stout Frenchman and his slender wife, leaving for Venice. Within minutes Ewan had handed his bag to the concierge and bought a copy of the *Herald Tribune.* Briefcase in hand, he was out in the street.

He headed towards the Piazza del Duomo. The paving stones were still wet from last night's rain, and the air felt soft and damp. As he stepped round a puddle, he remembered the flower sellers that had lined the pavement the previous day. Perhaps he could take Vanessa something? A bunch of violets or lily of the valley.

He found a café, crowded with people on their way to work. Half a dozen men in overalls, with orange hard hats dangling from their belts, stood at the bar, bantering back and forth over espressos. Ewan hesitated, uncertain whether to try and squeeze in amongst them, until a lithe young man, moving like a dancer between the tiny tables, beckoned him to sit in one corner, next to a bushy ficus tree. "Espresso, cappuccino, caffè grande, caffè latte?" he chanted. Ewan chose the last and asked for a pastry. In a few minutes the man was back with a caffè latte in a tall glass, a pastry that contained apples, a glass of water, and a reassuringly thick napkin.

"*Grazie,*" said Ewan. He tore open a packet of sugar. As the crystals fell into the milky coffee, he realised he had lied to Yvonne. He stared at the poster on the wall beside the ficus tree: it showed the rugged peaks of Valle d'Aosta against a sky of Titian blue. Why hadn't he minded at the time? Why hadn't he even noticed? He smelled the sandalwood fragrance of the hotel soap and, looking down, saw his fingers smeared with newspaper ink.

When he had read the paper cover to cover, it was still only eight-thirty. On a hectic day at Ginestra and Sedara, one could usually find someone to take a message by nine-thirty. Most of the people Ewan talked to made a point of getting in soon after ten. His own meeting with Marco was not until ten-thirty. A brisk walk, he thought, and perhaps another hotel, where he could wash his hands and sit in the foyer, working unobtrusively. As he tucked the newspaper into his briefcase, he had a sudden feeling of vertigo. What was he doing, skulking around the streets of Milan, moving from café to café? Already, without even speaking to Coyle, he was behaving like a criminal.

The meeting with Marco was in the same boardroom where Ewan had given his presentation the day before. They sat at one end of the long wooden table, files and charts spread around them, and tried to figure out where to raise the last $2.3 million. They were discussing insurance when the door of the conference room opened and a woman in a black dress came in and whispered something to Marco. She left the room and Marco stood up. "A telephone call for you," he said. "Very urgent. I will get the figures on Calogero."

Ewan, still engrossed in the chart before him, picked up the phone on the table. The only person who ever called in these circumstances was Yvonne. "Hello," he said. After a pause a hesitant British "Hello" came back to him. "I'm trying to find Ewan Munro," the man said. "This is David Coyle."

Ewan reached up to loosen his paisley tie. He heard Vanessa's voice from only a few hours before—"Whatever happens, don't speak to Coyle today"—but he was already doing so. Somehow Coyle had breached the wall of secretaries. "Ewan Munro speaking," he said. "I'm in the middle of a meeting."

"I'm sorry to interrupt." Coyle had a surprisingly mild voice. What was the accent? Birmingham, Ewan thought, and the small, useless insight made him feel a little better. "I was afraid of missing you. Sometimes you international business types flit off to another country between elevenses and lunch."

He paused to allow Ewan to respond, then filled the pause himself. "I'd like to talk to you as soon as possible. Let me see. There's a flight to Milan at one-fifty today."

The tie Ewan had just loosened grew chokingly tight. "I'll be back in London this evening," he managed to say. "I don't have a second while I'm here."

"Good, good," said Coyle as if their social calendars were falling nicely into place. "Perhaps I can meet your plane?"

"No, that won't be possible. Let me check my diary and see what I have on tomorrow." Keep talking, he thought, that was the strategy in presentations. Don't leave them time to disagree. He stared at Friday: a full moon was marked. "Lunch?" he offered. "I can meet you for lunch with a little rearranging."

"You're certain about the plane?" Coyle said wistfully. "I'd be happy to drive you wherever you're going."

"The plane is out of the question. I really do have to get back to this meeting, Mr. Coyle."

"Of course. How about breakfast? Safer than lunch. Last day of the working week tomorrow. Who knows what might come up, for either of us. Which would you prefer? Barnsbury or the City? It's all the same to me."

Out of the depths of his panic, Ewan suggested a coffee bar at Liverpool Street Station. He was not having Coyle come to either his home or his office. He hung up, and Marco came through the door as if he had been listening, waiting for the call to be over. He waved a file cheerfully. "Here's the Calogero stuff. It looks possible. Quite possible."

Good, Ewan was about to say, but the *G* proved insurmountable. Yes, he approached, but the *Y* rose like a pylon. Splendid, he thought, but the *S* writhed like a snake. He simply nodded.

On the plane, even *The Dark Forest* proved useless. Who cared if Leo was unmasked or Aunt Helen dropped dead? Ewan drank a gin and tonic, put on the headphones, and listened to music. A Beethoven concert carried him back to his first term at Edinburgh. Mollie was a year ahead of him and had slid into university life like Cinderella into her slipper. And Bridget, then in her final year, was living with a biology student and had her own fast friends. But Ewan was still passing through the lecture halls and cafeterias like an invisible man. At the time, he had thought he kept his secret pretty well, and said nothing to his parents on his frequent visits home. Later he realised they must have guessed everything about his loneliness. One night toward the end of November his father asked if he'd like to meet him for a drink at the Café Royal, just the two of them. He had never before issued such an adult invitation, and Ewan was thrilled.

He had made a point of getting to the Café early. He stood at the bar, nursing a half pint of bitter, and gazed around the old-fashioned room with its stained-glass windows showing men doing manly things—playing cricket, slaying deer, inventing the steam engine—until his father came in, brisk and ruddy from the cold. "Ewan, sorry I'm late," he said, clapping him on the shoulder.

Further along the bar two men abruptly set down their drinks. "Munro," spat one of them, a sallow-skinned man whose face Ewan could still recall, and then they were gone.

"What was that about?" he asked.

His father took out his handkerchief, blew his nose, and ordered a pint. "They offered me a wee gift to lose my specs, and I told them to get lost."

Ewan regarded him with amazement. "Does that happen often?"

"Not really," his father said. "Everyone who works for city planning gets the odd nudge, but they've more or less decided I'm a hopeless case."

A hopeless case, Ewan thought now; he, too, had aspired to that ironic understatement. No longer. He stopped the stewardess and asked for another drink. The pilot announced they would soon be over the Channel. Ewan doubted his father had ever had a colleague as attractive as Vanessa, but that was no excuse. In comparable circumstances, Ewan knew, he would have gone out to dinner, made excellent conversation, and let slip not one jot of useful information, irrespective of his companion's charms. "Oh, God," he muttered.

The stewardess put the drink down before him. "I'll have to collect the glass in ten minutes," she warned.

"No problem. Thanks."

When he stepped into the arrivals hall, Ewan's first impression was of a squadron of men holding signs with names— Smith, Pelletier, Bosola, Bekes. He moved forward, carried by the momentum of the crowd, embarrassed to look at so many faces, waiting, and none of them for him. He squeezed between two porters. Suddenly Vanessa was beside him. She was wearing casual clothes of a kind he had not seen her in before: jeans, a grey sweater, and a black leather jacket. Her fine, marmalade-coloured hair was caught back in a ponytail and, as usual after any interval, she was smaller than he remembered.

"Come on," she said, tugging his arm. "I'm parked right outside."

Whatever had occurred in the last few days had not compromised her posture. She glided through the crowds, and Ewan followed clumsily: the second drink had been a mistake. Soon he was sitting beside her in a small white car, heading into the city. "How was New York?" he asked when they stopped at a red light.

"Dreadful."

Perhaps because he'd so recently been thinking of his father, he heard his mother's crisp voice: "Ask a stupid question, get a stupid answer." He did not know what to say next. Once they were moving again, Vanessa relented slightly. "What about Milan?" she asked.

"Milan was actually okay. We got some things ironed out. I sat in a chair that belonged to Lucrezia Borgia."

"How did you manage that?"

"It belongs to one of the directors of the company I work with."

"Nothing like that happened in New York. Maybe I sat in a chair belonging to Donald Trump. I wasn't in good shape for dealing with the city."

He had not been to her house before—she'd always insisted on taking a taxi home alone after their dinners—and he was surprised when she turned into a new development of large brick terraced houses. They passed a group of children on their way home from school and pulled up beside a pink flowering tree. Ewan got out of the car with his bag and briefcase; the breeze caught his tie. He looked at the tree, wondering what kind it was. Then Vanessa was ushering him through the front door and up a flight of stairs to the kitchen. He set his bag and briefcase down near a radiator. "Would you like anything?" she asked. "I'm sure there's the usual things—tea, coffee, booze."

"Don't you live here?"

"No. This is my brother's house. My flat is on the other side of Chiswick High Road. He's in Dublin for the week, and I have a set of keys. I thought we'd be safer here."

"Good Lord, Vanessa, this isn't James Bond."

"If only it were." She braced herself against the counter. "Did Coyle try to reach you?"

"Yes." He tugged at the cuffs of his jacket, dreading the admission that was about to come.

"You talked to him, didn't you? Oh, Ewan, after I begged you not to."

"I'm sorry. I couldn't help it. They put the call through when I was in a meeting. I couldn't claim not to be there. I did do my best. I was out of the hotel by seven this morning."

"So what did he say to you? And you to him?"

In the house across the street Ewan saw a man washing dishes. "Nothing. He wanted to meet with me as soon as possible. He didn't say why. In fact that was the most sinister thing about his call; he assumed I'd know what it was about."

"Oh," sighed Vanessa. She hid her face in her hands.

Ewan longed to put his arms around her. Instead he said, "I think a cup of tea is a good idea." He spotted an electric kettle and moved to fill it and switch it on. Neither of them spoke while the water rumbled to the boil. Vanessa made tea and led the way through a double door into a large room furnished with a three-piece suite and several occasional tables. The windows overlooked a brown expanse of water, which, after a few seconds, Ewan recognised as the Thames. "This is splendid," he said, and recalled his earlier struggle with the word.

"Yes," said Vanessa. She perched in one corner of the sofa, motioning him to an adjacent armchair. He sat down. She poured the tea and passed him a mug.

"So," he said, "are you going to tell me what's going on?"

"I'm afraid I have to." She drank some tea and gazed out at the river. Ewan stole a glance at her admirable profile. In spite of her nocturnal phone calls, she looked wonderfully fresh. At last she said, "There's a good way and a bad way to tell this story, but I might as well tell you the bad way, because that, substantially, is what Coyle is piecing together. When we had dinner at The Ivy, you mentioned the Gibson Group merger. I was stunned you'd told me something so important—it wasn't as if I'd been trying to pump you. All this does have the redemptive quality of being unpremeditated. But once you'd told me, the information nagged at me.

"My brother, Patrick, is very hard up right now. His marriage fell apart last year, he's stuck with massive alimony, and his business is going bust. We thought it might be risky for him to buy the shares himself, but he had an old friend who was already playing the market and who had everything in place to make a purchase. Brian Ross is his broker."

"And what happened?"

"The obvious thing I didn't consider. Ralph, the friend, got greedy. I'd been thinking small scale, twenty, twenty-five thousand. Ralph mortgaged his house, raised three hundred thousand and bought the shares twenty-four hours before the merger went through. The Serious Fraud Office was bound to notice." She paused to slip off her shoes and curl her legs up on the sofa.

"I urged Patrick to go to Dublin; he had business there anyway," she went on. "That still leaves Ralph, though, and he's the weak link. He can't explain the purchase, and it doesn't fit with anything else in his portfolio. So far he's keeping mum, but Coyle is leaning on him." She stared down at her mug of tea, avoiding Ewan's eyes.

"Vanessa," he exclaimed, "how could you be so stupid?"

Her chin rose defiantly. "It didn't seem so stupid at the time. Every week I hear of someone making a fortune; why not someone I care about for a change? All I did was pass on a casual remark you'd made to me at dinner. My brother happened to mention it to Ralph, and Ralph decided to take action. Nothing very terrible. I didn't hurt anyone."

He stood up and went over to the window. Beyond the small lawn the Thames flowed with surprising speed; it must have rained here too, he thought. "You hurt me," he said. "Did you ever think of that?"

Before she could answer, he hurried on. "I've worked in the City for ten years, during which no one has had cause to question my integrity. In a few minutes of casual conversation, you wiped that out. I've no idea how a court of law would view your behaviour, or your brother's, but I'm fairly positive they'd find me guilty. The Gibson Group was in my charge, and by virtue of that I was privy to certain information, and because I was in love with you I squandered that information."

Love. He had said the word, though not in the way he imagined, more like an invitation to anger than a proffering of affection. He turned and saw Vanessa still sitting in the corner of the sofa, watching him, her legs drawn up under her. She was infinitely appealing. No, he thought angrily, she was like a child. If they were caught she would feel bad, she would understand then how she'd harmed him, but for now she was simply baffled by this mysterious talk of reputation and integrity—fool's gold in which only the eccentric believed.

She stood up and came over to the window, taking his

hands in hers. "Ewan," she said, "I'm sorry. You're right, I didn't think about you. If I had, if I'd had a brain in my head, I wouldn't have done it."

She looked at him, her greyish eyes wide, and he was filled with disgust at his own self-righteousness. Who was he to claim she had no moral sense? She had done nothing to elicit the information, save tuck her marmalade hair behind her ears and smile at him across a restaurant table. He was the one who had behaved like a child, trading secrets for love and not even admitting what he was doing. "I'm sorry too." He kissed her forehead.

They stood there for a moment, until Vanessa released his hands. "It's cold, isn't it?" she said. "I'm going to turn up the central heating. Help yourself to more tea."

By the time she came back, Ewan had fetched his notebook, refilled his mug, and returned to his seat. Somehow, he thought, they would find a way to undo the harm they'd done. "So," he said, "what next?"

Vanessa sat very upright in her boardroom manner. "The big question is whether to try to save Ralph."

Ralph, Ewan thought incredulously. "Why the hell should we do that?" he demanded. "If he hadn't been greedy, none of this would have happened."

"That's true, but there are a lot of ifs in this. If Ralph talks, we'll all be in trouble." She started to say something, broke off, then went on. "Coyle's hounding him like an axe murderer. I can see why people confess even when they're innocent. You get to the point you'd say anything."

"I don't plan to say anything," said Ewan stiffly, "but if Coyle asks, I'll have to tell him what I remember of our dinner conversation. Not to would be lying."

"And what about this conversation? He'll probably want to know what you were doing this evening."

Ewan paused, his pen hovering over his notebook. He realised from the heat in his face that he was blushing. "This evening is purely personal. It has nothing to do with Coyle."

"So our dinner was business? I thought we were going on a date."

She was wearing that little frown again. She had taken off her jacket, and against her grey pullover her face struck Ewan as strangely radiant. "You should have been a solicitor," he said.

"I'm just asking," she said, wrapping her arms around herself. "You're the only person I can trust. This would be an awfully inconvenient time for me to be fired."

They went to a local restaurant which served British food by day and Thai by night and ate pad thai and shrimp curry in coconut milk. Vanessa talked about a film she'd seen in New York. Ewan mentioned his trip to Mill of Fortune, and quite suddenly, he was doing what he had imagined on the plane from Edinburgh to London. "Guess what," he said. "I found a baby in a bus station."

"A baby in a bus station?" she echoed. "How do you mean you found it?"

"I went to the Gents in Perth bus station, and there was a baby lying on the floor, wrapped in a yellow poncho."

"So what did you do—hand it in at lost property? Do you want some more noodles?" She pushed the dish in his direction.

"Please." He hadn't realised until he began to eat how hungry he was. He and Marco had worked through lunch, and he'd dashed to the airport at the last moment. "No. It was a girl, and she ended up spending the weekend with us at Mill of Fortune. My sister took her to the police on her way back from driving me to Edinburgh."

"Why do you think she'd been left?"

"I haven't a clue. She was about four months old—or so

Mollie thought—healthy, dark-skinned. Maybe Indian. I'm going to ring the police tomorrow to see what's become of her." Guiltily he recalled his promise to Lucrezia. "First thing tomorrow," he added. He manoeuvred his chopsticks around another mouthful of noodles and waited for Vanessa's reaction.

"She was lucky you were the one to find her, given all the weirdos around nowadays. Perhaps she'll turn out to be the daughter of a rajah, and he'll offer you a fabulous reward."

"Actually I worry that we, Mollie and I, might seem like the weirdos, keeping her for an entire weekend. One thing led to another, my luggage was on the bus, Mollie lives way out in the country, the car wouldn't start," he faltered. There had been something, beyond geography or his own incompetence, that made it hard to return Olivia, but he could not bring it into focus. He looked over at Vanessa. "We did our best," he offered, lamely, for the second time that day.

She smiled. "It all sounds perfectly reasonable. It would be different if you'd found a lost two-year-old, desperate for her parents, or if the baby had needed medical attention. But someone deliberately abandoned her, and you did her a good turn by giving her a couple of days' food and affection."

"I hope so, and she did cheer my sister up. She was quite depressed until I arrived with Olivia."

"Olivia?"

"That's not her real name, just the one Mollie gave her because we were tired of calling her 'it.' I'm not sure why she chose Olivia." He fingered the checked tablecloth, remembering Mollie's odd insistence on the name.

"My best friend at school was named Olivia, but we always called her Ollie." Vanessa giggled. "I was called Vanilla."

"That's not bad. I was the kind of boy no one ever bothered to nickname. It was a source of great sorrow to me."

"Poor Ewan," she said mockingly. She set down her chopsticks. "You know what your story reminds me of? The time my brother ran away when he was eight. He left after lunch, but we didn't discover he was gone until suppertime. My father and the neighbours went out looking for him, and my mother and I stayed at home in case Patrick showed up. We played snap at the kitchen table, game after game. I'd never been up so late before. Then the door burst open and my aunt Tanya ran in. They'd found Patrick—he was fine—on the road to Swainswick.

"We were still laughing when my father appeared, with Patrick asleep in his arms. He just stood there holding him and said they'd found the body of a little girl in the woods. 'Oh, God,' my mother said. 'And was she . . . ?' She sat down at the table and began to sob. I didn't understand what was going on, nor why we weren't laughing anymore, but ever since that night I've felt that taking care of Patrick was one of my jobs in life."

"Lucky Patrick," said Ewan. He understood, of course he did—wasn't this how he felt about Mollie?—but he could not keep the bitterness from his voice.

The check came, Vanessa paid, and they were out in the street, walking back to the car. They had parked opposite a fish and chip shop, and as Ewan waited for her to unlock the doors, the smell of vinegar wafted over him. On winter evenings he and Mollie had used to stop on the way home from school to buy chips. An abyss opened. It would be very inconvenient for him, too, to be fired. Then they were in the car, driving back to the house. "That was a good meal," Vanessa said, and he forgot the abyss and thought instead about the remainder of the evening and how it might unfold. He made some comment about his local Thai restaurant.

The house had warmed up during their absence. In the kitchen, Ewan watched while Vanessa hung her jacket over a chair and poured two glasses of water. Thai food always made her thirsty, she remarked, handing him one. They stood drinking in silence. When he had finished, Ewan put down his empty glass, took off his spectacles, and rubbed his eyes.

He opened them, to see Vanessa standing right before him. "You look tired," she said. "Would you like to stay the night? It's a long way back to Barnsbury."

He stared at her, wondering what exactly she was offering, and she stared back, not smiling but as if she might be about to do so. All she had wanted, he thought, was to help her brother; was that so terrible? Vanessa took his silence for assent. She picked up his bag and led the way up another flight of stairs, to a small room with a double bed.

"The spare room," she said.

Ewan stood blinking stupidly in the soft glow of the bed-side lamp. He loved her, never mind Nina and Lucrezia Borgia. She was saying something about towels and bathrooms when he stepped forward and put his arms around her. He buried his face in her hair. "You must know how I feel about you."

"I thought you were angry with me," she murmured.

"Angry? No, I was just upset." He tried not to move, barely to breathe, for fear the slightest gesture might put her to flight.

She leaned against him. "Ewan," she said, "I've been so scared." Gently she moved out of his embrace until she was standing at arm's length, studying him with that calm, half-smiling look of hers. "I know this is awfully forward, but can I share your bed? Just for the company?"

Later Ewan thought of this day as his own particular Ides of March, a day on which he had failed all possible moral tests, but at the time he could think of nothing he wanted more than to sleep next to Vanessa, to smell her hair and hold her. She showed him one bathroom and went to use another. He brushed his teeth, put on his pyjamas, and climbed into bed. He had barely registered the chill sheets when Vanessa returned, wearing a nightdress of Victorian propriety, and climbed in beside him.

"You must do what you think right about Coyle," she said, and turned out the light.

Chapter 14

Time, Kenneth thought, the good old tickety-tock, was changing. Ever since he quit the infirmary, the days had tended to linger too long, congealing before him like the plates of food his mum kept waiting in the oven. This had been especially true in January, when the streetlights glowed soon after four and he had no dough to go anywhere. One evening he had wandered around Safeway until a shop detective threw him out. "I don't know whether you're loitering with or without intent," the man said. "But whichever it is, do it somewhere else." He had held on to Kenneth's arm the entire length of the cereal aisle, in a way that made Kenneth wish his pockets were crammed with steaks and booze. Now, since he'd dumped Grace on the floor of the Gents, the days were just the opposite, so skinny they slipped right through his fingers. He had barely got a grip on all the things he needed to do before night fell.

Time was something he understood because he'd done a project on it at school for Miss McBain. He was nine, and his year in her class had turned out to be his last of regular attendance. Being late for Miss McBain, even five minutes, was out of the question; if she had told him to come in on a Saturday, he would have been there. She was as upright as a ruler, and winter or summer wore a blouse, a tweed skirt, and a pair of thick-soled lace-up shoes. In fine weather she sometimes took them on biology walks up Kinnoull Hill. She strode along with her walking stick, stopping to point out a thrush's nest neatly woven into the fork of a tree or a caterpillar eating a nettle leaf. It probably wouldn't have been hard on these expeditions to skive off to the swings or the sweetie shop, but Kenneth would as soon have thought of trying to fly.

During the summer term everyone had to do a project. Miss McBain wrote the topics on slips of paper, and one by one the boys and girls came up to her desk to pick a slip out of her blue felt hat. Kenneth's was *Time*. He stared at it in bewilderment. Willy in the next desk had *Whales*; now, that was a proper topic. He waited after school to speak to her, but when at last she beckoned him over he didn't say anything, only held out his paper, trusting her to do the talking.

"Time," she said. "You lucky boy. There's so much to say." She made a speech about different ways of measuring time—the sun, clocks, calendars—and how he measured time too, by growing and by noticing the sequence of events.

"Like what?" he asked. He'd cheered up at the mention of clocks and calendars; they had those at home.

"Well," she said, "you chose this topic before you came to talk to me, and I made it up before you chose it. Before and after are ways of measuring time. Sometimes things happen at the same time, like you eating your tea in front of the telly."

He'd asked why some bits of time whizzed by and others dawdled. "I don't know," she'd said. "It always seems back to front. When we enjoy something it's over too soon, and when we don't it goes on and on. Maybe in your project you'll have an insight about that."

Her profession of ignorance had made a huge impression on him. He spent the whole weekend pondering this business of

time going fast and slow. Lots of things, he realised, were arranged like that—more of what you hated than what you
liked—and disguising your feelings made no difference. When
he presented his project, he revealed his solution to the discrep-
ancy: out-of-body travel. It was an idea he'd borrowed from his
mum, who claimed to do this on difficult occasions, beginning
with his own, untoward birth. Some of his classmates giggled,
but Miss McBain nodded seriously. "We'll have to give that a
shot," she said. "Not during school, though, boys and girls.
Thank you, Kenneth."

He had thought of her then as outside time, and this seemed
confirmed by his subsequent, rather infrequent, glimpses of her.
Last year he had run into her in Woolie's. He was about to
pocket a fancy Biro when, glancing down, he saw a pair of familiar shoes beside his grotty trainers. There she was buying half
a dozen pens, testing each one carefully on the wee pad the shop
provided. She looked exactly the same, if anything a little younger. He put the Biro back and moved away as quietly as possible. At the shop door he suddenly noticed they'd installed one
of those gizmos that beeped if you carried something through
without paying. Good old Miss McBain had saved him from another argy-bargy with a shop manager. How he loathed their
white shirts and bow ties.

Now time raced by like Easy Does It, although he wasn't
precisely enjoying himself. He hadn't meant to wait so long before his second phone call to the Laffertys. In fact he didn't realise he had until he went to collect his dole and counted off the
days on his fingers. There were reasons for the delay. The pub
with the special phone, The Blind Beggar, was a good twenty
minutes from Joan's flat, so he couldn't pop in on the spur of
the moment. And the situation with Joan was tricky. For one
thing, she refused to eat, he didn't know why. Maybe she
stuffed herself at the infirmary, but at home he never saw her
have more than a cup of tea. "You'd make a good Irish pris-

oner," he joked, "already in training for your hunger strikes."
She gave him a stony look and went on spooning baked beans
onto his plate. He'd started collecting her from work—a nuisance, but he wanted to be sure she didn't try to see her mother.
Impossible to tell what the old woman thought, a wizened
monkey in her sari, chattering in some weird language. She
could easily kibosh his plans. Lalit, he thought, you are my
main man. He looked fondly and often at the photo on the
fridge.

So when he was standing in line for his dole and saw the
date above the counter—Monday 13th April—it came as a
shock. Three days since he dumped Grace, two since he phoned.
As soon as he got his dole, he walked over to The Blind Beggar
and dialled the phone. No answer. He played a game of darts
with two blokes who turned out to be brothers. They both
worked at the swimming pool—leisure centre it was called
nowadays. "You can smell the chlorine on me night and day,"
one of them boasted. "It doesn't matter how much I wash."

He held out his arm, and sure enough, Kenneth got a whiff
when he sniffed the sleeve of his cardigan. He won the game by
seven points and tried the phone again. Still no answer, but he
wasn't fazed. Being out and about himself, seeing a steady
stream of people come into the pub for a lunchtime pint and
bridie, made it seem natural that the Laffertys were out too.
Then he had to go and see his mum. If he didn't show up on
dole day, she might change the locks. As it was, she winkled fifteen quid out of him before she even made him a cup of tea or
read his horoscope.

"Leo," she read, "a busy week. You have ample opportunity
to consolidate your position. Believe in yourself and don't back
down. Beware of vanity, your besetting sin."

"Let me see that," he said, reaching for the magazine. Except for the vanity—and what was besetting anyway?—it
sounded so appropriate she must be making it up, but no, there

it was, beside the little lion. He'd always been proud of his star sign. The only good thing his mum had ever done for him.

Finally, on Wednesday, he took Joan with him to The Blind Beggar. As soon as he said they were going out, she leapt up, and he knew she thought they were fetching Grace. She was into her raincoat in a trice. Outside, she streaked along the pavement, tugging him across the streets. At the sight of the pub her face went pinched. The place was much busier than at lunchtime. He stuck her in a corner by the cigarette machine and bought her a lemonade. No point in wasting a shandy on her in this mood. He carried his pint over to the phone. Joan was watching him, like a punter watches a horse, desperate to know his next move.

At the nearest table three old geezers were playing dominoes. The youngest, a lad of sixty or so, clacked down a tile. Opposite him, a chap with a hearing aid the size of a Walkman laid down a couple. Kenneth lit a fag. The pressure of Joan's gaze made that first drag particularly sweet. Ah well, time to get on with it. He took out his one-pence coins, okey-dokey, and rooted in his back pocket for the envelope where he kept his bits and pieces. There was the phone number tucked between a five-pound note and a bus ticket.

As he lifted the phone, he saw Joan lean forward, almost rise out of her seat. It had been drizzling on their walk over, and her skin matched the damp, ashy colour of her raincoat. Kenneth held up his free hand the way policemen do. She sank back, and praise be, someone answered.

He wasn't even sure it was the Lafferty woman until the second hello. Then a sponge wiped across his brain. All his ideas, every last one of them, vanished. After the several unanswered calls, he'd got out of the habit of making up speeches. The domino players were arguing, and the geezer with the hearing aid was slowly getting up from the table.

That was it, Kenneth thought, he should ask for the bloke. He did, and she said he wasn't there, and he began to lose it.

"Don't get high-and-mighty with me, bitch. I know you've got—" he shouted. But she had hung up. He squeezed the receiver so hard it made a small cracking sound. When he closed his eyes, the lids boiled red.

Hold on, Kenneth, he said to himself. No use killing the goose that lays the golden eggs. He put the phone down and found his cigarette where he'd balanced it on the edge of an ashtray, more ash than fag by this time, and took a quick puff. When he looked round again, Joan was standing up. Could she have heard him? He gestured for her to sit down and pointed to the Gents. Inside, there was a bloke ahead, and he had to wait. He leaned his forehead against the wall. It was icily, unpleasantly cold, and he soon straightened up. The white paint was speckled with graffiti. *Free Scotland/Fuck Maggie,* he read. *Bert Swanson eats haggis.*

While peeing, Kenneth had an idea, a small one that nonetheless made him feel better. It was gormless to have the phone number on a wee scrap of paper, especially when he was staying at Joan's and traipsing around. He'd write it on the wall of the lav: *For a good time call . . .* Then the number would be here when he needed it, no bother. And maybe someone else would have a go. That'd be a laugh. He stood on tiptoe and wrote it as high as he could above the basin.

When he came out he rang back. The line was busy, and he pictured plainly the empty cradle, the receiver dangling. I need to get a grip, he thought. He had the sudden fear he might be overlooking something obvious, like that time in London with Duncan. They had made money by hanging around King's Cross Station, where the trains to Scotland came and went, with a sign about needing the fare home to Perth. "We should put Inverness on the sign," Duncan suggested. "More charisma."

"Don't be daft," Kenneth said. "Perth's good enough for me, good enough for anyone." But one afternoon when Duncan had skived off, he made a new sign, with Inverness, and raised three quid more than usual. So much for Duncan and his bloody charisma.

The geezer with the hearing aid was back in his seat. Kenneth watched him lay down three tiles. It doesn't do to be stubborn, he told himself. You have to be flexible, inventive. Look at this business of bringing Joan along, for instance. Bloody stupid. It meant he was thinking of too many things at once. He didn't have the concentration to deal with the Lafferty bitch. Now at the cigarette machine a bloke was talking to Joan, probably asking for change, but she said nothing. Just hung her head. The bloke stepped away to the bar, and she sat there, head down, everything hidden by that pink headscarf, bad as those hats at the infirmary. What I should have done, Kenneth thought, was lock her in.

Next morning, as soon as Joan left for work, he made himself a cuppa and sat in the kitchen, laying his plans. You could only do so much on the phone. Tomorrow, Friday, was Joan's day off. He'd leave her here and go to Mill of Fortune. He wondered if he ought to get a partner, someone to watch his back, like in the pictures. But the only person he trusted was Duncan, and he was away in Glasgow. Besides, he wasn't dealing with the Kray brothers, just a bunch of toffs. That he knew they had Grace, and had kept her now for close on a week, was the only weapon he needed. If he hadn't been cut off during his last phone call, he'd have named his ransom price. Four thousand quid. He'd thought the whole thing through. If he asked for too much, they wouldn't cough up right away. But four grand—not to have your name in the papers as a pervert was dead cheap. They could hand the dough over, no bother. Along with Grace. Then he'd give her back to Joan and get the hell out of here.

He finished his tea and went to the bus station to check the times. The three o'clock race looked interesting, but he didn't stop at the betting shop. He felt he had just enough luck for one venture. To enter into others would be to invite disaster. Then he had the bus times and there was nothing else to do. At a loose end, he wandered down the High Street and into Kinnoull Street. As he passed the library, a lad in a natty black outfit swung through the doors. Watching him ponce down the steps, Kenneth reflected on his own wardrobe. What should he wear to Mill of Fortune? Neither his red jacket nor his anorak seemed right. Then he remembered the sports jacket he'd last worn to apply for a job at the infirmary, and made a detour to his mum's to retrieve it. She was out, thank God. On his way back to Joan's he stopped at the barber on Barossa Street, an Eyetie who did a nice job for three quid.

That evening he took Joan to the supermarket. "Got to stock up," he said. "I'm eating you out of house and home." He marched her up and down the aisles, putting stuff in the basket: soup, baked beans, sausages, eggs, margarine. In the bread aisle she suddenly froze. He didn't know what was happening. Then he saw her beady eyes fixed on this woman, dark like her, and a baby, dark like Grace; for a few seconds he even had the wild thought it could be Grace. But as they came closer he saw it was just an ordinary, spotty baby, dressed in blue. Tears were rolling down Joan's cheeks. He nudged her. "I suppose you want brown bread," he said.

No response. He eyed the nice white Mother's Pride, then put the biggest brown loaf he could find in the basket. "Never say I don't care about you," he said.

•   •   •

Friday morning, with the help of Joan's alarm, he was up at seven. Joan was watching as he got out of bed, but of course she didn't utter a peep. He went to the kitchen and put on the kettle. As he waited for it to boil, he greeted Lalit, his wavy hair, his bright white shirt. On impulse he made a cup for Joan, too, and carried it into the bedroom. "Here's some tea," he said, setting it down on the bedside table.

She lay on her side, looking at him blankly. Could she be poorly from not eating? "Listen," he said. "I'm going to get Grace. She'll be back here tonight."

She sprang up as if he had set fire to the bed. "Kenneth," she cried, flinging her arms around his neck. "You promise? Grace is coming home? You promise? Grace is really coming home?"

She must've asked twenty times. He laughed. "Yes, yes," he said. "Start warming the nappies." He pulled himself out of her clutches and went to the bathroom. He shaved for the first time since his last bus journey, borrowed Joan's deodorant, and combed his hair. The haircut was a good move. Through the closed door he heard Joan, noisier than she'd been in days.

He was ready to leave. In his mind he'd seen himself pocketing her keys and slipping out of the house while she was still asleep. Now, with all this good humour around, he felt he had to tell her what he was up to. "But why?" she said. "I will stay here. I will do what you tell me, but I do not like to be locked in."

He couldn't quite recall his reasons, and for a moment he was tempted to relent. Then he told himself not to be soft. "Grace," he said. "It's safer for Grace. Give me your keys."

"All right. When will you be back?"

"By dark. Maybe sooner. You have to be patient. Watch the telly and tell me what you see, okey-dokey? Good girl." He kissed her and was out of the door.

As he stepped into the street he saw the sky, clear blue with not an inkling of rain, and once again felt the spell of his own good luck. He'd given no thought to the possibility of bad weather. He stopped at the corner shop for fags and was at the bus station with ten minutes to spare. He didn't really need to, but out of nostalgia he used the Gents. There was something different about the place, and looking around, he realised what it was. They'd put up a mirror over the bloody basin. About time, he thought, giving his hair another approving glance. When he came out, the bus was waiting, with the same snooty woman driver as before. That trip already seemed so long ago she ought to be in retirement by now. She didn't recognise him, which was maybe no bad thing.

He spent the journey in a hectic trance. He pictured himself talking calmly to the bloke in a suit, the way he would've liked to speak to that snotty supervisor at the infirmary. He pictured money, a thousand dole cheques piled up and nobody telling him what to do. He wouldn't go mad with it either; he'd do what his horoscope said, consolidate his position. And the great thing was that he wasn't the one with anything to hide—well, from Joan, perhaps—but anyone else would think it was the toff who'd behaved badly, skedaddling with a baby, and he, Kenneth, was the hero, getting her back.

They reached the town. A couple of people got off at the caravan site on the outskirts. Then they were pulling up beside the Odeon, and he was following a woman in a brightly patterned headscarf down the aisle and out into the square. He walked along the main street, wondering where to ask the way. The chemists was the obvious choice, but he felt wary of a repeat visit, and it was too early for the pub. The butcher's with the hares hanging up outside caught his eye.

Inside, everything shone—the counters, the knives, the bald head of the butcher. "Good morning," he said. "What can I do for you?"

"I'm looking for Mill of Fortune. Some folk called Lafferty live there. Do you know it, by any chance?"

The woman in the chemists had said something else, a name he couldn't recall, but the butcher was already nodding. "Indeed I do. It's up Glen Teall. You'll be driving?"

"Yes." He would be soon.

"I'll draw you a map. I've always fancied myself a bit of a cartographer." He took a white paper bag from the pile beside the cash register, pursed his lips, and began to draw. Kenneth stared at the rows of chops, so neat they must have come from the same cow, and the chickens with their prickly flesh. This was what the country was for, he thought: making dead animals. After a few minutes the butcher summoned him. "We're here." He pointed to a square marked "Rae," then explained the route ending at a larger square, marked "Lafferty."

"How far is it?"

"Five miles?" His eyebrows rose into the expanse of his forehead. "Maybe a wee bit less."

"Thanks. Thanks a ton." Kenneth folded the bag in two and backed out of the shop, nearly colliding with an old wifie coming in.

Five miles, he thought, no bother. He stopped to buy a can of Coke and a Mars bar and set out across the bridge. Once he was on the road to Glen Teall, he walked briskly, sticking out his thumb each time he heard a car. A dozen passed him by. "Wankers," he shouted. Then a grey van stopped: a father and son, delivering potatoes to the local farms. "Where are you headed?" asked the father.

"Mill of Fortune."

"Och aye, the Lafferty place. It's right along here."

Strange, Kenneth mused, as he balanced on a sack of tatties, having a house with a name and everyone knowing about it. This only made the whole business with Grace even more peculiar. The chances of a bloke like that being in a bus station were tiny, but then so were the chances of him being there with Grace. He shifted, carefully keeping his jacket away from the dirt, and felt a sneeze coming on. Luck, he thought, ideas. He reached into his pocket and surprisingly encountered a Kleenex.

They dropped him off at the bottom of a small road. Fifteen minutes' walk, they said, keep to the left, an old stone house. He watched the van disappear; a puff of gravel and it was gone. He was alone, utterly alone, surrounded by this weird thing: maybe it was silence. He looked down at his hands and feet to reassure himself that he existed, and he did seem to, there they were, but everyone else, he thought, could be dead. His mum, Joan, Grace, Duncan, even the immortal Miss McBain, they could all be dead and buried in this sinister peaceful valley. A huge loneliness washed over him. He longed to be back in Perth, doing normal, boring things, like sniffing the chlorine on a bloke's cardigan. He was tempted to turn around right there and start walking back to the town.

Then he remembered his Coke and Mars bar. The chocolate was warm and soft, and the can made that satisfying little pop when he opened it. He stood there eating and drinking, and gradually the silence filled up with sounds: sheep and cows, birds, a tractor, something long and low that was probably a plane. He'd come this far, he thought; daft to turn back. He started walking up the narrow road towards Mill of Fortune.

He passed a modern wooden house, like pictures he'd seen of Switzerland, then the road curved to the left. He followed it through a pair of stone gateposts and saw ahead an enormous stone house, not a slate missing from the roof or a window broken, a pond with a wee wooden hut like a dog kennel, trees and bushes, several sheds. As he paused, taking all this in, the sounds began to empty out again. Keep going, he told himself, and walked purposefully round the house to the back door. A green car, with a dent in one fender, was parked outside. In passing, Kenneth kicked a tyre.

He knocked, a sharp rap. And then, not satisfied, slammed the palm of his hand against the wood. What if they were out?

Absence had played no part in his imaginings. Well, he would just bloody wait. He counted to sixty and knocked again.

The door opened. A bearded, dishevelled man whom Kenneth had never seen before stood there barefoot, tucking his red tee shirt into his jeans. He must have come to the wrong house. "Pardon," he said. "I'm looking for Mill of Fortune."

"You've found it."

"I wanted to speak to Mr. Lafferty?"

"Speaking," said the man, looking at Kenneth for the first time.

"You're Mr. Lafferty?"

"Sorry if I'm a disappointment."

Kenneth stopped uncertainly. Hadn't the woman in the chemists said something about Mr. Lafferty being a writer? "There was a bloke in a suit and a woman with very short hair. I thought she was Mrs. Lafferty."

"I wish. That's Mollie. As for the man, you're probably thinking of her brother. He was here on a visit recently and has a tendency to suits." The man—Kenneth couldn't think of him as Mr. Lafferty—stopped and blinked. "Who are you?" he said. "Are you selling something?"

Kenneth's fists tightened. "Really," he said, "I came about the baby."

"The baby?" The man swayed against the doorframe. "You'd better come in." He stepped back, and Kenneth followed.

This was more like it, he thought, staring round the large room, although why would a place this fancy have a stone floor? But maybe all the rich people had them instead of carpets or lino. How would he know?

"Would you like some coffee?"

He would have preferred tea, but it was no time to be picky. "That would be grand."

The man pulled out a chair at the table for him and poured

them each a cup. "Start again," he said, sitting down opposite. "I'm a little slow this morning."

"Your wife, or whoever she is, and the bloke in the suit have something that belongs to me—belongs to my girlfriend, that is. They've taken her daughter, Grace. She's going mad with grief. Mad with grief," he repeated, proud of the phrase. He had a sudden brainwave, reached into his pocket, and produced the photo of Grace in her cot.

The man gave it a sidelong glance. "Jesus wept," he said. He stood up and walked from the table to the sink, the stove, the window, back again, two, three times. Then he sat down and thrust a piece of paper across the table to Kenneth. "You'd better read this," he said.

Kenneth looked at it reluctantly. Pieces of paper often meant trouble, but the man clearly was not going to read it to him. He drank some more of the bitter coffee—no sugar to be seen—and bent his eyes to the note.

Friday, 6 am

Dear Chae,

In an odd way, certainly not the way you intended, you saved my life showing up last night. I have to go away— all much too complicated to explain—but I'll be in touch very soon, promise. Can you look after Sadie and Plato?

Love, Mollie

Kenneth read these words twice, with no sense of their meaning. "Who are Sadie and Plato?" he said.

"The animals," the man said. "What I'm trying to tell you is that I think she's vamoosed with your baby. There was one here last night. I didn't see her, but I heard her cry. And this morning she and Mollie and the car were gone."

"There's a car."

"That's mine. I'm sorry, I can't believe this. I think she's stolen your baby. Oh, Jesus, it's all my fault." He bent his head and made a snuffling sound. Could he be crying?

"Listen," Kenneth said sharply, "I don't have time for this crap. I came to get Grace. Where is she?"

"I don't know. I might by this evening. There are some people I can phone. This is terrible, but I'm sure the baby's safe. Whatever's happening to Mollie, she wouldn't hurt a baby."

He started to say something else, but Kenneth held up his hand, like he had with Joan, and it worked: the man shut up. This was a setback, Grace not being here nor the suit bloke, but not a catastrophe. Maybe he could even make it work in his favour, put the squeeze on the Lafferty bloke and then the other. Cash now and cash later. Almost like a job, he smirked. The secret was not to ask for money. No question of blackmail, just gifts, generous presents passing between people who understood each other.

That pacing business seemed a good idea. He stood up in turn and went over to the window. "Okey-dokey," he said. "I think a chat with the police is in order. I can't have that woman traipsing all round Perthshire with my daughter."

The man did not seem to remark Grace's metamorphosis. "No, please," he said. "Wait. I can get her back, I'm sure. Give me a little time."

"Time," Kenneth said suggestively, "is money." One of the nicest sentences he'd ever uttered.

Mr. Lafferty gave him a lift to the town, and Kenneth waited in the car while he went into the Bank of Scotland and came out with a sheaf of tens and twenties. No fifties, Kenneth had told him; more trouble than they're worth. He counted out the money, the entire thousand, trying to be nonchalant, and slipped it into the pocket of his sports jacket. The man thanked him profusely, several times, for waiting. They agreed that Kenneth would phone tonight at ten. "You'll be there," Kenneth said, "no more disappearing."

"Absolutely not. And I'll know where Grace is by then."

On the bus Kenneth kept slipping his hand into his breast pocket. Only some of the notes were new, most of them were used, but what they lacked in crispness they made up for in heft. Shifting in his seat, he felt something bulge in one of his other pockets: the two sets of keys. Briefly he pictured Joan's face in the bread aisle, gazing after the baby. She'd be upset, he thought. He realised he'd left Grace's photo on the table at Mill of Fortune. Then his fingers touched the notes again. He'd soon cheer her up. He remembered that dress she had admired in the shop window the night they went to the Koh-i-Noor. If it was less than fifty quid, he'd buy it for her. They could survive another day or two without Grace.

Chapter 15

In a lay-by north of Perth, Mollie stopped to install Olivia's car seat. As the woman at Mothercare had promised, it strapped in easily. Olivia fussed at being lifted off the pillow on the floor but, as soon as she was in the seat, with the door closed, settled down to stare raptly at the light fixture on the ceiling. Mollie lingered for a moment, breathing in the sharp morning air. The wooded hills were beginning to glow as the sun rose. A black lorry roared by, and suddenly the road was empty. In the fissure of silence came the call of a cuckoo, sweet, precise, and melancholy—cuckoo, cuckoo—urging her on.

Back in the car, Mollie discovered that the new seat had advantages besides safety. Olivia was much closer and faced backwards. Normally, after her first feed she grew drowsy, but today she kept an alert gaze fixed on Mollie and uttered a stream of sounds, right on the edge of speech. "Careful," Olivia said, and another time, Mollie was sure of it, "Music." She raised her small hands to grasp the shifting patterns of light cast by bridges, trees, clouds, other vehicles. From Perth, Mollie took the road to Stirling and on to Glasgow. She had a superstitious fear of going anywhere near Edinburgh, as if she were an iron filing on which that familiar city could exert an irresistible magnetism.

She was almost at Carlisle before she pulled into a restaurant to get breakfast for herself and to feed and change Olivia. There was a choice of stopping ten miles north or eighteen miles south of the border, and Mollie decided to have one last meal in Scotland. She lifted Olivia out in her seat—it dangled like a bucket from the handle—and walked across the car park. Inside, the restaurant was self-service, and she struggled round with Olivia and a tray until a cleaning woman in an orange smock offered to mind her. When Mollie returned a few minutes later the woman was bending over Olivia, singing "Rockabye Baby." Turning to smile at Mollie, she said, "What a pretty baby." She had a broad, pleasant face, with a tiny scar on her upper lip.

"She is, isn't she? I can't claim any credit, though. She's my sister's little girl. I'm just the aunt."

"Oh, but sometimes that can be more fun. All the nice parts, and you don't have to tell them to put their toys away." She patted Olivia's cheek. "Sweetie-pie, you be a good girl for your auntie."

Mollie sat down and watched the woman clear a pile of plates from the next table. She had believed herself perfectly happy at Mill of Fortune, only the two of them, but as she ate a bowl of muesli and a crusty roll with butter and honey, she was glad to be out in the world. The attention of other people cemented her relationship with Olivia and made it real. When she got up to leave, she waved to the cleaning woman and they called 'Bye to each other.

A quarter of an hour later she crossed the border and drove down over Shap into the Lake District. Compared with Scotland, the hills were strikingly bare; no trees, not even gorse bushes or bracken, just grass and scree. For mile upon mile Mollie passed nothing but sheep and the occasional shepherd's cottage set in the fold of a valley. The desolation of the land-scape weighed on her, and she was suddenly afraid that the car might break down. She thought she heard a strange clattering in the engine. Then Olivia cooed, and when she listened again, the noise was gone.

If she did break down, she could probably carry everything she had with her. In the back seat were Olivia's two carrier bags of possessions, *Pride and Prejudice,* Mollie's sponge bag, a towel, the jacket and cardigan that had been downstairs. For fear of waking Chae, she had not dared to pack any of the clothes she kept in the bedroom. Once the decision was made, she knew she must leave as early as possible. Passing Langdale Fell, she pondered whether there was anything she missed, besides her loom. The painting of Glen Teall that Chae had given her their first Christmas at Mill of Fortune? The 1920s handkerchief-print silk dress she'd bought in the Grassmarket to celebrate graduation? No, all that was fine; she'd buy more things, what-ever she needed. In the last few months she had been absolutely educated in the difference between want and need.

Mollie had noticed on previous visits to London that the city was not a place where one arrived, a distinct destination; rather it crept over the traveller in vague increments. There were fewer fields and then, by four o'clock, none. For a mile she passed semidetached mock-Tudor houses. She crossed a road, and these were supplanted by brick terraces. Soon the buildings grew denser; there were more shops and fewer houses and even the occasional black taxicab. The traffic was heavy but mainly heading out of the city. Mollie's shoulders ached from driving, and yet she felt perfectly alert as she came down the hill from Highgate into Archway and the Holloway Road.

She hadn't been to Ewan's for several years, in fact since coming to London with Chae for the publication of the novel before *The Dark Forest*, and she had planned to stop at a newsagents to buy an *A to Z*, but the route came back to her as she drew closer, street by street. By five-fifteen she was pulling up outside his house, into a space that had been waiting just for her.

She turned off the engine and sat bathed in the motionless silence. The street was lined with cherry trees, their branches heavy with blossom and the pavement beneath dappled with petals. Two women, one black, one white, both in nurses' uniforms, both carrying bags from Sainsburys, were walking towards her, talking. She watched them pass by, and their conversation seemed to leave a fragrance in the air, like the cherry blossoms: a good omen for her and Olivia.

She took the drowsy baby, still in her car seat, and climbed the five steps to the grey front door. As a precaution she rang the bell, though for Ewan to be home at five on a Friday afternoon was highly unlikely. Then she set Olivia down and retrieved his keys from her bag. There were three of them to get into the house, twisting different ways, and Mollie felt a little flare of panic before the third set of tumblers clicked and the door swung open. Stepping inside, she saw the wink of a red light—the burglar alarm—and quickly pushed the first four digits of Ewan's phone number.

She carried Olivia through the house. Everything was as she remembered. Ewan had had the house repainted in white and grey when he bought it; then their parents had died, and at Mollie and Bridget's urging he'd taken most of the old Edinburgh furniture. In the hall was the coatstand where Mollie had hung her school blazer. In the kitchen stood the round wooden table off which they'd eaten their meals, and in the living room was their parents' china cabinet, full of the Limoges tea set she had never been allowed to touch. Alongside these familiar objects were her own hangings. Ewan had staunchly bought two or three a year since she started selling them. One of her favourites, a dappled green meant to evoke the woods in spring, hung above the coatstand. She climbed upstairs to the first floor, where there were a bedroom and a study, and up another, narrower stair to the second floor and two attic bedrooms. The larger had a bathroom attached, and the beds in both rooms were already made up. "Olivia," said Mollie, "this is our new home."

"Mol," sang Olivia.

My name, thought Mollie.

She scarcely knew what to do first, but Olivia made clear her wishes. Feed me, she cried, change me, bathe me, talk to me. Mollie did, then she was hungry herself. A search of Ewan's cupboards, however, proved unrewarding. There was cereal, jam, and margarine, but no fresh food. A trip to the shops was definitely in order. It was still only six o'clock, and the slight risk of missing Ewan's return was far outweighed by the pleasure of establishing herself as a cohabitant, sharing equally in the chores, rather than a guest.

She popped Olivia into the sling and set out. The evening was mild, and the sparrows cheeped noisily in the cherry trees. Mollie saw that the daffodils, just budding in Scotland, here were almost finished. In several gardens she noted children's toys. Friends for Olivia, she thought. She soon found an open shop, a small supermarket run by an Indian family. She bought bread, milk, orange juice, apples, bananas, biscuits, cheese. The man at the cash register praised Olivia, and Mollie once more explained their relationship. He helped put her groceries in a bag and gently tweaked the baby's toes. "Who's a pretty girl?" he said.

Back at the house, she stepped into the hall without bothering to switch on the light. Sudden bright lights tended to make Olivia cranky, especially at the end of the day. She was lifting her from the sling when a figure came out of the kitchen.

In an instant she remembered the burglar alarm she had forgotten to set.

"Hello?" said Ewan cautiously. "Good Lord, Mollie. What are you doing here?"

He turned on the light, and she saw he was wearing his pinstripe suit and holding his briefcase, perhaps with the thought he might hurl it at an intruder. When he caught sight of Olivia, he set the case down abruptly. "Mollie," he said again.

"You gave me the keys." It was all she could think of to say.

Olivia, who had been dozing, woke. She squirmed in Mollie's arms and uttered a stream of sounds in which Mollie heard her own name and an account of their day together: the hills, the motorway, music on the radio, the cleaner who had played with her in the restaurant, the glimpse of distant furnaces as they passed industrial towns. "Here," she said, passing Olivia to Ewan.

His hands moved automatically to receive her, but he held her much too low, down around his chest, so that Olivia, deprived of her proper view, kicked with frustration.

Mollie took off her jacket and hung it on the coatstand. "I was getting some groceries," she said. "Just the basics. I'm sorry I didn't let you know we were coming." Her stomach heaved as if, unbeknownst to her, the house had slipped its mooring on the cherry-tree-lined street and set out to sea. There was no place to stand that was safely apart from the watery, sick-making motion. Beneath her the floor swayed. She took hold of the coatstand to anchor herself.

It helped, a little. Be careful, she whispered. She let go of the stand and managed to pick up the bag of groceries and lead the way into the kitchen.

A red-haired woman sat at the table. She wore a grey suit,

which, as she rose to greet Mollie, shimmered like the curtains in the kitchen at Mill of Fortune. "Hello," she said with a papery smile. "I'm Vanessa."

"I'm Mollie, Ewan's sister. And this"—she gestured behind her to the open doorway where Ewan stood—"is Olivia."

"Olivia," repeated Vanessa. She stood up and went over to Ewan.

Quickly Mollie put the groceries on the table. She felt worse, much worse. Do something, she told herself. Switch the kettle on. Cup of tea. Noise. Cry, she implored Olivia.

But Olivia was quiet, and she herself stood motionless at the table, and there in the doorway stood a man in a suit, tenuously related to her, a woman in a suit, not at all related to her, and a baby in a blue top and trousers, who was her whole life. When the idea came to her last night, it had seemed so absolutely simple. Ewan had said several times that she should think of his house as her home; and if it was her home, then it was Olivia's too. She gazed at him beseechingly. "Please," she said.

"How could you?" Ewan replied, his voice low and furious.

In answer, Olivia began to cry; perhaps he had inadvertently squeezed her. He stepped into the room and wedged her in a corner of the counter. Mollie took a step towards her, hesitated, and scooped her up.

She set about trying to calm her, though it was hopeless. Every molecule of air in the room was broken; nothing was neat and whole, and so Olivia wept. At the table, Ewan sat with his face in his hands, and Vanessa stood behind him, patting his shoulder. She had such small, pretty hands. At last she said to Mollie, "Could she be hungry?"

"I just fed her." Stupid, she thought. We're all upset. Why not Olivia?

"Still," urged Vanessa, "it might be worth trying."

Preparing the bottle, the small, exact ritual, did make Mollie feel a little better, and perhaps that betterness communicated itself to Olivia. After two or three adamant refusals, she seized the nipple; a few molecules knitted back together. Ewan and Vanessa went into the living room. Mollie could hear the low current of their voices but was curiously uninterested. Let the grown-ups talk.

One of her favourite childhood stories had been the tale of Thumbelina, who slept in half a walnut shell and padded from lily leaf to lily leaf. Now she tried to shrink herself into this room, this time. She smelled Olivia's milky breath and was convinced that all would be well. Maybe there were things she and Ewan needed to discuss; of course there were. She must be careful not to take him for granted.

She raised Olivia to burp her and saw by her eyes that she was nearly asleep. For the first time since she left Mill of Fortune that morning, Mollie allowed herself to think about Chae: the sweeping emotion of seeing him, the deceptive lure of their conversation, the ease of their love-making, and the seeming impossibility of explaining to him what a heinous crime he had committed. Looking down at Olivia, still drowsily sucking, she wished she had introduced her to him. When he next visited London, she would.

"Is everything all right?" Ewan was in the doorway.

"She's ready for bed. Perhaps she can use the sofa—we won't hear her up in the attic—unless you two need to continue your conference."

"No, no. That's fine," said Ewan. "I'll get some blankets."

He sounded more like himself. And I do too, thought Mollie, watching him leave the room. I'm tired from the drive. Goodness, nearly five hundred miles alone; no wonder I'm muddled. Within a couple of minutes he was back with blankets, a sheet, a pillow. They made a nest in one corner of the sofa and tucked Olivia in. Then there was nowhere for them to go save the kitchen.

"Do you have any booze?" Mollie asked. "I feel a drink would help."

"I agree," said Vanessa, with the first genuine warmth Mollie had heard her express.

"I'm sure I have something." While the two women watched, Ewan opened various cupboards. He soon assembled a half bottle of cooking sherry, an unopened bottle of Chianti, a bottle of vermouth and another of gin, each a third full, and a dusty green bottle with two fingers of Scotch.

"What a haul," Vanessa said. "I'll have gin with a splash of vermouth. How about you, Mollie?"

"Would it be greedy to claim the last of the Scotch?"

"Not at all. Ewan?"

"Oh, whatever you're having."

Vanessa chivvied him into finding glasses and even ice cubes. Soon they were all three seated at the round table, with drinks before them. "Cheers," Mollie said, raising her glass.

"Cheers," Ewan and Vanessa echoed in subdued tones.

"Did you both come straight from work?" she asked. "You look so respectable."

"Sort of," said Vanessa.

Mollie heard a clicking sound; it was the clock above the cooker, jumping to the next minute. Outside, a car went by in the petalled street. She almost wished Olivia would start crying again. Ewan stood up, silently left the room, and returned with his briefcase. He took out his notebook and sat back down. Mollie saw him turn to a clean page. He wrote a couple of words. "Mollie," he said, "we have to talk. You told me on the phone you'd given Olivia to the police."

She stared at the table. There was the familiar polished grain that had witnessed so many of her teenage rows: failing Latin, staying out late with boys, spending her entire allowance on music and make-up. "Yes, well, they didn't want her. No one wants her except me."

"Wait a minute," Ewan said. "Did you really go to the police station, or did you just think these things?"

"You asked," said Mollie, feeling herself go sullen. "You phoned them."

Ewan sighed. "I meant to ask," he said, "but in fact I didn't. I started to stutter, and the policeman thought it was a joke and hung up. I don't know what came over me; I talk on the phone all the time. Anyway, I apologise. I ought to have told you, but I was sure we were taking her back straight away."

I was right, Mollie thought, briefly pleased with her own acumen. She wondered whether to mention the man who phoned from pubs and called her Mrs. Lafferty and "bitch." But even as she phrased the thought, she knew such information would only make Ewan more insistent on handing Olivia over.

"I'm sorry, Mollie," he said gently. "I understand you're fond of her, but she has parents, a parent anyway. They're the ones who have a right to her. It's wrong for us to keep her."

"Wrong?" she burst out. "How can you say that? The only reason I'm here, alive in the world, is because your parents adopted me. Was that wrong? My biological parents, whoever they were, didn't give a toss about me. What would you say if they were to turn up, claiming their rights? If you didn't want me to keep Olivia, you should never have brought her to Mill of Fortune. You gave her to me, and now you're angry because I won't give her back. Well, you can't make me."

"But Mollie," said Vanessa, spreading her neat little hands on the table, "you can't go around keeping lost babies. Her parents must miss her, and she them."

"What do you know about it?" Mollie glared at Vanessa. Was this what Ewan liked, this porcelain doll? She took a sip of Scotch. "You're the girl who got Ewan in trouble, aren't you? You knew he fancied you, and you got him to spill his guts about some deal, and the next thing, he's getting awkward phone calls."

Here comes the silence again, she thought. She wasn't quite sure what she'd said, but why should she be the only one accused of bad behaviour? She drank more Scotch, recklessly.

After a moment she sneaked a look at Ewan. His face was stricken, and she was suddenly appalled. "Ewan, I'm sorry. I didn't mean to blurt things out. I'm such an idiot. I know I should have gone to the police, but I couldn't bear to. They'd just take her away and shove her in an orphanage. Or some ghastly people would be paid to adopt her."

She paused to run a hand through her hair, tugging hard, and remembered the old sixth-form debate about just laws. She had sat at this very table, arguing with her father and quoting Martin Luther King. "What I'm doing is against the law," she said firmly. "But it's not wrong, and that's what matters. Bad laws are meant to be broken."

Vanessa stood up. "I'd better get going. This is all a bit out of my depth." She turned to Mollie. "I've no idea what Ewan told you, but the truth is he was indiscreet with me and, unfortunately, I followed his example. The whole thing was an accident and will be sorted out by next week."

"You sound like a company memo," said Mollie, laughing. "Please, I'm sorry. I didn't mean to offend you. Don't go yet. I love your suit. Ewan and I will do a better job of talking with you around. You'll be our chairman, our mediator."

Vanessa hesitated, then tentatively resumed her seat. Mollie was about to demonstrate her good resolutions by asking where she was from and what she did, when the phone rang. She saw Vanessa and Ewan exchange an anxious glance. He went to answer it in the living room. "Ewan Munro speaking," Mollie heard him say. Now she would have liked to listen, but beside her Vanessa was almost quivering with eagerness, and for both of them to eavesdrop was intolerable. "How are things going?" she said quietly. "I don't know anything except that Ewan's fond of you and there's a bit of a mess."

"There doesn't have to be," Vanessa said. "At least I don't think so, if only Ewan would stop being such a goody-goody."

"I'm sorry. We were terribly well brought up. Ewan really took it to heart, unlike Bridget and me. Is there some way I can help?"

"No." She eyed Mollie more closely. "Well, maybe."

"Tell me."

They both paused, to make sure Ewan was still safely on the phone. In a soft voice, Vanessa explained that all she needed was for him to be a little absentminded. "He'd have no problem with anyone else, but it's mixed up with the fact that he likes me. He doesn't trust himself to behave well, so he's determined to get us both in trouble. Perhaps if he realises you're depending on him, you and Olivia, he can relax his scruples."

"Are you in love with him?"

Vanessa's hair swung back and forth in denial. "He's so proper I didn't even realise he was in love with me, until this business. Actually I'm seeing someone in New York. I haven't told Ewan yet. First it didn't come up, and now it's fraught with complications. Besides"—she gave Mollie a sheepish look—"I do like him."

In the living room, Ewan was saying, "Certainly not."

"I'll do what I can," said Mollie, "but you have to help out with Olivia. It's no worse than what you're doing."

She smiled, and presently Vanessa smiled back. "All right. I'll do what I can too."

" 'Bye," came Ewan's voice.

Simultaneously Vanessa asked if Mollie wanted another drink, and Mollie asked where she'd grown up.

"Not yet," Mollie said.

"In Bath. My father runs a restaurant there. I go back whenever I can. It's still the most beautiful town I know."

"I feel like that about Edinburgh."

They both turned as Ewan came through the door. Mollie

noticed that his tie hung loose and his hands were clenched into fists. "M-m-m-m-" he started to say, like Olivia. He gave up the struggle and simply stood there.

When at last Ewan spoke, he asked for her keys. She gestured towards her bag, on the counter next to the toaster, and he took them out and put them in his inside pocket. He left the room, and Mollie heard him locking the front door. She wished desperately she were holding Olivia, but the swaying motion of the house had begun again and she did not trust her legs to carry her to the living room. Ewan returned. Still he did not sit down but remained standing as if only an upright position would enable him to deliver his difficult message.

"We're going to Mill of Fortune tomorrow," he said. "That was Chae on the phone. A man came for Olivia. Her real name is Grace, and he wants her back."

"Chae?" she exploded. "You can't trust him. Look at what he did to me with Leo. Why do you think I left? Of course there's a man. But he doesn't care about Olivia. He doesn't love her, I can tell. It's something else he's after. Money. I bet it's money, like you two."

"So you knew about the man," Ewan said.

"Yes, fuck him." She was shaking, as well as the house. Who was this banker in a suit ordering her around? Only her little brother. Fuck him too. She heard something. Had Ewan spoken? Had the table? She examined each in turn. The sleek wood had grown oddly smug and duplicitous. As for Ewan, his face had a strange plastic sheen, and it came to Mollie that what she'd taken to be her brother's intimate, revealing flesh was a mask. Who knew how he really looked?

Then Vanessa was standing over her, one cool hand on the back of her neck, saying, "Here, put your head down. Lower . . .

that's right. Everything's going to be fine. Breathe deeply. One, two. There."

Ewan had helped her up the stairs. Vanessa had carried Olivia. She had turned on the electric blanket, sent Ewan to make hot milk, and run Mollie a bath. Mollie had meekly, even pleasurably, submitted to their caretaking. By the time she was in bed between clean warm sheets, with Olivia beside her, everything was fine again. The bed lay solid and firm beneath her; the ceiling hung motionless above. She would talk to Ewan in the morning. Of course he couldn't understand until she explained properly, but once she had, he would.

She woke to the sound of Olivia whimpering. Immediately other bewildering noises broke in upon her: the grind of brakes, several sharp toots of a horn, the washing-machine slurp of a taxi. Where am I? she wondered. Then as she climbed out of bed and reached for Olivia, she remembered she was at Ewan's and felt safe. No dark countryside here. She carried the baby down the carpeted, silent stairs to the kitchen, where a small lamp was lit on the counter, and prepared a bottle.

In her sleepy state she made the milk a little too hot and had to hold the bottle under the cold tap before offering it to Olivia. But Olivia, who had roused her, ignored the milk. She lay in Mollie's arms, tossing restlessly, her tiny fists clenched against unknown demons. "There," Mollie whispered, "it's all right, Olivia. I'm here. Wake up. Have some milk."

Olivia frowned; her face, coppery in the dim light, darkened to blackberry. "Cunt," she said.

Mollie screamed.

Olivia's eyes were shiny little turds. Her lips peeled back over glistening toothless gums.

Then a kind of scrim seemed to cover Olivia's face or Mollie's eyes, to gather and thicken and disappear. Already Olivia was reaching for the bottle, and Ewan and Vanessa were standing in the doorway, both still dressed in their suits, asking if anything was the matter.

"No, no, nothing," Mollie stumbled. Her hands were trembling, but whoever it was she held in her lap, she was not yet ready to surrender.

Chapter 16

Shortly after eleven Mollie returned upstairs with Olivia. A few minutes earlier her piercing scream had brought Ewan running to the kitchen, with Vanessa right behind him. In response to his anxious questions, Mollie claimed nothing was wrong; she was just startled. But the mere sight of her sitting at the kitchen table in her nightdress, wide-eyed, wild-haired, and muttering, was profoundly wrong. As he backed out of the room, Ewan recalled reading somewhere that Bedlam had once been one of the tourist attractions of London.

He and Vanessa sat down again in the flowery armchairs on either side of the living room fireplace. Music from a passing car rippled by. Upstairs, a toilet flushed. "This is one of the strangest nights of my life." Vanessa sighed. "What exactly did Chae say?"

"He was at Mill of Fortune, and when he woke up this morning Mollie was gone and someone was pounding on the door. He opened it to find a man he'd never seen before, demanding a baby."

"Was he Indian?"

"No, he was white and rather unpleasant. Chae had to pay him not to go to the police before we could bring Olivia back." Suddenly Ewan remembered the curious phone call during his visit to Mill of Fortune; he described what he'd overheard to Vanessa. "Mollie was very odd about it. She came up with some bogus story about a farmer and the right-of-way. At the time I was sure she was lying, though I'd no idea why. Now I think that must have been Olivia's father." He reached up to remove the tie he had loosened earlier. "I should call her Grace," he said, running the silk through his fingers. "It's just so confusing."

"But how could Mollie have done this?" Vanessa frowned. "I mean, I understand not wanting to hand a baby over to bureaucracy. But if she knew Grace's father was searching for her, even if he is a nasty piece of work, then her behaviour makes no sense at all."

"That's what I'm just beginning to grasp," Ewan exclaimed. "We're not talking about sense. Last night at dinner, when you asked why I hadn't taken Olivia to the police, there was some additional factor over and above the practical issues that I couldn't quite get hold of. The real reason was Mollie. From the moment I got into her car, she was scheming to keep Olivia. And, stupidly, I went along with it."

"Don't," said Vanessa. "Nobody could've guessed the lengths she was prepared to go to."

They moved on to the problem of how to get Olivia back to Mill of Fortune by seven the following evening. Clearly Mollie was not about to drive north again.

"We could fly," Ewan said doubtfully. He had a vision of Mollie in the confined space of a plane, making some terrible scene.

"I'm not sure Mollie's up to public transport," Vanessa said. "Of any kind. Besides, you'd still have to get from Edinburgh. I wonder if maybe I should drive you. After all, we have her car."

She looked at him questioningly, and as he looked back, it occurred to Ewan that at some point since they met at Heathrow, they had entered into a bargain, a quid pro quo, about Coyle. The mere thought gave him a clammy feeling; if Vanessa had intimated, even by a gesture, that such an arrangement existed, he could not have borne it. But she was perfect. She smoothed her skirt and assumed matters were settled. "Lucky I only had one drink," she said. "I'll go and fetch a change of clothes."

"Isn't it a bit late?"

"No, at this time of night I can get to Chiswick and back in under an hour. You might need support in the morning."

She stood up, and Ewan did too. "Thank you," he said, the tie dangling foolishly from his hands. "I don't know how I'd manage without you."

"Don't be silly. I've never been to Scotland before. It'll be fun." The childishness that came over her when she was frightened had vanished; she was all businesslike efficiency. He handed her Mollie's car keys and watched her clip down the front steps in her high heels and drive away without a second's hesitation.

Alone, Ewan returned to his armchair. The chairs were another Edinburgh inheritance, and fleetingly he conjured up their true occupants: his parents, as he had so often seen them, sitting on either side of the fire, each deep in a book. Thank goodness they had not lived to see two of their three children behave badly.

His mind turned to the meeting with Coyle, an event which only yesterday he had dreaded and which now he recollected almost with relief. Ewan had gone directly from his night with Vanessa to the coffee bar at Liverpool Street Station. In the panic of their initial phone call he'd forgotten to ask Coyle how they would recognise each other, but as he stood there, craning around the crowded room, a man appeared beside him, saying his name.

Coyle in person was quite different from the saturnine figure Ewan had imagined. Small-boned, thinning sandy hair, thickish glasses, a sharp nose. The kind of man Bridget would have called a train spotter, who probably lived with his parents in Hounslow. Ewan felt slightly better. "It's good of you to meet me on such short notice," Coyle said. "I appreciate it."

They both got coffee and what claimed to be croissants. "How was Milan?" Coyle asked. He's trying to soften me up, thought Ewan, and by way of retaliation he repeated the remark he'd made to Vanessa about the Borgia chair. "Really?" Coyle put down his coffee cup. His sharp nose seemed to quiver. "That's quite amazing. I'm a bit of a Dante scholar. Of course he was a couple of centuries earlier." He carried on about Dante's difficult involvement in Florentine politics. As he waved his hand, Ewan noticed a fat gold wedding ring.

Then Coyle explained that he was talking to people involved with the Gibson Group because a large transfer of stock had taken place shortly before the merger went through. Ewan frowned and asked who the buyer was. "A man named Ralph Marsden," said Coyle. "A high-class dentist who plays the market as a hobby."

Ewan waited. That was one thing about stuttering; it taught you an inevitable patience. "So," Coyle said, "he could be a very lucky dentist. But the deal has all the marks of special info: mortgaging the house, borrowing from the father-in-law, and, of course, dodging my calls. His broker, Brian Ross, claims he was simply following instructions. The reason I wanted to see you so urgently is that I'm going to Marsden's office today, and I was hoping you might throw some light on the situation."

"Brian and I have been friends since university," said Ewan. "We did speak a couple of times about the Gibson stuff, but I'm certain we maintained confidentiality." He put on his primmest Edinburgh voice, and Coyle at once began to apologise.

"No, no, good heavens. You Scots have a reputation for discretion, bar none. Do you have any thoughts, though? Someone who might've been privy to the deal, any odd people showing up for meetings?"

Ewan fiddled with his shirt cuffs and pretended to consider. "I honestly can't say," he said at last. "This thing has been in the works for nearly a year. Maybe what I should do is go through my office diary; it might jog my memory. And there is the whole problem of faxes. One never is quite sure who's reading them."

"Don't I know it." Coyle nodded. "Well, I really would appreciate your checking that diary, Mr. Munro, and getting in touch with me if anything occurs to you."

Outside in the shopping precinct they exchanged a brief, dry handshake. Coyle was turning away in the direction of the underground when he stopped and, as if the idea had just occurred to him, said, "I don't suppose you have much contact with people at the Marlowe Company?"

No, Ewan started to say, and could not speak. He simply shook his head.

"Thought I'd ask," Coyle said with another quick twitch of his nose, and disappeared into the underground station.

An hour later in the office, Yvonne announced that the woman from the Marlowe Company was on line two. In the instant of hearing Vanessa's panicky voice, Ewan decided not to mention Coyle's last question. The conversation had gone well, he reported, but Coyle was still determined to talk to Ralph as soon as possible. Vanessa gave a stifled groan. "What's he like?" she asked.

"Small, with a Birmingham accent. A Dante fan," he added.

Yvonne was pointing to the other phone, and hastily he suggested they meet at the Lord Nelson after work.

In the taxi from the pub back to Barnsbury, Vanessa had been kittenish with relief. There was no word from Coyle. Ralph, she believed, had heeded her admonition; so long as they both kept silent, they were safe. Swept up in her jubilation, Ewan made a joke about shuffling off that mortal coil and failed to notice the signs of his sister's arrival. They had been looking up film times in the newspaper when Mollie came back with the groceries.

Now Ewan stared at the hanging above the fireplace and realised there was nothing to celebrate. Very likely Coyle was going to get Ralph; Ralph would betray Vanessa; and she in turn would betray him. What, after all, would prevent her? To his surprise, the people whose disapproval he most feared were Coyle, who had seemed to believe an Edinburgh upbringing put him above suspicion, and Yvonne—as if these two had become his surrogate parents.

At school one winter there had been a craze: any lie could be cancelled by crossing one's fingers. Did you take my gym shoes, George? Course not. Then the shoes were produced and the crossed fingers triumphantly displayed. At the age of ten, Ewan had scoffed at the notion of morality that lay behind this game. But at thirty-three he had succumbed hook, line, and sinker.

A soft knock interrupted his reflections. He hurried to the front door and found Vanessa, a bag in one hand. She'd changed out of her suit into jeans and her leather jacket. Before he could stop himself, he pulled her close and kissed her.

"Ewan," she said.

"Sorry."

He led her inside, locked the door, and returned the keys to his pocket. Beneath the hall light she looked tired, and he could see as a fact, indisputable as her supple posture or her small even teeth, that she did not love him, that she liked him, that she thought him a nice person—all those irredeemable phrases that from anyone other than the beloved count as praise and from the beloved are the most damning. And in the midst of this revelation Ewan was appalled to hear himself say, "Vanessa, will you sleep with me? I mean like last night. I just want to hold you."

"All right," she said, and followed him upstairs without another word. Something about that quick agreement, Ewan thought, was like a knife in the heart. Another knife, he corrected wryly.

He would have claimed not to have slept a wink, but proof to the contrary was furnished by his waking the following morning. Vanessa lay remote on the far side of the bed. He held his own breath and caught the slow sound of hers. By the glowing numerals of the clock it was only five past six. He stole from beneath the covers, determined to let her sleep as long as possible. If they left by eight, they could still be at Mill of Fortune in plenty of time for the rendezvous. He washed, put on his dressing gown, and went downstairs. In the kitchen, Mollie was already feeding the baby. Her eyes passed over him as if he were an empty television screen.

"Well, we're up early." Ewan's voice came out in that jolly register he knew Mollie loathed, and to make matters worse, he clapped his hands. Quickly he bent to the morning tasks of filling the kettle and finding tea bags. For several minutes he moved around the room, pretending they were just two taciturn, sleepy adults. Then the tea was brewed, and there was no choice but to set a mug before Mollie and sit down.

She drank some tea, still ignoring him. Ewan remembered how once, when he'd borrowed her bike without asking, she had refused to speak to him for an entire week. He leaned over to see Olivia. She was wearing the same blue top and trousers as the day before, and beamed up at him. When he reached out his hand, she gurgled and grasped his finger. "She looks like she had a good night," he said, trying desperately to sound normal.

Still nothing.

"Mollie, what is it? Are you angry? Talk to me."

"Grr," said Olivia.

Mollie bent over her. For a moment Ewan wondered if he had indeed spoken. It was so early, he was so tired. He touched the side of his mug to feel the heat. "Mollie," he tried again. "I know you think I'm letting you down. But Olivia has parents, and they want her back. We can't just shanghai her."

"Why not? Why can't we keep her? See how happy she is here, with us. She's learning to talk. And she loves music. The king's daughters promised her she could stay with us. Why should we give her up to some lout who left her in a toilet? All he cares about is money. And booze."

She continued ranting. Ewan had never seen his sister, or anyone, in such a state. Words were pouring out of her and, even more disturbing, a mysterious bitter smell, which made him edge back his chair. He longed to wake Vanessa, who, whatever her shortcomings, behaved badly in the usual ways, but it was still only six thirty-five.

"Olivia needs love. Every day you can see her learning and growing. And—"

"I've nearly finished *The Dark Forest*."

Maybe it was not the most sensible interruption, but it did get Mollie's attention. She came to an abrupt stop, an almost visible slamming on of the brakes, and swerved into a new topic. "So you understand?" she demanded.

"Understand what?"

"How miserably Chae treated me."

"No," said Ewan. "Not really." Nothing in his life so far had prepared him for the storm of Mollie's emotions.

"I'll never forgive him," she spat. "Those stupid pots, as if that would deceive anyone. The birds keep pecking away. She wears my clothes. She has my dreams. The part about Leo and Maudie, the part where he fucks her—did you read that?"

She was clutching the edge of the table, her eyes bulging with passion.

Ewan nodded, and his acquiescence seemed to calm her slightly.

"Babies, what does Chae know of babies? He wouldn't give me one. He has no sperm. He thinks Leo . . . but no, that's not it." She stopped and sighed. "The whole thing makes me feel crazy."

Ewan gazed at his tea; the light above the table bobbed in the surface. Mollie was revealing a part of herself that ought to be kept hidden, and he was torn between wanting to pay the closest attention and feeling duty-bound to turn a blind eye. If he ignored her shameful indiscretions, he thought, later it would be easier for her to do the same. But what was all this about no sperm? Then he remembered Mollie telling him casually, years ago, that Chae had had a vasectomy. "He sounded devoted to you on the phone last night," he offered.

"Devoted," Mollie muttered.

"His girlfriend. Affair." Each word was worse than the last. He hurried on. "Perhaps that's all over with?"

"What girlfriend?"

"Didn't he have a girlfriend, a woman friend? Wasn't that why he left?"

"Ewan, he left because of the fucking book."

"You mean—"

"Christ!" She slammed her fist against the table so hard their mugs jumped. "He stole my life. Do you think I could live with a thief?"

She spoke with furious impatience, as if she'd forgotten that for two months she had allowed, even encouraged, Ewan to believe Chae had left her for another woman. He was dumb-founded. Over and over she claimed to have been abandoned, but it was she who had left. Or, rather, made Chae leave. All the transactions of the last few weeks flipped from red to black, from round to square. Ewan was still staring at Mollie when Olivia uttered a sound and his sister's face went pale. Before he could ask what was the matter, Vanessa breezed into the room.

"Good morning, everyone," she said. "I hope you slept as well as I did." She smiled at the three of them. "I was afraid I was holding things up, but I can see that's not the case."

Ewan took in that she was washed, dressed, had her bag in one hand and her jacket over her arm. "Is there any coffee?" she asked.

"I'll make some," Mollie said. As she stood up, the acrid odour engulfed Ewan, filling his nostrils and tickling the back of his throat. He gave a surreptitious cough and reached for his tea.

Chapter 17

Kenneth wandered out of the bus station and saw a taxi idling at the curb. In his entire life he'd ridden in no more than half a dozen, always with other people, either crammed in with a bunch of mates, someone's elbow jabbing into his ribs, or, once or twice, with his mum. Now he stared at the white Austin with a sign on the side advertising a Chinese restaurant and thought, Why not? He climbed in and asked for The Blind Beggar.

"Mind going by the South Inch?" the driver asked. "It's a bit longer, but the traffic's no as bad."

"Fine by me," said Kenneth. The longer the better. He sat back and gazed appreciatively at the park and the river. If he had had a pen, he would have written his name on the seat beside him, just to prove he was here. This was the life.

When they drew up outside the pub, the meter said three pounds sixty. Kenneth proffered a twenty-pound note with a flourish. Disappointingly, the driver's wedge-shaped face did not change an iota; he pocketed the smooth, clean note and handed back three crumpled fives and some coins.

Inside, the swimming pool brothers were at the dartboard

and there was a chick behind the bar, with her sleeves pulled up so you could see her pretty arms. Kenneth ordered a nip and a chaser at two fifty a go. Eager to get rid of the smelly notes from the taxi, he bought a round for the brothers and the barmaid. They all thanked him. When he went to take a piss, he saw his inscription, *For a good time . . .* and the Laffertys' phone number. Someone had added, *Oh yeah?* and a third hand had written, *Out of this world.* Kenneth chuckled.

By three he was wasted. The barmaid had to tell him several times before it dawned on him that he was to be included in the general exodus. Outside, the street was reassuringly noisy, not like that creepy country road where he'd been this morning. Even the hardness of the pavement when he tripped and fell was okay. He lay there scrutinising the gutter. There was a Mars bar wrapper and too many cigarette butts to count; he started anyway, got to six, stopped and started again.

"You okay, mate?" one of the swimming pool brothers was saying. And he was on his feet, which did, after all, seem preferable.

"You'd better go home," said the other brother.

Home, thought Kenneth, and pictured his mum's dusty pink sofa, a place to which he could find his way in almost any state of inebriation. He set out past the row of furniture shops, the laundry, and the seedy hotel. Quite suddenly he was climbing the stairs to her flat. He knocked at the door and stared at the nameplate, Singer, left by some long ago tenant. "Singing," he chanted. "Sewing."

Ideas were swarming, so many he couldn't identify them. I'm too brainy, he thought, that's my trouble. The Singer nameplate receded, and there was his mum, dressed in her pale-brown trouser suit. Something about her head seemed different, though. For a moment he wondered if she was wearing a hat, all those tight orange curls. No, probably Rita downstairs was the culprit. "Mum," he said, "you look fab."

Behind her blue-framed spectacles, her eyes narrowed. "You've been drinking."

"A wee dram. Nothing to mention. Can I come in?"

She stepped back reluctantly. Kenneth moved towards the kitchen, then, remembering other needs, swerved to the bathroom. He took a piss and, as an afterthought, threw up in one tidy heave. Amazingly it all landed in the bowl. At the basin he ran water over his hands, splashed his face, and rinsed his mouth. He avoided the mirror. It was one thing for his mum to look different, another if he were to find his own reflection gone AWOL. In the kitchen, she was waiting. "Where are you getting the money to drink, then?" she said in vinegary tones. "You'll never get another job if you carry on like this."

"I have a job," he said indignantly. Putting the frighteners on someone was definitely an occupation. "Temporary," he added.

"Lorries?"

"No, not lorries." He had an inspiration. "I've moved into PR. Public relations. Just for a couple of days."

"PR?" She snorted with laughter. "You gormless wonder."

This was chronic. Look at her stupid hair. He beat a retreat to the sitting room, where, without bothering to turn off the TV or draw the curtains, he lay down on the sofa and, in the comfy atmosphere of cigarettes and dust, fell instantly asleep.

When he woke, the curtains were drawn, or at least it was much darker. He raised his head experimentally, one inch, two, then saw his mum watching from her armchair. "You know what, Kenny?" she said. "You were talking in your sleep. At one point I could hardly hear the telly. I'm so pleased. It means you were dreaming."

"I never dream," he said automatically. His mouth was sandpapery, and he swallowed. "What did I say?"

"It wasn't easy to follow. You kept saying 'grace.' And Lally? Lully? Some nonsense word. You said 'no' a lot. Something about water. Oh, and you mentioned Miss McBain. Remember, she was that teacher of yours in primary school, the old battle-axe."

Kenneth did not bother to answer. He stared at the furry pink fabric and grappled with the notion that he'd been dreaming. Daydreaming he understood; it could even be useful. You pictured a situation and figured out what to do next. He'd done a fair bit of that lately. But the other kind of dreaming was different, and he had been proud of never succumbing to this peculiar habit. He wanted to argue, tell Mum she was daft, but even as the protest rose to his lips, dark shadows from the last hour crowded in upon him. Yes, Grace had been there, he recalled, his little breadwinner, but grown larger, and that bearded guy, Mr. Lafferty, who had turned out to be surprisingly understanding. So this was dreaming, bits and pieces of your day coming back to you. He shifted, and Joan's blue sari rose out of the sofa—she, too, had been there. And someone else, whom he didn't recognise, a figure so indistinct he wasn't sure if it was man or woman. He felt immediate indignation. What the hell was some stranger doing in his brain? It confirmed what he had always suspected: this dreaming was a weird, chancy business, not something he wanted to go in for.

He buried his face against the dusty cushion. He'd have liked to forget Joan. She had food, water, a toilet, a telly. Why not leave her be? By tonight he should have news of Grace. By tomorrow the baby herself. Now that he thought about it, it was amazing, that woman's kidnapping Grace. Real *News of the World* stuff. What would happen, he wondered, if he went to the police? There was that copper who sometimes picked him up after football matches. Wallace, he thought; Willy Wally they called him mockingly. It would be nice to go to the nick, seek out Wallace, and report a crime, be the law-abiding one for a change: have blokes say please and thank you and bring him a cup of tea.

As if he'd spoken aloud, or his head was transparent, he smelled tea. "Cup of tea," said his mum.

Slowly, cautiously, he tried moving his head and his feet in different directions. It seemed to work. His feet were on the floor, his head resting against the back of the sofa. He drank some tea, bitter as usual. She had a theory about sugar and seldom put in enough. That made him think again of Joan, more warmly. She would never give him three spoons and claim it was four.

"Last night I dreamed about cows," his mother said. "I don't know why. I haven't been near one in ages." She recounted the dream in laborious detail. "Maybe it had something to do with my father. He was always fond of cattle. Or it could be the massage Rita gave me with the shampoo. She rubbed especially hard behind the left ear. That's where the childhood memories are stored."

Kenneth drank his tea and nodded. She had talked this way for years, as though her dreams contained vital messages. For the first time he felt something like sympathy. He did want to know who that stranger was and what the hell they were doing messing around in his head. Forget it, he told himself. His stomach growled. He'd pick up some fish and chips. Then Joan wouldn't have to cook.

He moved his hand to his pocket. There were so many notes it was almost like carrying a book, a book with a single, wonderful page repeated over and over. Not safe, though. With his free hand, the one not holding the tea, he explored the side of the sofa and found a narrow space between the cushions. Once his mum left the room, he'd slip the money down there. Just keep a hundred pounds for current expenses. He'd seen people get lucky on the horses or a bonus at work—not this lucky, mind you—and piss the whole thing away in a weekend. Stupid buggers. Well, he wasn't going to be one of them.

As usual, an idea cheered him up. "Perhaps the cows are telling you you need to go somewhere," he said to his mother. "You haven't been out of Perth since you visited Nelly. It's only a few quid on the bus to Edinburgh. You could have a nice day out. Buy yourself a spring bonnet."

"Kenneth, are you okay? Just because you have a dream doesn't mean you turn into Mother Teresa."

He grinned at her. "Why do you never put enough fucking sugar in the tea?"

Time had done one of its odd things again, humped up and sprawled out. When he got downstairs it was already dark, with the streetlamps casting their dingy glow. He counted the pubs as he walked, so he could tell Joan how many he'd passed up to see her. Fourteen by the time he reached the Chip Inn round the corner from her flat. He got two plaice and chips—thirty pence more than the haddock but well worth it, another thing he could point to as evidence of good behaviour. He scoffed a few chips on his way up the stairs; they were thin and hot. Whenever he was a bit wobbly, fish and chips was one of his standbys—according to his mum, the grease helped bind the stomach together. Almost immediately he did feel better.

Outside Joan's door, he was about to knock when he remembered he was Lord of the Keys, both sets. He juggled the fish and chips, found the keys, and on his second attempt got the door open. Stepping inside, he nearly collided with Joan. She was standing in the hall. At the sight of him her face widened from surprise to dismay to horror. Before he could proffer the fish and chips, she began to scream. "Grace, where is she? Where is Grace?"

It was like a fire alarm. The first impact of the noise, echoing up and down the stairwell behind him, was so overwhelming it was impossible to think or act. He tossed the fish and chips on a chair, shut the door, grabbed Joan's wrists, and shook her. "Shut up," he said. "Shut bloody up. How can I tell you where Grace is if you're making this goddamn racket. Grace is fine. She's in the pink."

"You liar," Joan screamed. "You said she would be here. You said this evening."

He slapped her, briskly, on the cheek and suddenly thought of the neighbours. Mrs. Kemp downstairs had a phone and might just call the cops. Then Kenneth would have to explain it was a domestic argy-bargy, which did not fit with his earlier fantasies of re-encountering Wallace as an honest citizen.

His hand was stinging, and Joan only screamed louder. She wants the cops to come, he thought, stupid bitch. He held on to her wrist and clamped his other hand over her mouth. "Listen," he said, "if you want to know about Grace you keep quiet. Okey-dokey?"

He kept his hand there until she nodded. Slowly he took it away. "Come into the kitchen," he said. "I got us some plaice and chips." He picked up the two packets and carried them into the kitchen, then scooted back to lock the door and pocket the keys. Joan was standing beside the table. She was wearing regular clothes, jeans and a sweatshirt, which made her look smaller and dumpier. There was a dark mark on one cheek where he'd smacked her. A pity, but at least it didn't show as much as if she were white.

"Okay," he said, "I'm going to explain. These people have Grace, nice people, big house in the country, a dog, a car, really la-di-da. They gave me a cup of coffee. They took Grace by mistake. They're sorry, but they're looking after her. They gave me some dosh. Here."

He pulled out a couple of twenties and laid them on the table so she could see the purple picture of the man, his name was Michael Faraday, and the Queen, without her specs, and the metal strip they wove into the paper. "There'll be more of this. Lots more."

"Grace," she said.

"Ten o'clock tonight I'm phoning the bloke. He said he'd have her by tomorrow. I told him we'd go to the police if he didn't get a move on. I mean, she's our kid, not just any old baby. Come on. Let's have some grub. Then you can ask all the questions you like."

He sat down, unwrapped a packet, and began to eat. When he looked up, Joan was still standing there. She was not crying. He couldn't think of a word for the expression on her face, but probably there was one. At school once he'd had to find "melancholy" in the dictionary and been appalled by how many words there were, hundreds of them, thousands. The ones he read nearby—megrim, melic, melinite—were for things he'd never heard of: a small flounder; meant to be sung; a French explosive. The experience had made the world seem even larger and more confusing. He never wanted to see a dictionary again.

He'd finished his fish and chips, and Joan was still standing there. "Aren't you hungry?" he said. She didn't answer, so he reached for her packet and started in on that too. The chips were a bit cold but nicely sodden with vinegar, and the batter was crispy.

When he had eaten everything, he got up and washed his hands at the sink, drying them on a tea towel. His stomach felt thoroughly, even overly, settled. He sat back down again. "That was grand," he said. "What's the time?"

"Eight-thirty."

"Okey-dokey. Time for a cup of tea and some telly. Then we'll go to the Blind Beggar and sort this bloke out. Grace will be back in no time, you'll see." Joan was onto something, he thought, the old brain clicking away. There was money in being an outraged dad. He should watch her and take lessons.

Some of what he said must've got through, because finally she put on the kettle and threw the fish and chip papers in the rubbish. She made tea and went so far as to pour herself a cup. "Come sit with me," he said. "There's no fun watching alone."

At first he thought she was going to refuse. Another of those dictionary expressions came over her face. Then she followed him into the living room and sat in the farthest possible corner of the sofa. A hospital program was on, docs and nurses rushing around in a way they never had at the infirmary. Across the room he spotted Grace's carry cot and felt a tug of what was maybe fatherly feeling. Bloody cheek, those nobs nicking his baby. Hang on to that, he admonished, don't let it out of the starting gate for nothing. Now, instead, he pondered the pleasant subject of money.

At nine-thirty Joan stood up, left the room, and came back in her raincoat. For a moment he thought she was cold. Then she stepped over to the television and switched it off. "We must telephone," she said. "Get up."

He started to bluster it wasn't time yet, who the hell did she think she was, bossing him around, but it *was* time, and her screams came back to him. If Mr. Lafferty made any trouble, he'd pass the phone to Joan. She'd soon sort him out. He stood up and felt the reluctance of his body for any further gyrations. The fish and chips were like a stone in his stomach. He shifted his jeans, trying to loosen the waistband. It was better, then worse. If they saw a taxi, he decided, they'd just hop in.

There was not a single taxi in sight. Joan marched him along at a ferocious pace, taking his arm to drag him across at traffic lights. By the time they entered the pub, his head ached and his stomach was distinctly dodgy. The place was jammed with a darts tournament, and Kenneth stood swaying in the doorway. Why was he here? he wondered. Christ, he could afford a regular phone. Joan jerked his arm. "Telephone," she said.

He shook her off. "In a sec." He lined up at the bar. After five minutes he got a shot of Teacher's for himself and, on impulse, one for her too. Might loosen her up a bit. He added plenty of water. She took the glass silently and stood there while he drank. He watched one of the darts players, a skinny bloke with a long ponytail, which he tossed back before each throw. Though Kenneth couldn't see the board, he had the impression the bloke was playing well. Then something distracted him. Was it a new smell, a new record on the jukebox? He sensed a profound shift in the barometric pressure of the pub, but no one else seemed aware of the change. He felt Joan motionless beside him, and it came to him that it was her waiting that was fouling things up. If he didn't make that phone call, one or the other of them might just drown in these strange vibrations she was giving off.

He squeezed round the darts match to the phone. When he got there he realised he couldn't faff about, searching for the scrap of paper. He ducked into the Gents, catching a searing look from Joan, and came out mouthing the number. His palms were wet from heat or nerves, he wasn't sure which. Maybe the latter, because the first time he dialled he got a recording saying the number was out of service. The second time the phone scarcely rang before Mr. Lafferty said, "Hello."

"Have you got Grace?"

"Tomorrow. I swear she'll be here by tomorrow evening. I know where she is. Everything's under control."

Through the crowd Kenneth saw Joan pushing and shoving her way towards him. "My wife," he said—had he called her that before?—"my wife is in a terrible state. She's talking about going to the police."

"Don't," Mr. Lafferty gasped. "We'll do—"

At that moment Joan seized the phone and in a high-pitched voice, almost a wail, said, "Where is my baby? What have you done with her? Where is she?" over and over, leaving no chance for the bloke to answer. Kenneth sipped his whisky. Good old Joan, he thought, going for an Oscar. He slid three more pennies into the coin slot.

At last she fell silent, and he got restive. "What's he saying?" he whispered hoarsely, but she didn't respond. Her face was bent over the phone as if she could pour herself down the receiver and emerge at Mill of Fortune like a genie out of a bottle. Kenneth grinned. That would give Mr. Lafferty a shock. He seized the phone back.

"You see what I mean," he said. "She's in a right old state. What did you tell her?"

"I said Grace will be here by seven tomorrow. You can fetch her then. You'll all be together again tomorrow night."

"And what about the . . . ?" He hesitated. "Money" was too crass a word, even if Mr. Lafferty had already made a deposit.

"Don't worry. We'll take care of her. Tell your wife the baby is safe. Absolutely safe and well." Before Kenneth could explain that that wasn't his worry, Mr. Lafferty said goodbye and hung up.

Kenneth hung up too. Then, noticing the slippery palm print, he picked up the receiver, wiped it on the sleeve of his jacket, and put it down again. "Shite," he said. "Banks are closed on Saturday."

He had been speaking to himself, but Joan must have heard. She stared at him with glittering eyes. "You did it for money," she hissed. "You stole Grace for money. Like a slave trader."

He didn't have a clue what to say. He wanted to boast of his cleverness, to let her know that all this new largesse was due to his ingenuity. Christ, what could you do with a baby? If you let them, they ate money and crapped shit, but he'd found a way to turn the process around, to get something out of Grace, and he was dying for applause. The noise of the pub throbbed around him, and the lights grew dazzlingly bright. Patience, he thought. Soon he could explain everything. For now, keep her calm so she doesn't rock the boat.

"Joan," he said, "what happened was an accident, several accidents." Mention Grace: that was what she had a bee in her bonnet about. "The main thing is Grace's okay. This time tomorrow she'll be home, bawling her head off. We won't be able to go out on the town at the drop of a hat. Come on, let's have another drink. We're here, we might as well enjoy it."

She pulled away as if he had one of those diseases you can catch from standing next to a person. Who gives a fuck, he thought. "Have it your way," he said. "Let's go home."

"I want to fetch Grace. To go to the man's house."

"Joan, he doesn't have her. I was there this morning, and she definitely wasn't there. They're bringing her back tomorrow. Didn't he tell you? I'll collect her then. Okey-dokey? There's no point in going now."

She said nothing, simply went on staring at him, without affection, without regard, with an absolute, merciless desire to know whether he spoke the truth. He looked back at her—the mark on her cheek was almost gone—and did his best to make his face open and friendly as he had that morning, hitching a lift to Mill of Fortune. "Let's go home," he repeated. "We need a good night's sleep."

In the street there was still no sign of the taxi he'd imagined. They started walking, past the spot where he had fallen that afternoon, past the fourteen pubs. As they waited to cross Kinnoull Street, Joan spoke. "I am coming with you tomorrow," she said.

Kenneth stumbled over the curb. Not a bad idea, he thought, taking her along. He wouldn't have to deal with

Grace, plus it would up the ante. Hysterics have their price. Meanwhile, the night lay before him, and he hoped he didn't do this dreaming stuff again. Once was enough, more than. He hated the way people came and went in his head without permission, hated the way they left their shadows. "Wait a sec," he called to Joan, and took her arm.

Chapter 18

By eight a.m. the four of them were in the car, retracing Mollie's journey of the day before. Mollie and Olivia sat in the back, Ewan beside Vanessa in the front. Normally when he was up this early on a Saturday, it was to go to the Chapel Street market. Now, as they drove down the narrow streets, he envied the pedestrians, whom he imagined on innocent errands: off to buy mushrooms picked in Kent that very morning or smooth brown eggs laid in Sussex the night before. His own errand was of a grimmer nature. The last twelve hours had proved beyond doubt that something was deeply awry with Mollie. Although she had raised no active struggle against departure, indeed had collected her few possessions and filled Olivia's bottles with automaton-like efficiency, Ewan felt the effort of imposing his will upon her. The smell that had hung around her earlier was gone, but he waited apprehensively for its return.

As for Vanessa, sharing a bed with her for a second night had turned out to be more misery than pleasure. He had been poignantly aware that her feelings fell far short of love or even lust. When he rested a hand on her sleeping shoulder, she twitched him off as if he were a gnat buzzing through her dreams.

They passed an Odeon in East Finchley showing the film the two of them had planned to see the night before, and suddenly, as the red and white striped marquee flashed by, Ewan thought he could not continue this charade. He must have clarity, at least in one area of his life. On Monday morning he would phone Coyle and tell him what had happened. Not the part he knew from Vanessa, but his own indiscretion. There was no reason to become a criminal twice over.

Then Vanessa asked him to turn on the radio, and reaching for the knob, he realised that his so-called integrity was now a luxury beyond his means. Here was Vanessa helping him drive his mad sister back to Scotland; he could not reciprocate with betrayal. Whatever the cost, he was committed to mendacity.

For a moment this knowledge caused him such pain that he did not notice the raucous music flooding the car. Some small but essential organ had been cut out of him. He was no longer his father's son.

"Ewan," Vanessa protested, "I wanted one of those Saturday morning programs about the relationship between oysters and mussels or the history of jade."

"Sorry," he mumbled. He found Radio Four, where a gardening programme was in progress. "Take the lupin," a man with a Yorkshire accent was saying.

"Oh, good," Vanessa said.

"How's Olivia?" Ewan asked.

"Asleep."

Mollie's voice was so curt he glanced around. He could see little—her face was tilted towards the window—but the visible crescent of cheek had an unpleasant greenish tinge. More striking than her pallour, however, was her posture: she was leaning towards the door as if she could not bear to be close to Olivia strapped in her car seat. This, too, is my fault, Ewan thought. He had failed to grasp the most fundamental fact about his sister—her yearning for a child—and construed her response to the baby as simply the way women were. Then he had compounded his offence by allowing her to become Olivia's main caretaker. For the rest of the day, he vowed, he would be more helpful. Too little, too late, yet better than nothing.

When they stopped near Nottingham for coffee and petrol he moved to act on his resolution, but Mollie, with a resumption of her former possessiveness, had already lifted Olivia out of the car and was carrying her towards the restaurant. She and Vanessa seated themselves at a table while Ewan went to get coffee and biscuits. Waiting to pay, he watched the women chatting and wondered how they had achieved this easy footing; their only time alone together had been during Chae's phone call.

He came over, and Vanessa said brightly, "I was asking Mollie about her weaving. The pieces you have are so beautiful. They remind me of the Rothkos at the Tate—the soft greys and browns."

Ewan unloaded the tray. "I got lots of biscuits. These kinds of trips make me ravenous."

"These kinds of trips?" echoed Mollie.

"Cars," he said, awkwardly. "Should I have got something for Olivia?"

Mollie shook her head.

"She's sleeping like Rip Van Winkle," Vanessa said. "If she keeps this up for another few hours, we'll be set. I'm longing to see Scotland."

"I'm afraid it's not very picturesque to start with," said Ewan. "The first major sight we come to is the ruins of Lockerbie." He unwrapped a chocolate biscuit, took a bite, and saw that Mollie was crying. He put the biscuit down on the neat square of foil. "Oh, Mollie, I know this is a ghastly day, but everything will be fine soon, I promise."

At the next table, a woman and a girl, both in purple anoraks, were staring. Ewan felt a flush of embarrassment. His sister was making a scene. Then he despised himself for caring, even for a moment, about the opinions of others. The main thing was that Mollie was in pain. Once they got back to London, he would take her to a doctor, someone who specialised in what the Victorians had quaintly called nervous disorders. Nowadays there were drugs to ease the spirit's suffering, just as penicillin relieved the body's. Meanwhile, in the harshly lit restaurant, he took her hands in his. "Whatever happens," he said, "I want to help. Please don't be so sad."

Vanessa went off in the direction of the Ladies, and he moved over to put his arm around Mollie. She was blubbering incoherently about love, betrayal, about Chae not giving her a baby.

"There, there." He did his best to be soothing. But when she claimed that Olivia hated her, he could not contain himself. "Olivia doesn't hate you," he said sharply.

"No, listen to her," said Mollie. "Next time she's awake, you just listen."

The day wore on. At eleven they were making excellent progress. Two hours later, for no discernible reason, the reverse was true. They would never escape this dour, industrial landscape. It had begun to rain relentlessly, and Olivia howled. They stopped at two motorway cafés in a row to try to placate her with food and changing. Mollie clutched her, wild-eyed, her own face still streaked with tears. At the second stop, Ewan said, "Why not let me have a go with her? You know what they say about a change being as good as a rest." With Vanessa aloof and Mollie hysterical, he felt acutely helpless.

Mollie thrust Olivia into his arms and raced towards the cafeteria, followed by Vanessa. Ewan walked around the car park, holding an umbrella over himself and the baby, and recited the story of the three pigs. On his fourth rendition, just as the wolf blew the house down, she quieted, and he carried her inside. Mollie and Vanessa were buying fruit salad. "We're fine now," he said.

"Well done," said Vanessa.

Mollie said nothing, nor did she reach for Olivia. When they returned to the car Ewan offered to sit in the back, and she silently acquiesced. As Vanessa accelerated onto the motorway he remembered they would have to repeat this whole trip again tomorrow, minus the baby. Perhaps he should suggest that Mollie use the return ticket from his original train journey. But no, that would leave him to drive back alone with Vanessa and their cargo of delicate compromises.

He was rescued from this daunting prospect by the sight of a man's glove on the floor. That had been the other major revelation of the last twelve hours: it was Mollie, not Chae, who had ended their relationship. On the phone Chae had said he still loved her. Now, Ewan thought, if only they could be reconciled. He adjusted the cuffs of his shirt—already the white cotton was slightly soiled—and cautioned himself not to presume that Mollie would return to London. Once Olivia was safely united with her parents he would take Vanessa out to dinner, leaving Mollie and Chae alone together.

Near Beattock the rain ceased. A few miles later they passed the small town of Moffat. He leaned forward and asked Mollie if this wasn't where Great-Aunt Ethel had come to take the waters. "I have this memory of her in our living room," he added, "showing us how she could touch her toes since she'd been to Moffat."

"That's right." Mollie nodded. "She said the well was awfully smelly."

"Probably the sulphur," Vanessa said. "Some of the springs in Bath have quite a pong."

Bad move, thought Ewan. "One of my neighbours is a chiropractor," he offered quickly. "She claims that hot springs are about as beneficial as hot baths."

"Nonsense," said Vanessa, but before she could remonstrate further, Mollie interrupted.

"I'd like to sit in the back," she said.

They stopped at the next lay-by. As he walked round the car, Ewan saw a sign by the side of the road with a list of towns: Glasgow, Stirling, Perth, Dundee. How on earth was he ever going to apologise to Olivia's parents?

Mollie stared at her brother's wispy hair lying neatly above his white collar. Like everyone else, he had betrayed her—My home is yours, she thought sardonically—-but all those past betrayals paled in comparison to her fear of Olivia's treachery. She turned to look at the baby. She was asleep, her lips pursed, her eyelashes curved against her plump cheeks; yet what if she were to raise those beautiful eyelashes, as she had the night before, to reveal something vile and vicious?

Mollie bent so close that Olivia's breath whispered on her cheek. I must be going mad, she told herself. She's four months old, a helpless infant. Look how sweetly she sleeps. But there, right at the corner of her eye, wasn't that the edge of a mask, no different from Ewan's and fitting even more perfectly?

She had scarcely taken in the maelstrom of confrontations that lay ahead. The man on the phone—Olivia's father?—was about to reclaim Olivia. She and Ewan would be accused of kidnapping, or worse. If Olivia was wearing a mask, it was only because these last few days had been so fraught. When the two of them were once more alone together, she would become her angelic, transparent self. The only real terror, Mollie thought, was the terror of separation.

The man wanted money, and didn't Ewan have money? Then she remembered Chae. Her brother had his own complicated problems, but Chae was in her debt. And if they were together, then the arguments against single parents would disappear. Yes, that would work, and it would leave Ewan free for Vanessa. Though hadn't she mentioned a boyfriend? Besides, you had only to see the two of them together to know she was untouched by Ewan. Like Chae, she found his virtues absurd.

She pulled her gaze away from Olivia and saw that they were nearing the town. On the left was the Grahams' farm, and just ahead the caravan site. Her skull tightened as if all the bones had simultaneously edged closer together. A list—a list would calm her. She was searching her bag for paper and a pen when the car suddenly swerved. From the road ahead rose two rooks, their beaks stained with blood. They had been feeding on the corpse of a rabbit. Mollie shrank down in her seat. Her hand, she discovered, was holding her cheque book. On the back of a cheque she scribbled: *1. talk to Chae.* When she couldn't think what to put for *2*, she reached into the bag for her make-up.

In the dusty mirror of the compact she saw a human face: two rather heavy eyebrows, two dull eyes, the lids shiny, the skin beneath drawn, a mouth, the lips thin and pale, though none of these features seemed to belong to her. So I, too, am wearing a mask, she thought. All the better for playing my part. She raised her hand to tap one cheek. Yes, she could feel that, surprisingly enough. She began to put on eyeliner, remembering the dexterity with which her teenage self had performed this task on the bus to school each morning. She rubbed in foundation, applied lipstick—Ginger Flower, it was called—and considered the result. More mask-like, she decided, better, and blotted her lips on a tissue.

That night Kenneth had another dream. He was stoking a wood stove in a hovel, and he kept having to go out and find more sticks. Joan was there, draped in a red dress, the one he had planned to buy her if it wasn't too dear. She began a zany dance, disappearing into the dress and emerging again. He came in with another load of sticks. They were no longer alone. Behind Joan, near the stove, stood a shadowy figure who had some dreadful power over him. Before anything else could happen, thank Christ, he opened his eyes. An unfamiliar expanse of gold-patterned wallpaper lay before him. Then he spotted the dresser with its bottles and gewgaws and remembered Joan.

Maybe he'd dreamed of the red dress because he himself was dressed. He was wearing a tee shirt and jeans. The former for warmth and the latter because he needed a safe place to keep the keys. The previous evening he had dimly grasped that Joan was so desperate she might do anything, including running away to find Grace.

Suddenly he was struck by the silence. The usual car noises, of course, and someone hoovering downstairs, but nothing hu-man nearby. Could Joan somehow have escaped? The idea brought him to his feet. He tiptoed round the bed. From the doorway he surveyed the empty hall with its four doors. The door of the flat was closed, still locked, and the bathroom door was ajar. That left the living room and the kitchen.

He stood for a minute, listening, and had a twinge of that weird loneliness he'd felt walking up the track to Mill of For-tune. Was this what life was like—you had a new feeling and it kept coming back, like this dreaming shit? Quickly he stepped into the kitchen.

Joan was seated at the table, her head resting on her arms. In spite of his noisy entrance, she did not stir. What if she was dead? Fucking hell. He'd never seen a dead body, although once in a London park he and Duncan had come across an old codger sprawled under a bush. They'd been about to throw stones at him when they both saw the funny purple colour of his face and, without speaking, hurried away. Later they'd had a good laugh: fancy being scared of a bum sleeping off a bender.

Joan's shoulders rose and fell. She was just sulking, as usual. Something about the room was different, though. He scanned the tidy counters, the cupboard, the orange bread bin, the fridge. That was it: Lalit no longer smiled from the fridge. During the last week the snapshot had been his friend and ally. Hadn't he even said Lalit's name in his sleep, according to his mum? He stepped across the room and shook Joan's arm. "What've you done with the snap?"

She raised her head, barely. "Snap?"

"Your brother on the fridge." As he spoke, he noticed that not only Lalit's but all the photographs were gone.

"Your eyes are evil," Joan said, putting her head down again. "Your gaze hurts my family. That is why we suffer, because I let you gaze upon them."

Evil? Bloody hell. She sounded like she'd been at the kirk. "What rubbish," he said. "How about a nice cuppa?"

While he waited for the kettle to boil, he leaned against the sink, studying her. She was wearing the same navy sweatshirt as the evening before, and he realised he hadn't felt her come to bed. She must have sat up all night, silly cow. He'd get her to wash and change before they went out. He and Duncan always collected more money on the days they shaved. He made tea and put a cup beside her. "We're fetching her today," he said. "Quit being such a mopy Mary."

From Joan's bowed head came a muffled reply. "You have no heart."

"Okay, be that way." He slammed out of the room.

On the box two women were discussing primary school education. Kenneth slumped on the sofa and pondered his plans.

No point being too finicky. The Laffertys had nicked Grace and must pay for it. Joan would raise the stakes. The only danger was she'd be so glad to get Grace back she'd blow off everything else. It was up to him to turn her motherly gushing into dosh. They'd be like those detectives in the films—the hard one and the soft.

He pictured himself saying, "Excuse me, my wife and me"—no, my wife and I—"we've suffered mental anguish." Mental anguish, that was good. Then Mr. Lafferty, maybe the bloke in the suit too, would reach into their pockets and haul out wads of notes and hand them over with smarmy apologies. Yes, he thought, draining the tea to the sugary half-inch at the bottom that was his favourite part, money and apologies. Once again he flashed on the bored way the infirmary superintendent had given him the sack. Now, finally, he would have his revenge, and didn't they say revenge was sweeter than wine?

"Nearly there," Ewan said. "We turn right in about half a mile. Look how the daffodils are just coming out here. In London they're already dead."

"Daffodils," murmured Mollie.

Glancing over his shoulder, Ewan stifled a gasp. Before, his sister, though pale, had looked more or less herself. Now her cheeks were an unlikely beige, her eyes outlined thickly in black, her lips smeared. And as he took in her bizarre appearance, the acrid odour, which once or twice since Perth he had almost smelled, rushed over him in a wave.

Speechless, he turned away and rested his hand on Vanessa's thigh. "We take the next left," he said, leaning closer to inhale the comforting fragrance of her shampoo.

"What an amazing place," she said.

"Perhaps there'll be time to show you the sights before it gets dark. Here are the gates."

They passed the pond, and Ewan remembered the ducks. He never had found out the name of the fourth one. Thank goodness, he thought, Chae will be here. Whatever Ewan's reservations about him in daily life, his presence this evening seemed eminently desirable. He directed Vanessa to the back of the house. She braked hard, and they all rocked slightly in their seats.

Before any of them could move, Chae appeared. He opened the back passenger door and leaned into the car. "So this is Grace," he said. "What a beautiful baby. Hello, everyone."

While Chae extricated Grace, Ewan went round to Vanessa's door. "You've been terrific," he said, kissing her cheek.

"I agree." She smiled, then climbed out and began to bend and stretch.

Ewan opened Mollie's door. In one hand she clutched a piece of paper on which something was written; he could not read what. "Here we are," he said.

Her garish face remained expressionless. Without hesitation, however, she got out and went to join Chae. "You haven't met Olivia, have you?" she said. "Chae, Olivia. Olivia, Chae."

"Actually," Chae said, "her name is Grace."

Ewan waited to see how Mollie would respond to this direct attack. Perhaps she grew a little paler, but she did not protest, only suggested they go inside. In the kitchen Sadie bounded around and Plato chirped a few notes. Vanessa asked where the bathroom was and disappeared up the creaking stairs.

While Mollie and Chae fussed over the baby, Ewan stood near the stove, trying to keep out of the way. His presence in this familiar room filled him with renewed amazement at the events of the last week. He had found a baby in a bus station and unwittingly kidnapped her, gone to Milan, sat in a chair belonging to Lucrezia Borgia, slept with an Italian pianist in one way and Vanessa in another, met the deadly Coyle, discovered his sister had kept the baby, and accepted the offer of the woman who had betrayed him to drive them back here in a desperate effort to avoid grief and scandal. He watched Mollie, as she measured out formula, and wondered if she had ever really believed she could get away with keeping Olivia. He wanted to say it was ludicrous and then, remembering his own recent behaviour, thought, no, all it took was a small talent for forgetfulness, and anything was possible.

Kenneth was glad to see the snooty driver of his two earlier bus journeys had been replaced. A lard bucket of a bloke was squeezed behind the wheel. "Cheers, mate," he said, handing Kenneth two tickets and his change.

"Cheers," Kenneth said.

Usually he sat near the back, but today he nudged Joan into a seat only a few down the aisle. At his insistence she had washed her hair and changed her clothes, all without emerging from her silent cloud of rage. Now she stared straight ahead while he tried to read the newspaper. He'd bought the *Sun*, hoping there might be news of that American kid, the one who'd given him the idea of making money off Grace in the first place. Today, after twenty minutes' battling to turn the pages against the swaying bus, he found nothing. Lowering the paper, he caught sight of the graffiti on the back of the next seat. *George loves Lindy forever,* he read, and, more inspiringly, *Remember the Krays.*

Four thousand quid, he mouthed, and felt a slight choking. Could he actually say the words aloud? "Four thousand quid," he said, tugging Joan's sleeve. "What'd I say?"

"Four thousand quid."

It was a lot, no question, but look how easily Lafferty had given him a thousand. Look at what a house like that cost, or even that stupid car in which he'd given Kenneth a lift to the town. They had the ready, no mistake. And faced with a choice between gaol and handing over a piece of it, they'd hand it over in a flash. Anything else would be mental. He slipped his hand into his breast pocket and encountered the reassuring, slightly rough texture of a twenty-pound note.

By the sepia light of late afternoon, Ewan took Vanessa up the hill to St. David's Well. Since his last visit the leaves on the beech trees and horse chestnuts had unfurled like little green flags, and the rhododendron buds were swelling. Sadie ran ahead in rapturous circles. Vanessa strode along in her jeans and leather jacket, seeming quite at home. She remarked, disconcertingly, how handsome Chae was. "I suppose," Ewan said. This was not a topic he cared to pursue. "What kind of state do you think Mollie's in?"

"Completely messed up where the baby is concerned, though in other ways she's rather together." She stepped over a fallen branch. "It's interesting how different the two of you are."

"We are?" he exclaimed, and wished he hadn't.

"Well, she's a bit of a hippie, but I think she has more of an edge than you do. More of the killer instinct."

"Not something I've ever really aspired to," Ewan said, but Vanessa either missed or ignored his irony.

On a rock beside the path lay a speckled eggshell, almost whole. Ewan spotted a clump of primroses, and they both bent to examine the pale-yellow flowers. Walking along again, he confided his hopes about Mollie and Chae. "That's why I dragged you up the hill, to give them some time alone together. And us too," he added awkwardly.

Vanessa made a noncommittal sound.

"I'm so grateful to you for helping."

They moved to opposite sides of the path to avoid a patch of mud. "There you are," said Vanessa. "Mollie would never say

that, because it isn't true, is it? We both know I'm not really
doing you any favours. You're in one sort of mess and I'm in
another."

Oh, God, Ewan thought. "We go to the left here," he muttered, and took the lead for the short walk to the base of the
crags. At the well, Sadie drank and darted off after a noise in
the undergrowth. Vanessa expressed surprise that this small pool
of water, only a few feet deep, was called a well. Ewan explained
that it never emptied, never froze, and told her about the
legend.

"We must wish," she said.

She had no money, and he had only five-pence coins in his
pocket. "It won't matter to the king's daughters," he said.
"They deal in another currency."

They threw their coins. As they watched the ripples fade, he
reached for her hand. "I love you," he said, "but I hate all this.
In the car I was thinking how much I want to talk to Coyle. I
don't mean I'm going to. I just mean I want to. This duplicity
makes me feel terribly far from myself."

"I'm sorry," said Vanessa. "If I could give the money back
without damaging anyone, I'd do it like a shot, but we both
know I can't. We have to go on."

"Like Macbeth."

"Good grief, Ewan. We're not talking about killing people.
This is like cheating on the underground—not immoral, just
slightly illegal."

"That's what Mollie says about Olivia."

She pulled her hand away. "Don't be ridiculous. It's part of
Mollie's delusion to believe that stealing babies is okay. What I
did isn't remotely comparable. I don't think it even counts as
theft."

"You may be right," said Ewan, thrusting his empty hands
into his empty pockets. "I suspect most people would agree

with you, maybe ninety-nine percent. Unfortunately I don't. I believe there's an equivalent of the Hippocratic oath for bankers, and I've broken it. So have you."

"Okay," said Vanessa. "For the sake of argument, suppose you're right. There are other ways to make amends than by confessing. You can be extra scrupulous on behalf of your other clients."

"You don't love me, do you?"

"Oh, Ewan, it has nothing to do with you." She hung her head. "I'm seeing someone else, a market analyst I met in New York last spring. I'm sorry, I should have told you, but the relationship is so shaky. And I do like you."

Ewan strove to keep his face as still as the water in the well. "I'm sorry," she said again. "Don't you think we should get back?"

Far above them in the treetops Ewan heard the rustling of the evening breeze. He saw the fine lines on her forehead, the shadowed skin beneath her eyes. How lovely she was. Yet, just for an instant, he glimpsed a future in which she would be no more to him than another clever stockbroker. "What did you wish?" he asked.

"I wished that everything would be all right. Pretty cosmic." She grinned. "And you?"

"I didn't know what to wish for. Everything I want for myself or other people seems too complicated, so I asked for Grace to be fine. If she survives, the rest of us will too."

"She will." Vanessa raised her face and kissed him, a friend's kiss on the cheek.

In the drowsy warmth of the stove Mollie sat feeding the freshly bathed Olivia. Chae straddled a nearby chair and watched. Since Thursday he'd trimmed his beard, but the neatness only made him look more haggard. While she filled the bottle, he had put on a tape, something classical and sad: Chopin, she guessed. During her weeks alone in the house she hadn't even turned on the radio except when Chae showed up unexpectedly. Now the notes shaping the air were a mark of his return.

"Mollie," he said, "we need to talk."

"Yes." This was the first, the only, task on her list, but instantly the plates of her skull squeezed closer. She stared down at Olivia and waited.

"The other night," Chae continued, "you said I'd stolen from you twice over. If I did, you have to believe it was an accident. When I'm writing, characters come to me and I don't question their origin. Remember after you read *Debts and Trespasses* you said I'd got my mother just right. You could have knocked me down with the proverbial feather. I thought Peggy was pure invention, and then, as soon as you said that, I realised I'd taken almost everything from life. It was a weird feeling." He spread his hands to indicate the extent of the weirdness.

"Of course I knew Maudie had one or two things in common with you, but I honestly had no idea how much I'd borrowed. Even the part about Edward . . . this must seem incredible, but I was sure I'd made it up. It wasn't intentional. Jesus, it was barely conscious. More like you in your weaving coming back to certain motifs again and again."

"It's nothing like that." Mollie tilted the bottle to ensure Olivia's milk supply. "You told everyone my secrets—things I didn't even know myself. When I read about Maudie wanting a child, I recognised this longing that had tormented me for years. I hated you for knowing what it was and not telling me."

"Forgive me," Chae said. "Please."

For a moment the only sounds were the piano notes and the low melody of Olivia's sucking. On the table stood a vase of flowering currant. He must have picked them while we were in London, Mollie thought. She looked down again at Olivia, whom she had dressed in one of the new sleepers from

Mothercare. What was that vivid red called? Pomegranate? Persimmon?

"Please forgive me," Chae repeated. He leaned back, balancing the chair on two legs. "Whatever else I write, you can read it first. I'd like us to live together again. I'll do anything you want."

Mollie felt a surge of triumph. He had said the very words she needed. She shaped her face into a smile. "If you really want me to forgive you, help me keep Olivia."

The legs of Chae's chair clattered to the floor. "Mollie, she's someone else's child. She's not Olivia. Her name is Grace. We can't keep her. It isn't possible."

"You just said you'd do anything. I heard you. Olivia heard you. Well, this is my anything. You can write about me from now until kingdom come. All I want is Olivia."

"But—"

"I'm not mad," Mollie said carefully. "I know she has parents. But they don't want her. They'd never have left her in the first place. And they'd have reported her missing. They want money. When I spoke to the man on the phone, that's what he was working up to. I could feel it. Olivia shouldn't be for sale, but if she is, we'll buy her. You still have the money from your book—Maudie's money. We can say we're married. They'll see this house and know we can give her a good life." She stopped, thrilled at her own rational eloquence. She had managed to say it, the whole spiel, about books and money and marriage and Olivia.

Chae tugged his beard and studied the floor. "It's true," he said slowly, "the father asked for money, but I don't think that means he doesn't want the baby. He wants her and he wants cash. Like someone who's ill asking for compensation—they still want to be healthy. Listen, Mollie, I didn't know you felt this strongly. If it means this much to you, we can adopt a baby."

Mollie stood up. She held the squirming Olivia out towards him. "People aren't interchangeable," she said. "Do you want to live with anyone? No, you want to live with me. And I want to live with Olivia."

Chae looked at Mollie, then at Olivia, wriggling in her arms, then back at Mollie. "All right." He sighed. "You can have the money. I'll stand by you."

She leaned to kiss him, and to her surprise, he flinched. Had it come to that? His eyes were brown, like Olivia's, only lighter. Bending close, she saw the pupils shift, but no, she would not look, not this time. The windows of the soul—who knew what one might see, peeping through a forbidden window?

"Why don't you take a bath," Chae said, "and let me finish feeding the baby? We've nearly an hour until they get here. Once you're done, I'll go and change. I think it's important to be at our best to meet them. You know," he trailed off, "to talk and explain."

Mollie's first instinct was to refuse, but she felt the ache in her muscles, the crinkliness of clothes in which she'd travelled five hundred miles—no, a thousand—and besides, it was part of her plan to have Chae fall in love with Olivia. She handed the baby over and climbed the stairs. They creaked loudly, one by one, but she hurried on, refusing to listen. In the bathroom the steam poured out of the tap and hung in talkative clouds. She undressed quickly and climbed into the bath. This was no time for voices. She lay back and let her head sink until the water sealed her ears. Unbidden came the image of two black birds feasting on a rabbit.

The taxi pulled up outside Mill of Fortune. Kenneth paid the driver and watched him reverse out of the yard. Once again he faced the dull green door. His stomach churned. Four thousand quid. Crikey. Briefly he was tempted to forget the whole bloody scheme and just enjoy the grand he already had. Then he sensed Joan standing beside him in the near darkness, waiting for him to make a move, and he knew the daft thing would be to give up. He was in charge, no question: Colonel Kenneth. He stepped forward to knock at the door.

His first thought when it opened was that Lafferty was wearing smarter togs than before. Like Joan's docility, it was a mark of respect, which made him feel better. They shook hands. Lafferty looked enquiringly to Kenneth's left. Oh, yes, "This is Joan," Kenneth said.

To his surprise, Lafferty offered her his hand, but she paid no attention. "Where is Grace?" she squeaked.

"She's here." He nodded over his shoulder. "In the kitchen."

Before Kenneth could move, Joan rushed past them. "Grace!" they heard her cry.

He and Lafferty followed. In the kitchen the suit bloke and the short-haired woman who'd met him off the bus that first day were sitting around the table, plus a chick Kenneth had never seen before. They were all watching Joan, who was holding Grace and crying.

Kenneth stopped, flustered. He hadn't expected so many people. The bloke in the suit stood up, held out his hand, and spoke loudly, to be heard above Joan. "I'm Ewan Munro."

More handshakes.

"I owe you and your wife an enormous apology," the bloke went on. "I found the b-b-b-b- Grace on the floor of the Gents. I assumed she'd been abandoned. My b-b-b-"—he gave up on "bus"—"was leaving, and I got confused and took her with me. Then there was a bit of a mix-up."

How pink-faced he was, Kenneth thought. Somewhere nearby a dog barked. And what a din Joan was making. He was tempted to tell her to shut up. Instead he said, "My wife's quite upset."

He and the bloke turned to look at Joan, who was kissing Grace's hands and head and saying strange foreign things. Lafferty fetched a bottle and poured whisky. There was an awkward pause, as if they were waiting for a toast. Then they drank anyway. Good stuff, Kenneth thought. Now, about the dough—but before he could speak, the short-haired woman leapt out of her chair.

As soon as she laid eyes on Kenneth, Mollie felt vindicated. He was nothing but a punk, a lager lout, a hooligan, completely unqualified for fatherhood. The woman, like the birds and the voices, she vehemently ignored. When Ewan had finished his incoherent remarks, she came forward. "How do you do," she said. "I'm Mollie Munro. We spoke on the phone."

"Yeah," Kenneth said vaguely. He swirled the whisky round in his glass.

"About the baby. I wondered . . . we wondered . . ." He was staring at her now, rather than at his whisky, and into his clear, cold eyes she said the simplest words she could find. "We want to keep her. To give her a home. Of course," she hurried on, "we'd recompense you."

"Mollie," said a voice, two voices. Chae was at her elbow. So was Ewan. But she did not look at either of them, only at Kenneth. To her delight, his eyes kindled.

"Recompense," he said. "Like compensation?"

"Exactly. Money, in fact."

"Yes, well, it's something to consider. We've suffered a lot, losing Grace. Mr. Lafferty knows that. The coppers would find this business very strange."

"We'd be happy to compensate you," said Ewan stiffly. "It was a mistake, and we're terribly sorry. Whatever we can do—books, clothes for Grace."

" 'Clothes for Grace,' " spat Kenneth. "You think we're going to keep quiet for a nappie and a pair of booties? You've got to be fucking joking. You can't nick a baby."

"Ewan, shut up. Don't listen to him." She smiled desperately at Kenneth and turned to Chae. "Help me."

"My wife has become very attached to your daughter," Chae mumbled. "If there's anything, any way—"

"Ten thousand pounds," Mollie blurted. And, to be quite clear, used the name she had never before uttered: "For Grace."

Kenneth's face flared as if she had slapped him. "Ten grand," he whispered. Far more than he had imagined. "Ten grand." He narrowed his eyes at the woman and gave a small gasp. From her first words she had seemed familiar, not just from the chemists; now he recognised her. She was the figure of his two dreams, the one that was always in the shadows. In the dream he had thought she had power over him, but it was the other way round! He was the powerful one. "You have that kind of dough?" he said.

"Yes, Chae, my husband, has it from his book. We can show you a bank statement."

"Okey-dokey," said Kenneth, smoothing the lapels of his jacket. "I think you may have yourselves a deal."

He was about to offer his hand to the woman when someone stepped between them. "Stop," Joan cried. "You . . . you shitty bastard. Grace is mine—mine, not yours—and no one buys her."

To prove her point, she made the same gesture Mollie had earlier, holding the baby out before her. Ewan saw the unmistakeable kinship in their brown eyes, their dimpled chins, their short upper lips. Mother and daughter: how could he have separated them? But his immediate duty was to poor Mollie, who was getting into deeper and deeper waters. He glanced over at Vanessa, where she sat alone at the table, watching the five of them as if they were in a play. For a few seconds he forgot everything else and allowed himself to take comfort in her presence. During those seconds several things occurred.

Joan was holding Grace, and Grace was smiling. She was waving her arms and legs in graceful Tai Chi motions and burbling those sounds right on the edge of speech.

"Ahhh," she said. And "Mmm. Mmm."

Mollie, hearing her own name, lunged. Somehow she got the baby out of Joan's grasp. She brandished her high, like a banner in her deep-red clothes. Grace, startled at this sudden change of ownership, fell silent. Her eyes opened wide and she blinked, her dark lashes fluttering over her brown eyes. Then she stared straight at Mollie and made a short, glottal sound.

"No!" Mollie screamed.

And even as her mother reached for her, Grace was falling, falling towards the stone floor. There was a dull thud and the worst silence Ewan had ever heard.

"Oh, my God," said Vanessa softly.

Joan dropped to her knees beside the baby.

Mollie watched the room fill with green light and felt herself growing smaller and smaller, dwindling.

"Fuck," Kenneth said, emptying his glass.

Chae just stood there.

Ewan gazed at Grace. Once again she was lying on the floor, much as she had been when he found her eight days ago. But now one arm was bent beneath her. She seemed to be unconscious. He remembered his wish at St. David's Well and yearned for her to utter the smallest sound. He knelt down, meaning to help, but Joan was already doubled over the small red figure. Far away he heard Vanessa say "ambulance" and call Chae to give directions on the phone. Grace's dark silky hair was shadowed by something darker still. Someone knelt beside him, and he knew, from the smell, that it was his sister.

"Don't touch her," he said to Grace's mother. "We mustn't touch her until the doctor gets here. We might hurt her."

"Doctor?" said Kenneth. "No need for that. It was just a wee bump. She'll be fine. Come on, Joan, hang on a sec so we can think what's best."

But Joan ignored them both, calling out in a loud voice to Krishna, to Kali. She put her face close to Grace's so that her hair hung down around them like a shining tent.

It was hard to see what she was doing, but Ewan guessed: she was trying to catch her daughter's soul before it flew too far, to bring it back and slip it safely home between Grace's slender ribs. Meanwhile her slim brown hands shuttled up and down the quiet body. Surely, he thought, such love could not be denied.

He kept staring at Grace's red-clad legs, all he could see of her. Wait, was that a sound? A whimper? But no, it was just the wind, or Mollie murmuring, or a noise escaping his own tight throat. Joan moved to press an ear to the baby's chest. Suddenly Ewan saw her hands grow still. Dread swarmed in every corner of the room, and he knew the awful answer: Yes, love could be denied.

In one gentle movement Joan picked Grace up and rose to her feet. Ewan wanted to protest again—don't move her, the doctor—but every letter of the alphabet loomed higher than the Tower of London. She walked to the door. On the threshold she turned to face them: Ewan, Mollie, Kenneth. The baby limp in her arms. Blood blotting her coat. She was not crying. Ewan almost wished she were; tears would have dulled her gaze.

"Why?" she said. "Why did you harm us? Grace and I, we did you no wrong." Her eyes rested impartially on the three of them. "You are bad people," she said.

And it was, Ewan thought as she stepped through the door, no less than they deserved.

Chapter 19

Later, in the long list of things Ewan blamed himself for, the one he kept coming back to as the most puzzling and grievous was his failure to recognise Mollie's condition. He had known she was distressed, but proximity had blinded him to the true extent of her altered state. Indeed, he had even begun to share it. What else could explain his incredible laxity towards Grace? After a lifetime of returning library books by the due date, of writing meticulous cheques whenever he used a friend's phone, he had behaved as if he had found an apple labelled "Take me" at the bus station rather than a living, breathing human who, in her helplessness, had a particular claim upon him. Or so Yvonne remarked, furious, when he told her what had really happened in Scotland.

The events following Joan's departure were mired in sorrow and confusion. Ewan continued to kneel on the floor until Vanessa returned to say that an ambulance was on its way. Then he stood up and went to raise his sister, still kneeling like a penitent in her grubby black clothes, but the sight of her face stopped him. Together with Chae, he manoeuvred Mollie into the car, and Chae drove her to the hospital. Throughout this

Kenneth swore steadily. At some point he had poured himself a second large whisky.

Each terrible moment blotted out all the other terrible moments. As soon as the rear lights of the car disappeared, Ewan could think only of Grace and her mother, wandering the dark countryside. He set out in search of them. Vanessa and Kenneth stayed at the house; the latter protested Joan was a grand walker. Halfway down the drive, Ewan had a ghastly premonition. He made a detour to the pond and, standing by the empty duck house, called Joan's name. He was so afraid he could barely push his voice out into the clotted air—"Joan, Joan"—but no one answered his cries. The surface of the water lay smooth and untelling.

He was almost at the road when suddenly he understood that once again he was repeating his major error of the previous week: not informing the proper authorities. He turned and ran back to the house, his leather-soled shoes slipping on the gravel. When the police operator answered, he burst out that a woman and her baby were missing; the baby had been in an accident.

"Let me see," said the operator, in glacial tones. "An ambulance just reported picking up a mother and child near Glen Teall. Foreigners of some sort?"

"Yes, yes, Indian. How is the baby?"

In the pause he heard paper rustling. Answer me, he wanted to shout, but instead made himself count the stairs: one, two, three, four was especially crooked, five.

"I have no details, sir." The operator's voice thawed slightly. "But a police car has been dispatched to Mill of Fortune. It should be with you shortly."

She hung up, leaving Ewan no option save to do the same. Back in the kitchen he told Vanessa and Kenneth what he'd learned. At the first mention of police, Kenneth got to his feet. "Well, then, I'll be pushing off."

"You can't leave," Ewan exclaimed. "What about your daughter?"

"She was Joan's kid," he said, seeming to take the worst for granted. "I was just trying to help out after you nicked her." He scrutinised his empty glass. "I'm a bit short for the bus home."

Ewan regarded him with loathing. If anyone was to blame, besides himself, it was this layabout in his scruffy sports jacket. He took thirty pounds from his wallet and made Kenneth write his name and address on the back of the leaflet about bauxite mines before he handed it over.

Then Ewan was alone with Vanessa and a small pool of blood, no bigger than the palm of his hand. As he paced back and forth, he saw it was already thickening, darkening. He would not clean it away. Not until he had news of Grace. It should stay here, like the blood of Rizzio staining the floor of Holyrood Palace.

While he paced, Vanessa sat at the table, crying quietly. A week ago Ewan would have done almost anything to cheer her up. Now her distress seemed trivial compared to what had happened to Grace. And to Mollie. He circled the loom, noticing it was dressed in blue and yellow yarn, different from the piece that had been there last weekend.

Gradually Vanessa grew calm; she asked what they should say to the police.

"You know what to say," Ewan retorted. "You were here." He could not bear the undertones of conspiracy.

"But what about Mollie?" she pleaded. "And you? Aren't you going to get in trouble?"

"I don't see how anyone can hold Mollie responsible; she's clearly having some kind of breakdown. Whatever she did was done out of affection for Grace. As for me, I've done enough harm. I plan to do the only thing I can: make a clean breast. It won't save Mollie, or Grace, or Grace's mother, but maybe my s-s-s-s-" He stopped, defeated by the sinuous *s*, unable to find a synonym for "soul."

From the parlour, where she was still shut in, Sadie barked. Ewan hurried to the back door. A black and white police car, headlights blazing, was pulling up outside. A mechanical voice grated on the night air—the driver was talking on the radio—and the passenger door opened. The light from the kitchen glinted off the buttons of the tall, stocky policeman's uniform as he stepped forward.

"Constable MacIntyre," he introduced himself in a lilting Highland accent. "Are you the one who telephoned?"

"Yes," Ewan croaked. "And Ms. Lawson." He gestured towards the house. "How is the baby, Constable? Please."

At first it seemed that the policeman, like the operator, was going to ignore Ewan's pleas. He fiddled for several seconds with his breast pocket, getting out a notebook. "Unconscious," he said at last.

Alive, Ewan thought—and could admit now how much he had feared the contrary.

"An arm appears to be broken," the constable went on in his mellifluous tones. "But they won't know the full extent of the injuries until they examine her at the hospital." He opened the notebook. "Your name, sir?"

Ewan told him, and spelled it. As he did so, the brightness of relief gave way to massive darkness: what did unconscious mean? what was the full extent of the injuries?

The other policeman finished his radio call and got out of the car. "Might we come in?" asked Constable MacIntyre. Silently Ewan ushered them inside.

The following morning Ewan shared a taxi to the town with Vanessa. She was going on to Perth station to catch the train back to London. Another entry in his catalogue of self-reproach was the discovery of a regular, reasonably priced taxi service from the town to Perth. He could easily have taken Grace back that first day. When the taxi pulled up at the hospital, Vanessa squeezed his hand and begged him again not to speak to Coyle. He kissed her but promised nothing.

At the hospital reception he got Mollie's room number and asked about Grace. "The Indian baby and her mother," he said, shamefully ignorant of their surname. The receptionist directed him to a plump-cheeked nurse at the next desk, who'd been on duty the night before.

"Oh, yes, that was quite a palaver," the nurse said, looking up from the folder she was reading. "The mother made an awful scene when we tried to examine the baby. Couldn't speak a word of English."

Ewan did not bother to correct her. "Is the baby all right?" he asked, gripping the edge of the desk.

"She won't be doing the Highland fling anytime soon, poor wee thing." She patted the folder, as if it were in need of consolation. "Her arm's broken and she has a fracture near the base of the skull. Some sort of accident, the police said. Are you a friend of the family?"

Ewan nodded.

"Well, she's still in a coma. We moved her to the ICU at Edinburgh Royal a couple of hours ago."

"I'm sorry. I'm very sorry. It's all . . ." He saw the nurse's cheeks pucker in bewilderment and broke off. "Sorry," he said again, meaning this time for his outburst. He thanked her and headed for the stairs.

Mollie had a private room on the second floor. The door was ajar, and when Ewan pushed it open, Chae rose stiffly from a chair beside the bed. "Ewan," he said, "I was afraid you were never coming. It's been an awful night. You know Grace's mother was here?" He wrung his hands. "I heard her crying, hour after hour."

Over Chae's shoulder, Ewan glimpsed Mollie sitting bolt upright in bed, wearing a demure blue nightgown. He was about to ask how she was, when a small whitish stain on the pocket of Chae's shirt caught his attention. Could it be from Grace? And then Chae was asking if Ewan would mind staying with Mollie while he went to collect some things from the house.

"Of course not," Ewan forced himself to say.

" 'Bye, Mollie. I'll be back soon." Chae kissed her cheek. "There's a nurse down the hall," he told Ewan, and hurried away.

Ewan shifted his briefcase from hand to hand. Could he fetch the nurse immediately? Mollie stared fixedly straight ahead, seemingly unaware of his presence. All the animation with which she had addressed Kenneth was gone, as if whatever demon had frightened her into dropping Grace had driven out every other emotion. Ewan loitered in the doorway until the curious glance of a passing nurse drove him inside.

As he drew near the bed, he gazed at Mollie in amazement. Out of context, he might not have recognised her. Even her eyes, still faintly rimmed with make-up, were different, lightened to the grey of a seagull's wings. Then he heard a familiar sound and, looking down, saw her hands pleating and unpleating: she was cracking her knuckles. In some deep part of herself, he thought, his sister was unchanged, and at last he found the courage to sit down and talk to her.

"Mollie, can you hear me?"

Perhaps she paused in her cracking.

"The baby—Olivia—she's only unconscious. They think she's going to be all right." Ewan was dismayed to hear himself give a cheerful version of Grace's condition. Late last night, as he finally wiped away her blood, he had sworn never to lie again, if she would make a full recovery. And here he was, already peddling falsehoods.

"I'm sorry I failed you," he went on. "I didn't understand about Olivia. That you really loved her. I thought . . ." What had he thought? He could no longer recall the chain of pathetic rationalisations by which he had justified his behaviour. Mollie's knuckles cracked again; the bones of her wrists stood out like golf balls. Had she been this thin a week ago? "You mustn't blame yourself," he concluded. "I'm the one who's responsible. Me, with my stupidity."

The night before, making this claim to Constable Mac-Intyre, he had begun to tremble uncontrollably. If Grace had fallen from a slightly greater height, with a little more force, he would have been a murderer. Now he studied Mollie and hoped, desperately, that somewhere behind her blank stare his words were reaching her. She probably just needs lithium, Vanessa had said in the taxi, but Ewan could not help feeling that Mollie, like himself, needed absolution.

On Monday, Ewan took the train back to London. He had wanted to visit Grace in Edinburgh, but Chae had said, "Good God, man, are you out of your mind? You don't steal a baby and then go and sit at her bedside." Ewan had blushed, grateful for this bluntness. At home his first act was to phone Coyle. They arranged to meet the following morning in the coffee bar at Liverpool Street Station.

Ewan arrived early and was hunched over a cup of coffee, trying to focus on the share prices in the *Financial Times*, when a voice said, "Good morning. Sorry to keep you waiting." There was Coyle, as neat, affable, and sandy-haired as before.

They shook hands. Coyle ordered a coffee and sat down. Across the small table he studied Ewan, his eyes alert behind his thick glasses, his sharp nose attentive. "You look exhausted," he pronounced.

"I am a bit tired." Disconcerted by this unexpected sympathy, he busied himself folding the newspaper.

Coyle made a couple of comments about the restructuring of building societies; not necessarily as beneficial as people claimed, he thought, but overall a move in the right direction. Ewan nodded, unable to feign even slight interest. Then Coyle asked if there was something he wanted to talk about, and to his own amazement, Ewan plunged into an account of the last ten days, all the same twists and turns that had baffled the policemen. Coyle listened, his forehead furrowed, while Ewan described the events leading to that moment when Mollie seized Grace from her mother and dropped her on the stone floor.

"So she's in intensive care—they're still not sure of the extent of the damage—and Mollie's mad, and it's all my fault."

"A tragedy," Coyle said, shaking his head. "A terrible tragedy. But what makes you think it's your fault?"

"Who else is there? If I hadn't taken Grace from the bus station, she'd be fine. And Mollie too, probably. Or better anyway." "If"—that small word which had never given him any trouble—had become the gateway to a tortuous labyrinth: if he hadn't been worried about Coyle and obsessed with Vanessa, if he hadn't had a cup of tea at the bus station, if he hadn't stuttered on the phone, if he had paid proper attention to the people around him . . .

Coyle stirred his coffee, and took a sip. "You did behave badly," he said, "not telling anyone about the baby. But you had no idea how far gone your sister was, nor that there was someone like the father in the picture. Being a stockbroker doesn't prepare you for this kind of scenario."

"The thing is," said Ewan, "I did have the information about Mollie. It was in that wretched novel."

Surprisingly, Coyle had heard of *The Dark Forest*—he

thought his wife had read it—but as Ewan tried to explain about Leo and Maudie and Chae's vasectomy, he frowned and tapped his coffee spoon against his saucer. "Well," he said when Ewan paused, "this is a bit too convoluted for me." He pushed back his chair. "I'm going to get another coffee. Would you like one?"

Ewan watched him make his way to the counter. What was he thinking of, spewing out family secrets as if Coyle were his confessor or best friend. He retrieved his notebook and looked at the list of topics he had drawn up for their meeting. *1. Confess. 2. Vanessa. 3. Repercussions. 4. Resignation?* So far they had covered none of them.

"I bought some buns." Coyle deftly laid a plate of pastries and two cups of coffee on the table.

"Thanks. You've been very patient, letting me ramble on. What I really wanted to talk about was the Gibson Group. Last week you asked whether I had any contact with the people at Marlowe's." He stared down at his own neat handwriting. Yes, it had to be done. "I do occasionally see Vanessa Lawson."

"Ah." Coyle sounded pleased. "I thought it had just slipped your mind—that she worked for them."

"You don't need to let me off the hook." Now that he had begun, Ewan was almost eager to unburden himself. "I was in love with her. Or thought I was. A month ago we had dinner and got into shoptalk." As he described his own fatal indiscretion, the future he had glimpsed at St. David's Well came into being. That he gave away nothing Vanessa had said or done did not seem to matter; still she slid further and further down a long tunnel, until, by the time he finished, he could barely make out her pale face. "I should have told you," he said.

"You're telling me now." Coyle bit into his pastry.

"So what will happen?"

"I'll talk to Ms. Lawson. I already had my suspicions."

"What about me? Will I have to resign?"

Coyle hesitated. His Adam's apple bobbed, and he began to tap his spoon again. "I doubt if that will be necessary," he said at last. "There's no evidence that you were conspiring to defraud, certainly no evidence that you planned to profit, at least in monetary terms. It'll be up to the Serious Fraud Office, once I finish my investigations, but I imagine I'll be recommending clemency in your case. Being a little careless with a colleague is, unfortunately, all too common." He ran his finger round his plate, seeking the last crumbs.

"Your real problems," he went on, "lie north of Hadrian's Wall. That poor mother. Especially with a child too young to talk, it's terrible when they're ill. You feel so helpless."

"Do you have children?"

"One so far. Max. He's learning to walk. I hope to follow Dante's example and have three." He smiled. Then the smile disappeared as he focused his full attention on Ewan. "What I don't quite get is why you didn't just take the baby back right away."

"It all had to do with cars," Ewan said. He described the location of Mill of Fortune, the various misadventures, and his own long-ago near accident on the Caledonian Road.

"If I were you," said Coyle, "I'd learn to drive."

On Friday Ewan flew back to Edinburgh. As he followed Chae through the airport doors, the memory of the last time he had been there, saying goodbye to Mollie and Grace, leapt at him like a rottweiler. Instead of his fellow passengers, the porters, and taxi drivers, he saw, between one footfall and the next, Mollie's scream, Grace's fall, Joan's final condemnation. He had to stop until his vision cleared and he could safely cross the road.

Once they were settled in the car and heading towards the

Forth Road Bridge, Chae asked about Grace. Ewan reported she'd been moved from intensive care into the children's ward; her arm was healing nicely, but her eyesight remained affected by the fall.

"What does that mean—affected?" Chae braked at a zebra crossing and motioned a man in a green jacket to proceed.

"I'm not sure. They don't like to give out information unless you're a family member. I only know this much because I got a chatty nurse on the phone." He tried to remember her exact phrases: something about cerebral edema and intracranial pressure. "They do seem hopeful she'll make a full recovery, once the trauma recedes. How about Mollie?"

"Same story really," Chae said. "Waiting for the trauma to recede. Today we took a walk round the building. She's reached the stage when she needs things to do. I'm trying to find a way for her to start weaving again, maybe a hand loom."

"Does she remember anything?"

"Not consciously, but she often wakes up in a state. Two days ago I wore a red tee shirt, and she threw a complete wobbly." He signalled to overtake a bus and gave Ewan a quick glance. "I never should've written that damned book."

"There are lots of things we should never have done." Chae's guilt left his own vast supply absolutely undiminished.

At the hospital he met with Mollie's doctor. She's the opposite of motherly, Chae had warned, but Ewan was pleased to find himself in the presence of a tall, angular woman who reminded him of his statistics tutor at university. "Your sister is responding, Mr. Munro," she said, "but slowly. She's travelling in a far country, and in my opinion we should respect her reluctance to return. She needs to grow stronger before she'll be ready to come to terms with recent events and her part in them. I'd suggest you not mention the baby but otherwise talk to her as you always have."

"Actually," said Ewan, twitching his shirt cuffs, "I've never been very good at talking."

"Then this is your chance to improve." She looked at him with the same severe expression his tutor had worn when he confessed to not understanding standard deviation. "Don't think of yourself. Think of her, and tell her the truth as best you can."

Upstairs in her small white room, Mollie was still staring straight ahead. She gave no sign of recognition when he came in. "Mollie," he said, "it's me, Ewan. How are you?"

She turned to look at him, and her gaze snagged on his paisley tie. She reached out to touch it. "What's this—a noose of flowers? I don't like seeing you with a noose around your neck."

"I can take it off. See, it's quite easy." He unknotted his tie and slipped it into his pocket. Mollie's eyes followed his movements. Her lips parted, and he thought she would ask to see the tie again, but with a visible effort of will, she closed them.

"I spoke to Bridget yesterday," Ewan said. "She sends you her love. As soon as you're better, she wants you to visit her in Boston."

"No, not there. Not Boston. Is she all right?"

"She's fine. Very busy as usual."

"So I didn't give her cancer?"

"Cancer?" said Ewan, bewildered. "Of course not. You can't give someone cancer. It's not that kind of illness." He passed on Bridget's news: she'd just printed the program for a conference of women scientists and was running fifteen miles a week.

"Fifteen miles," Mollie exclaimed. "I bet it's not hilly like round here."

Ewan's first impulse, to contradict Chae and the doctor, subsided. What Mollie said might be odd or nonsensical, but the terrible stoniness, the utter lack of affect, was gone.

She reached for the glass beside her bed, sipped some water,

and gave a little sigh. "You know what Olivia told me? Everything in life is to do with plumbing. That's how they enter and
leave our houses, through those hidden pipes." She pointed,
with obvious pleasure, to the washbasin in the corner of the
room. "Mother came to me last night."

"She did?" Ewan said. Then he wondered, was this lying?
Should he contradict her? The doctor had not prepared him for
these dilemmas.

"I don't mean our mother," said Mollie sharply. "I mean
mine. She was fine. She said that orange-haired woman wasn't
good for you."

"Vanessa?" he suggested.

"Vanessa," she agreed.

By the time he left the hospital it was after eight and already
dark. Chae had invited him to stay, but Ewan had taken a room
in a bed-and-breakfast, claiming it was more convenient. The
truth was he could not bear the thought of being at Mill of Fortune. Now he walked the main street of the town, searching for
a place to eat. He was trying to recall which pub served evening
meals, when he heard footsteps and saw a young man in a red
jacket coming towards him. For a moment, in the dim light, he
thought it was Grace's father. A few more steps and the illusion
vanished. This man had fair hair and a scraggly beard. As he
passed, he bade Ewan a soft good evening.

Ewan ate lukewarm shepherd's pie at the Melville and went
back to his tiny room. With its single bed, basin, and chair,
there was nothing to do save go to bed. Once there, he turned
to *The Dark Forest*. Mollie had told him everything he needed to
know, but he was loath to leave the book unfinished. He
skimmed through Leo's departure from Larch House and moved
on to the last chapter.

• • •

Soon after my trip to the States I landed a part in *What the Butler Saw* and, in the frenzy of rehearsals, mostly forgot my recent adventures. I would've forgotten entirely if Maudie hadn't bombarded me with letters. Two nights after we opened—mixed reviews—I came home to find yet another 100% recycled billet doux on the doormat. I left it lying there and went to the kitchen for a beer. I hadn't answered any of her letters, and after reading one that began, "Leo, the last few weeks have been the most important of my life. Loving you, I feel alive again," I had stopped even opening them. As I drank my beer, I worried matters were getting out of hand. In Boston I had daydreamed of seducing Maudie and having Roman find out but now I just wanted to put the whole episode behind me. I was wondering if I should call her to explain—I could already imagine my contrite speech: carried away by your beauty, etc., owe it to Roman, etc.—when the phone rang. I went to answer, expecting one of my theatre friends. We often talk late after shows.

"She knew," said my brother's voice.

"Roman, what are you talking about?" I said feebly. With Maudie's unopened letter a few yards away, I thought he was saying he knew. My mind whirred uselessly. Was there any possible excuse for screwing his wife?

"I got a letter from Aunt Helen today. Listen. 'I liked your little brother. He had me fooled for five minutes but as soon as we sat down for tea and he asked for lemon instead of milk, I realised what was going on. Still he gave me a good run for my money.' She goes on to say she's changing her will—but not how."

"Shit, I'm sorry." In my amazement I forgot my earlier fears. How could Helen have known and I not noticed? I remembered the odd scene in Art Savage's office when

she was so full of beans. Then I remembered my Edinburgh shopping spree. Jesus. "The sly old bag," I said. "I
never had a clue."

"Well, clearly she was a much better actor than you."

"This was your great idea," I protested. "We just
didn't take enough account of our audience. We'd have
fooled a younger person. Only an octogenarian would remember for ten years how you take your tea. Maybe she'll
make you her heir anyway. The part of her letter you just
read didn't sound angry, more like she got a kick out of
the whole thing."

"Oh shut up, Leo. We're talking about half a million
dollars." Before I could say more, he slammed down the
phone.

What happened next, I learned from Maudie. Roman
had been ranting—I was an idiot in general, and he was
an idiot to have trusted me—and she had chosen this moment to announce she was in love with me and was leaving him. It must have been a wild scene. As for me, after
that phone call, Maudie was the last thing on my mind. All
I could think of was Roman opening his credit card bill.

The following morning I had an audition for a com-
mercial—fish fingers; they said no after thirty seconds—
and went directly from the studio to the theatre. When I
arrived home at eleven that night, Maudie was sitting on
the stairs.

"Jesus, Maudie," I said. "What are you doing here?"
For answer she flung her arms around me and burst into
tears. Several minutes passed before she calmed down
enough for me to get the door open. In the kitchen I
poured her a glass of water and we sat down. She blurted
out what had happened.

"I thought he was going to lock me up to stop me
leaving," she said, "but when I told him I was pregnant,
he didn't dare."

Of course it was all in her letters. I asked how she

could be sure so soon, and she pulled up her tunic. "See." She pointed with her free hand. "See the veins, how blue they are."

From a hasty look they did seem awfully blue. I stood up and wandered round the kitchen, trying to figure out my lines. I could feel Maudie watching me, her face still wet with tears. This was much harder than the speech I'd imagined the night before.

At last I sat down again and reached for her hands. "Maudie," I said, "you have to forgive me. I can't do this. Roman loves you. I could never get over taking you away from him. He would always be between us."

"No, the baby would be between us. Leo, don't you understand? We love each other. That's why I got pregnant the first time we made love."

"You got pregnant because I was careless," I said. And that was just the start. She argued true love; I argued jet lag, lust, inebriation. At two in the morning I threw her out, shouting that she was my brother's whore. She pounded on the door until I threatened to call the police.

From the safety of my living room window, I watched her wander down the street, a small, disconsolate figure. After she turned the corner, I got a beer and sat down, but I couldn't stop thinking about Maudie. It was a cold night and she didn't even know London, for Christ's sake. Finally I stood up, drained my beer, and fetched my jacket. My flat is half a mile from King's Cross Station, and that was where I headed. It seemed the logical destination. I went in the side entrance and saw only the usual drunks. I came out at the front. A single taxi was idling by the bus stop, and there, on the far side of the Euston Road, was Maudie.

In spite of the late hour there was plenty of traffic. As I stood watching, a white car pulled up. I saw her bend down to talk to the driver. Then she lurched into the street. The white car screeched away and another car narrowly missed her. A lorry driver shouted something. I caught the word "bitch." Somehow she reached the island in the middle unscathed.

While Maudie waited for the light to change, a scene like the one she had just escaped was enacted on my side of the street. A woman in a skirt scarcely wider than my belt was hailed by a motorist. She too bent down to the window. In this case negotiations were successful, she climbed in and the car sped away. Maudie continued across the road. She passed within a few yards of where I stood and I fell in behind her. Inside the station she made her way to the line of phones. I saw her rummage through her pockets for change and begin to dial.

Please, let her be calling Roman, I thought. Please. And as if my thoughts had reached her, she stopped dialling, put the phone down and ran her hands through her hair. She picked up the receiver and began again.

• • •

As Ewan closed the novel he heard from the hall the sound of a toilet flushing and then, from the wall behind his head, water running into a basin. Plumbing, he thought, the source of wisdom. How perfect that Aunt Helen had known all along. Not for her Isaac's gullibility. For want of a lemon, a kingdom was lost. But at least Maudie had the baby. Or she would, if she didn't get hit by a car, if she didn't have an abortion, if she didn't meet someone like Kenneth, or—Ewan paused— like himself. If indeed she dodged all the arrows Fate lets loose upon her human subjects.

And for the first time since that night at Mill of Fortune, he was able to reach back across the dreadful moment when Grace had slipped from Mollie's grasp. What he pictured was not her dimpled smile, nor her imperious needs, but their first few minutes together on the bus, when he had tucked her downy head beneath his chin and they had both fallen asleep.

The police, after filing an accident report, decided not to press charges. For their very different reasons, neither Joan, Kenneth, nor Mollie would offer testimony, and they remained unimpressed by Ewan's protestations that he was to blame for everything. He did find a local sergeant who, like Coyle, agreed he had behaved badly, dabbling in kidnapping, possibly child abuse, but nobody was interested in bringing a case against him, partly because of Kenneth's mysterious involvement, partly because Grace showed every sign of making a full recovery. "Think yourself lucky," the sergeant said. "If that baby had snuffed it, you'd be mopping out your cell right now." Ewan nodded, but the sense of how easily his luck, and everyone else's, might have been otherwise still made him tremble. After some discussion, he and Chae had decided to offer Joan money through a solicitor. Not compensation, not payment, but simply in order to free her of financial worries during this difficult period. The solicitor suggested two thousand pounds as an adequate sum. Reluctantly Ewan agreed; he wished it were more.

In the weeks that followed, the people whose lives Grace had briefly knotted together went their separate ways. Mollie continued to travel in her own strange country. Chae waited at Mill of Fortune for her return. Ewan visited her most weekends and passed on Bridget's good wishes without mentioning Boston. Vanessa left Marlowe's for what were termed personal reasons and went to New York. Joan spent many hours chanting to a little statue of Shiva; she no longer spoke or responded to English. Her mother had accepted the money on her behalf, and as soon as Grace was well enough they moved to Preston to live with Lalit. Kenneth bought a secondhand car with the thousand pounds, worked at the swimming pool, got himself fired, and spent the summer picking raspberries. Like Ewan, he blamed himself for Grace's accident, but his angle of reproach was different. What he could not get over was his gormlessness in bringing Joan to Mill of Fortune. Although he had no further need of phones, he continued to frequent The Blind Beggar. Regulars there soon became familiar with his lament that Joan's maternal crap had kiboshed his whole scheme.

A NOTE ABOUT THE AUTHOR

Margot Livesey grew up in Scotland. She now lives in Boston and London.

A NOTE ON THE TYPE

The text of this book was set in a film version of Garamond
No. 3, a modern rendering of the type first cut by Claude
Garamond (1510–1561). Garamond was a pupil of Geoffroy
Troy and is believed to have based his letters on Venetian
models, although he introduced a number of important dif-
ferences, and it is to him we owe the letter which we know
as old style. He gave to his letters a certain elegance and a
feeling of movement that won for their creator an immediate
reputation and the patronage of Francis I of France.

Composed by Creative Graphics, Inc.,
Allentown, Pennsylvania
Printed and bound by The Haddon Craftsmen,
Scranton, Pennsylvania
Typography and binding design by
Dorothy S. Baker